REST HER SOUL

REST HER SOUL

A James Buckner Novel

Christopher C. Gibbs

iUniverse, Inc.
Bloomington

Rest Her Soul
A James Buckner Novel

iUniverse books may be ordered through booksellers or by contacting:

*iUniverse
1663 Liberty Drive
Bloomington, IN 47403
www.iuniverse.com
1-800-Authors (1-800-288-4677)*

ISBN: 978-1-4759-5055-7 (sc)
ISBN: 978-1-4759-5054-0 (hc)
ISBN: 978-1-4759-5053-3 (e)

Library of Congress Control Number: 2012917101

Printed in the United States of America

iUniverse rev. date: 10/03/2012

The germ of this book was planted while sitting before a campfire in Australia's Red Center. Thanks, ladies, for the idea. And thanks again to David Gibbs for the title and Jeanne Buckner Gibbs for the photo on the back. Readers curious about geography will find Highland County bordered by Iron, Crawford, Washington, and Dent Counties. The town of Corinth lies about one hundred miles south of St. Louis.

 1

James Buckner leaned forward in the saddle, his face against the horse's neck, his eyes focused intently on the bare, rocky slope, searching for a scuff mark, an overturned stone—something that might mark the trail. He felt the animal heat and the rough hair against his cheek, smelled the sharp, familiar scent of horse sweat. He only half heard Robert Carter's question.

"I said, who you votin' for?" Carter's saddle creaked as he shifted his weight and repeated his question.

Buckner kept his eyes on the ground. "Local, state, or national?" he muttered.

"President, naturally."

"I don't know. Haven't decided. Being chief of police is about all the politics I can handle."

"Haven't decided? It's only a couple weeks away." Carter sounded surprised. "You'll go for Smith, I s'pect. He's the Democrat."

"I guess he is." Buckner sat up, and the horses continued slowly up the bare, gradual slope.

"You know he got a gun," Carter said.

"Al Smith?" Buckner said, grinning.

"Amos," Carter said. "Used it robbin' the store."

"Yes," Buckner answered. "And I can't figure it. Amos's never gone off like that, has he?"

"No," Carter replied. "But he like to gamble, and he like to drink, and that can be a bad combination."

They rode in silence for a while. The air was hot for Missouri in October—still and heavy with moisture and a threat of storm. Buckner's faded khaki shirt was sweat stained.

"So I guess you'll be going for Hoover, then," Buckner said. He stopped abruptly, got down on one knee, and bent close to the ground.

"Huh! That's a good one," Carter scoffed. "What makes you think they gone let a colored man vote?"

"The Fourteenth Amendment?" Buckner grabbed the stirrup and pulled himself up and then remounted. He pointed to the crest of the hill, toward the thick crown of trees touched with autumn colors, russet and yellow among the evergreen. "He's up there. A few minutes ago. These tracks are fresh. We just missed him."

"Fifteenth Amendment," Carter corrected. "Sheriff Foote don't care nuthin' 'bout no Fifteenth Amendment."

"Foote's busy running for state assembly, according to what I hear," Buckner said. "He's a Republican. Down this end of the county, he might just need your vote. Besides, Foote may be sheriff of Highland County, but I say who votes in Corinth."

"I hear the Klan been burnin' crosses where Smith goes campaignin', him bein' a Catholic. And wet."

"None of that around here, either," Buckner said. "I won't have it."

They continued up the slope to the woods. Mixed pine and scrub oak shut out the sun and the scant trace of breeze. The air stilled—heavier, hotter … closing on them. They paused and listened, and heard nothing—no birds, no rustling of small animals, nothing. A few yards ahead was a broad, shallow depression full of pine needles and freshly fallen leaves. Buckner gestured for Carter to stay where he was and then rode to the opposite side of the depression, again watching the ground carefully. He stopped on the far side, nodded, and smiled. "All right, Amos," he said. "Come on out. But I want to see that pistol come out butt first."

Nothing. Silence.

Buckner said, "Amos, Officer Carter is with me, and he's carrying his service weapon. In about a minute, I'm going to tell him to take a shot at that copperhead I see crawling through the leaves."

Instantly, a hand and arm rose from the leaves. In the hand was a nickel-plated revolver, butt aimed at the sky. The arm was followed by a large, thickly built black man wearing faded overalls and a collarless shirt with the sleeves cut off at the elbows. Carter dismounted. He took the pistol, unloaded it, and pocketed it along with the bullets. Then he handcuffed Amos's hands behind his back and remounted.

Buckner pointed west and down the hill.

"Let's go, Amos."

"Don't I get to ride?" Amos asked. "I ain't feelin' none too good."

"You don't get nuthin', nigger," Carter said.

Buckner cleared his throat loudly.

Carter muttered something under his breath, and then aloud he said, "Start walking, if you please, *Mister* Monroe."

They started through the trees and heavy underbrush and then continued down the long, rocky slope to the wide valley and the road that led back to the small town of Corinth. Church spires and the town hall clock, visible from the ridge, disappeared behind trees as they rode down. Buckner and Carter followed Monroe, their horses' steel shoes clattering on stone. Behind them, to the east and south, the mine and smelter works that dominated the company town of Taylor grunted and puffed under a thin brown haze. Ahead of them, in the road that ran up to Taylor, sat a Model T Ford.

"I guess when you stole Miz Longstreth's flivver, Amos, you should've asked her if it had any gasoline in it," Carter said, laughing.

Monroe did not answer.

Carter turned to Buckner. "I still ain't sure how you tracked him across all this rock and into them trees," he said. "When I was growin' up in Virginia, we got by lots of times on game I shot, and if I didn't bag nuthin' we was as like to go hungry, so I got to where I was a pretty good tracker." He waved an arm, taking in the ground around them. "They ain't a mark anywhere that I can see."

"It's just something you learn how to do," Buckner said. "Like anything else."

"Well, somebody must've taught you. Was this when you was in the calvry?"

"Yes. Sergeant Riley at Fort Huachuca, last part of nineteen eleven, most of nineteen twelve." Buckner laughed. "I was always after him to teach me how he did it. He'd say to me 'You think too much, white boy. Can't read sign if you think too much.'"

"White boy? He one a them Buffalo Soldiers?"

"Mescalero Apache. He came into the barracks one day and said, 'Let's go, white boy.' First Sergeant had given him permission. We spent most of the next six months in the desert south of the post, him trying to teach me, and me trying to learn."

"Well, he taught you good."

"Been fifteen years and more," Buckner said. "And I'm out of practice. When I was in France, we always pretty much knew where the Boche were, and for the past two years I've been mostly polishing the chair in my office with the seat of my pants."

As they passed the Model T, Carter said, "I'll have somebody run me out here with a can of gasoline and bring it in for her."

"Sure," Buckner said. "No wonder you're her favorite police officer."

"Yeah." Carter laughed. "I'm hell with all the little old white ladies in town."

"Makes you a good cop," Buckner said. "Folks got to trust you or they won't talk to you, and if they won't talk to you, you can't do your job."

They picked up their pace as they turned onto the Corinth road, and they were back in town within the hour. Walter Greene stood waiting for them at the door of his livery stable. "I'll take care of the horses, Buck," he said. He was watching Amos. "Looks like you got your hands full with old Amos here." He chuckled. "He musta been pretty drunk. Never known him to go holdin' up stores like that."

"Right, Walter." Buckner was used to Greene trolling for gossip. He ignored him. "Thanks. And send the bill on over to my office."

He and Carter escorted Monroe to the town hall, which sat in a small grassy square. Benches sat along all four sides of the square, and as usual they were occupied by the elderly men who came and went with the seasons, basking in the summer sun, disappearing during winter. Today several of them carried rolled umbrellas and looked warily at the sky.

Buckner glanced up at the town hall clock in its stubby tower. The original town hall in Corinth, Missouri, had been burned down by raiders in 1863, and he'd heard different views on which side they claimed to be fighting for. The new town hall, anyway, was squat and square, red brick, and three stories high. The truncated clock tower on the top remained unfinished, since the town had run out of money prior to completion, and the workmen refused to continue without getting paid. Buckner thought the tower diminished the effect of the entire building, but everybody said they were used to it by now, so regular attempts to raise funds to top it off always failed. The result was an ugly but functional building in the center of a small plaza in the center of town.

As the three men started up the steps, the big double doors banged open and a slim man in a lightweight, gray worsted suit and silver homburg charged out. He halted abruptly.

"Mornin', Mist' Elroy," said the prisoner.

"Mornin', Mister Dutton," said Officer Carter.

The man barely glanced at them; he merely nodded and focused his attention on Buckner. "I need to talk to you," he said.

"All right," Buckner said. "Go ahead and talk."

"Not here."

"What about my office?"

"Mullen says there's already somebody waiting in there to talk to you—obviously somebody more important than me."

"Or maybe somebody that got there first. Can you wait a while?"

"I've got a business to run, for the time being, anyway, and I don't have time to sit and cool my heels while you're chatting up the local bigwig." And Elroy Dutton pushed past them, strode down the stairs, and walked purposefully across the plaza.

"Gosh," said Carter as they escorted the prisoner into the building and down the stairs to the police department. "That was something."

"He seem pretty mad," Monroe agreed.

"He never comes over to this side of town to see me unless he's really stirred up," Buckner said. *And I'll just have to wait and see what it is*, he thought. He knew Dutton ran the most successful speakeasy in Corinth. It was over on the other side of the Iron Mountain train tracks—the black side of town—but that did not stop plenty of people heading across the tracks from the white side of town to sample Dutton's fare and enjoy the music provided by his band.

But since this made Dutton one of the town's most successful businessmen—black or white—Buckner understood. It also meant he believed he could demand the police chief's attention whenever it suited him. *Lord knows*, Buckner thought, *he's done it often enough.*

At the bottom of the stairs, Buckner pushed through two swinging doors that opened into the police department. Carter and the prisoner followed.

"That was quick," said Michael Mullen, the desk officer.

"Nothing to it," Carter said, grinning. He removed Monroe's handcuffs.

"You got a visitor," Mullen said. "In your office. It's Mr. Powers. From up at the mine."

"He'll have to wait," Buckner said.

"What're the charges?" Mullen's pen hovered over the open booking ledger.

"Well, there's assault on your dad over at the store. Amos pointed a pistol at him," Buckner said. "Caught him just as he was opening up this morning."

Carter took out the .32 and the three rounds he'd removed from it and put it all on the desk. He added, "And there's a count of robbery for cleaning out the till."

"There wasn't more'n five dollars in there," Monroe protested. He dug out a handful of bills and coins to make his point.

"Which you stole," Buckner said.

Monroe put the money on the desk next to the pistol.

"And then you stole Miz Longstreth's tin lizzie, and that's grand theft," Carter said. "And you pointed that popgun at her too."

Mullen was writing. "All right," he said. "That's two assaults with a deadly weapon and two robberies. Is my daddy all right?"

"'Course," said Monroe. "I wouldn't hurt your daddy. I just needed some money on account of I lost everything I had shootin' craps with some of the boys last night, and if I didn't have nuthin' to show my wife, she'd give me hell 'cause she don't like me gamblin'. An' I guess I musta been pretty drunk las' night."

"I guess so," Carter said.

"Fine, then," Mullen said. "Anything else?"

"That'll do to hold him," Buckner said. He had been a policeman long enough that the boneheaded reasons why some people committed crimes no longer surprised him. "I'll lock him up. Mullen, you get word to his wife that we've got him. Carter, you do the paperwork."

"Uh, Chief," Monroe said. "I'd just as soon you didn't tell my wife 'bout me shootin' craps, though. Since she gonna gimme hell for sure 'bout bein' drunk anyway."

Buckner ignored him and took the keys from the hook behind Mullen's desk. He led the prisoner around the corner to the hallway that ran past his office and on down to the department's three cells. There had once been a turnkey who spent all day perched on a stool, chewing tobacco and spitting into a coffee can, but after Buckner took over as chief of police, he decided a turnkey was a luxury the department could no longer afford. Only the stool remained.

"Can I get something to eat, Chief?" Monroe asked. "I ain't et since yesterday."

"Yeah, it'll take a while, though." Buckner closed and locked the door.

"Tha's all right," Monroe said, smiling sadly. "I be right here." And he sat on the bunk to wait.

Buckner went back around to the front desk. Mullen had finished entering the new prisoner and was handing Carter several report forms.

"You know, if you'd just leave a stack of these back there next to the typewriters, we wouldn't have to come to you every time we want one," Carter said.

"The way you all go through them," Mullen replied, "there wouldn't ever be any there and you'd be out here pestering me for more forms, only I wouldn't have any because I would have put them all back there."

"Did Powers say what he wanted?" Buckner asked as he returned.

"He wouldn't tell me. But he's pretty upset."

"All right. And what was Dutton going on about?"

"He wouldn't tell me anything either," replied Mullen. "Said he'd only talk to you. He did say something about somebody out to get him."

"Probably some woman's husband," Buckner said.

"No, it's about business I think."

"All right. I'll deal with him later. You find Amos's wife. I think she takes in laundry at their place. Have her bring him something to eat. Tell her we'll pick up the tab. And ask Judge Norden if he'll keep bail as low as possible so she can afford it. He's no good to her and the kids—or to us either—while he's locked up here. Just tell him it's a first offense, and with his family here in town, I don't believe he's going to run off before he's tried. If Judge Norden insists, I can explain it to him. Right now, though, I better see what Mr. Powers wants."

Buckner had known Josiah Powers for almost ten years. He hadn't known him well, but he had met him from time to time at the big round table in the back room at Coy's Drug Store, where Powers and the others sat and smoked cigars after lunch and made decisions about what should happen in Corinth. He had certainly seen Powers in all seasons and all kinds of weather and had never seen him break a sweat. The man always seemed calm and collected. His vested suits were always sharply pressed. His crisp shirts gleamed; his cuffs and high collars shone fresh and spotless. He never hurried, taking everything in measured strides, with careful consideration and carefully chosen words. His gray eyes, behind the rimless pince-nez, always glittered with self-confidence. In fact, Powers had a way of making Buckner feel scruffy and out of uniform, as though the commanding officer was inspecting the troops and he had just rolled out of his bunk after a hard night in town.

So Buckner was surprised to see a slightly wild-eyed Josiah Powers. He was hatless. Soot and dirt stained his badly wrinkled suit, his sweat-streaked face, his hands. He was pacing back and forth in Buckner's tiny office like a caged bear.

"I need help, Buck," he began at once. "And I need it pretty darned quick." His tie was undone, and one end of his collar stuck up into the unshaven skin of his neck. He didn't seem to notice.

"All right," Buckner said. "Do you want to set a spell and catch your breath? You look all in." He could smell smoke—and worse—coming off Powers in waves.

"No, I don't want to catch my breath. We've had a fire."

"At the mine? Underground or above?"

"No damage to the works, thank the Lord." Powers glanced upward. "It was that boarding house that sits just a few houses down from my office."

"Yes, sir, I know the one. Anybody hurt?"

"No … no." Powers shook his head impatiently.

"That's good news, anyway. What can I do for you?"

"I need you to come up with me right away. Right now."

"Sir, I'm mighty sorry to hear about the fire, but I don't see … What I mean is, Taylor and the mine are both way outside my jurisdiction. And I don't know anything about fire investigation. Have you contacted Sheriff Foote—"

Powers cut him off abruptly with the blade of one hand. "He's no good for this, Buck. Let's go upstairs and talk to Allgoode about it."

"All right, but I still don't see—"

"You have to come, Buck." Powers was almost pleading. He caught his breath and finished in a rush. "We found a dead body."

Buckner nodded. That was the other smell. He had recognized it immediately, and felt the tremor of the bad memories that came with it … memories of the mud and the stink of the trenches in France. Memories that made him, scarcely realizing he was doing it, reach one hand around to touch the back of the leg he had very nearly left on the wire fifty yards from the German lines.

"You said—"

"No, not from the fire. It was in the cellar, buried in the cellar wall." Powers was trembling now, his eyes blinking rapidly, his breathing shallow and harsh. Buckner was afraid the man might faint. "It was horrible. I've never …" He stopped in mid sentence.

"Who was it?" Buckner asked.

"I have no idea," Powers said. "We haven't touched it. Nobody has touched it. On my orders. "You've done this sort of thing before, Buck. Foote hasn't. Nobody around here has."

"Yes, sir," Buckner said. "I guess that's true. But I really …" He stopped because Powers was heading for the door.

"Come on," Powers said. "We'll go talk to Allgoode." The man was through the door and moving quickly down the hall. Buckner followed. As he passed Mullen at the front desk, he muttered, "Allgoode." Mullen nodded.

The Corinth police department occupied the entire basement of the town hall. The mayor's office was on the top floor, three flights up. The climb usually set Buckner's bad leg on fire, so he made it as seldom as possible and went slowly on those occasions when he couldn't avoid it. He preferred to let Mullen communicate with the mayor's office via the paperwork he was so good with. This meant Buckner could often avoid dealing directly with the mayor for days—even weeks—at a time, since Allgoode was as disinclined to come down as Buckner was to go up.

Mayor Allgoode had company. By the time Buckner arrived, Powers was already in the office speaking to both men.

If Powers was cool, Buckner thought of Charles Allgoode as moist. His face glowed with a light film of perspiration, and his palms were always sweaty. His smile glistened, eager to please. Corinth was a small town, and being its mayor was only a part-time job. Allgoode spent a few mornings a week in the office; he spent the rest of his time at his farm implement store. The store was the source of most of his income, and that was important to the men who ran Corinth—the men who ate lunch and smoked cigars in the back room at Coy's—since the office of mayor didn't pay much and could be filled only by someone who didn't really need the job. While in theory this was supposed to attract mayors who had a feeling of independence, in practice it meant the mayor was usually the sort of man who agreed with the men who ran Corinth, and so tended to stay in office for years, usually until he died—or stopped agreeing with the men who ran Corinth. This had not happened in living memory, however, so Allgoode was only the fourth mayor since the War Between the States. He was a young man, and at the rate he was going, Buckner figured he should make it to the middle of the century.

"You'll probably want to hear this, too, Fred." Powers spoke to a handsome man in a light gray suit and vest much like his own. The man was Fred Linderman, owner of the biggest bank in town, so of course he was a luncheon regular. It had originally been the German-American Bank when his father established it in 1857, but Linderman, in a burst of patriotic fervor, had changed the name to Corinth National Bank in 1917. He had simultaneously made adjustments in his own name. In the ten years since, both the bank and Fred Linderman—born Wilhelm Friedrich Lindermann and named after Kaiser Wilhelm I—had prospered.

"Hello, Joe. Hear what? You still working on saving souls up there? Can't be going to good, 'cause you look like hell." Linderman chuckled. He acknowledged Buckner's presence with a nod.

"Hear what, Josiah?" Allgoode echoed.

Buckner noticed that, as usual, the mayor was ignoring him. Communications from the mayor's office were almost entirely the work of his secretary, Marie. Allgoode's excuse was that it was more efficient, but Buckner realized it saved him from these face-to-face encounters, which always made him perspire more heavily than usual. Buckner suspected it was more than that, though. After all, selling farm equipment had to be a lot simpler than handling government issues. Persuading a man he needed the latest seed drill or disc harrow probably didn't make him sweat as much. Of course, with the nation's farmers still suffering from the post-war slump, he probably needed the extra income that mayoring provided.

"I've got a serious problem up at the mine," Powers was saying, "and I believe Buckner is just the man who can solve it for me. The way he solved Bill Bust's murder last year proves that. But he says it's not in his jurisdiction." Powers sighed and sank into the only remaining chair. In the company of men more like himself, Powers seemed to calm down considerably. He went on with his story. "Now I'll be the first one to admit that our operation up in Taylor isn't as big as some I could name over in Washington County, but small as we are, we're plenty important to the Company—and plenty important to the economy of Corinth."

Mayor Allgoode made small clucking sounds and waved his plump white hands. "We're all aware of the importance of your operation, Josiah, and the Company's always been a good neighbor. What is the problem, exactly?"

"Yes, spell it out, Joe," Linderman added. "I'm sure we can spare Buck for a couple of days. That is, as long as we don't have a crime spree or anything. Right, Charles?" He chuckled some more.

"Yes," Allgoode said. "Things have been pretty quiet since the bank robbery—"

"Attempted bank robbery," Linderman corrected with a raised finger. "Attempted."

"Yes, of course. Attempted. Totally unsuccessful, thanks to our fine police department. Right Buck?"

Buckner smiled and nodded. The attempt had cost the life of one of Linderman's employees as well as the lives of the robbers. Buckner briefly considered reminding Linderman of that fact. Instead, he waited for them to quit dancing around and get to the point. *They all seem to think I'm an experienced crime investigator,* Buckner thought. They really had no idea what a deputy sheriff or a police chief did. As a deputy, he'd spent most of the time serving writs, transporting prisoners, following up complaints about wandering livestock, and doing paperwork. Things had not changed much since he had taken over as chief. One way or another, though, he was pretty sure he would be going up to Taylor to see about this dead body. The Company's lead mining and smelting operation in Taylor did its banking through Fred Linderman's bank. The railroad spur that connected the mine and smelter with the outside world joined the Iron Mountain in Corinth. Tools, spare parts, stock for the company store—all came through local firms. The possibility of Allgoode ignoring the request for help was so slim as to be invisible.

"Maybe if you told us what the problem is, Josiah," Linderman suggested gently.

"Yes, yes, of course." Powers collected his thoughts and then continued. "You see, we've found a dead body."

"What?"

"Where? How? Who is it?"

Powers told his story. "I want to emphasize," he concluded, "that I'd like to keep this a local matter."

Allgoode and Linderman understood at once. "Of course," Linderman said.

"No point in troubling New York with a matter like this." Allgoode stated the obvious. The Company had mining operations across the United States and Latin America, and a regional office in St. Louis, but headquarters was in New York City. The late war, which had closed down so much of Europe's mining, had brought unprecedented profits to the Company. Buckner knew Josiah Powers had gained a reputation for running the Taylor branch quietly and efficiently, and he suspected that Powers had no intention of remaining there forever. He had larger ambitions, and didn't want this corpse raising questions about his fitness for high position in the Company.

"What about the county sheriff?" Buckner said. The others turned to look at him, surprised at this interruption. "After all," he continued, "Taylor is an unincorporated village under the sheriff's jurisdiction. That's the only reason I was up there back in nineteen' ... back when Elmer Aubuchon was sheriff and I was his deputy down here."

"I don't know ..." Allgoode began.

"Sheriff Foote's pretty busy right now," Linderman said.

"Yes, running for state assembly," Powers added.

"And he's never appointed a deputy to take over the substation down here since ... uh, since that new deputy ... uh ..." Allgoode struggled to remember.

"Roy Kelly," Buckner said.

"Yes, of course, Roy Kelly. Got himself shot a while back," Allgoode said.

"I doubt he ever will," Linderman said. "With all the deep-dyed Democrats and unreconstructed Rebels down this end of the county, I don't expect he's interested in wasting resources where it won't win him many votes."

"He's got other deputies," Buckner said.

"They're all out campaigning," Powers said. "And he's never in his office these days. Won't answer the wires I've sent him. I tried telephoning right away, soon as we found the body, and I'll try him again, but I honestly don't think he's the man to handle this. Buck is, though. Besides, it's not as though Taylor is a long way off. He could leave one of his men in charge here, and he'd only be a telephone call away."

"Excellent idea, Joe," Allgoode said, glancing at Linderman, who gave a nod of confirmation. "Mullen, perhaps, or Durand, although I would personally prefer Mullen. He's so efficient. Always sends me the neatest reports. Never a mistake in them." He smiled happily. "What about it, Buck? Be another feather in your cap if you solve this—when you solve it—and you'd be doing the town a real service. And after all, that's pretty much the chief of police's job, the way I see it."

"Shotwell," Buckner said.

"Shotwell?" Linderman responded.

"You mean, to be in charge while you're gone?" Allgoode was astonished.

"Yes."

"But ..." the mayor continued. "He's a ... I mean ..."

"Shotwell," Buckner repeated. "I need Mullen behind the desk. Shotwell's my best officer, a natural leader. The other's look to him anyway, so he's just the man for the job."

"Buck, I know you've always said we have to have Negroes on the police force—"

"There are Negroes on the forces in St. Louis and Kansas City," Buckner said.

"Yes, yes, I understand that."

"I'm just doing my best to make Corinth a progressive, forward-looking town."

"And we appreciate that, Buck, we really do." Here the mayor got supporting nods from Linderman and Powers.

"They live here and they pay taxes here, so they ought to have cops here too," Buckner said. He knew he was just repeating the argument Elroy Dutton had presented when he had first suggested that Buckner hire black officers. But he also knew it was as good a reason as any to give it a try.

"Yes, of course."

"All very good points, Buck," Fred Linderman put in, smiling his banker's smile. "But you keep assigning them to patrol over on this side of the tracks."

"And you've got white officers patrolling over there," Allgoode added. "You wouldn't believe the complaints I get about that from the business owners over there. They say white policemen scare away their customers."

Buckner opened his mouth to reply, but Powers cut him off. "If we could postpone this discussion of Buck's hiring practices, I've got a dead body to deal with."

"Of course, Joe, of course." Linderman's voice was calm, soothing.

"And, uh ..." Allgoode struggled with his confusion. "Of course, you'll be staying here in town at night, won't you, Buck? Of course you will. And only driving up to Taylor to look into this, uh ... this matter during the day, right?"

"I guess so." Buckner looked at Powers, who nodded reassuringly to the mayor. Buckner continued. "And don't worry. Officer Mullen will still be sending those nice, neat reports."

Powers was up and moving briskly. "Thanks, Charles, I appreciate it. Fred, be seeing you. Come on, Buck. Let's go." And he was out the door. Buckner gave Allgoode and Linderman a brief smile and followed along. Marie, Allgoode's secretary, looked up from the fingernail she was buffing and grinned at Buckner as they rushed through the reception area. He winked back without breaking stride. Powers was already talking as Buckner caught up with him at the top of the stairs. "Take one of the police department's Fords," he was saying. "That way you'll have plenty of freedom to move around. We'll set you up in a spare office down the hall from me—telephone, all that." Powers paused and looked over his shoulder before continuing softly, almost whispering. "Of course, Buck, since this will be outside your normal, ah ... purview, shall we say, I feel you should be compensated appropriately."

"We can talk about that later, Mr. Powers. Let's see if I can solve your problem first." Buckner hesitated and then went on. "I want to warn you, though."

"About what?" Powers was rebuttoning his collar and restoring his necktie to its proper place.

"Mr. Powers, I haven't conducted all that many serious investigations. And that thing last year with Mr. Bust—I honestly just got lucky. I do know that these investigations sometimes take you off in funny directions, but once they get rolling, they kind of get a momentum of their own. Makes them hard to stop."

"What makes you think I want to stop it? I need to get this resolved—quietly and right now."

"Yes, sir. I'll do what I can. I just wanted you to know."

"Fine. Let's get to it."

Powers led the way downstairs. The two men shook hands and parted at the front doors. Buckner watched Powers walk down the steps to the automobile waiting for him in the no-parking zone in front of the town hall. Buckner continued down to the department.

"If he thinks this isn't going to get to the New York office, he's in for a big surprise," Buckner said. Mullen nodded, said nothing, waited. Buckner looked around and said, "Where is everybody?"

"Carter's finishing up the arrest report on Amos and then he's going home to bed, since he's been on nights all week. Shotwell's back in the squad room getting ready to go out on patrol. Everybody else is on the street."

"Right. Get them in."

Buckner went to the squad room. It had been a storage room until Buckner told Mullen to get it cleaned out months ago. He had gotten right to it, moving boxes of files, with Willis Johnson's help, to a dusty corner of the attic. He then installed typewriters he had bought secondhand up in De Soto and refurbished himself, plus a table and some chairs scavenged from other rooms in the building that nobody seemed to be using. All this so the officers wouldn't keep using his desk to write up the reports Buckner had begun insisting everybody complete.

Shotwell was pecking away at one of the typewriters as Buckner entered. The smell of dust and paper was overlaid with the smell of stale coffee and cigarette smoke. Half-empty cups and overflowing ashtrays littered every level surface.

"One thing, Buck," Shotwell said. "Did you explain to the mayor that I'd be taking over, or is this going to be a surprise?"

"I told him. And Fred Linderman too. He was there at the time."

"And they didn't object to a Negro running things?" Shotwell was skeptical.

"Nope." Buckner grinned innocently. He had hired Shotwell and Carter because, as the new chief of police, he needed officers. He needed officers because he had fired most of the department's incumbents for incompetence or corruption, and then the rest had left voluntarily. Elroy Dutton had suggested Shotwell and Carter, pointing to their army experience. That was true enough, as far as it went, but Buckner suspected Dutton wanted them to patrol "his" side of Corinth, where they would show him their appreciation for having regular employment in the struggling postwar economy. When Buckner instead assigned them to the white side of town, and white officers to patrol across the tracks, Dutton and the other black business owners had been just as upset as the white business owners. Black men in blue uniforms brought back bad memories of Reconstruction times, especially to people who had supported the South.

Buckner had simply shrugged and explained that qualified white men had not exactly rushed to join the new department, and that everybody should just get used to it. And, in fact, they were getting used to it … mostly. Buckner's predecessor had filled the department with thugs—bullies with guns and clubs and the itch to use them. Nobody had been sorry to see them go. And if some of the new batch were the wrong color, they were also honest and respectful and seemed genuinely interested in helping people on both sides of town. That made it easier for people to accept them, or at least put up with them, and that made it easier for the new men to do their jobs. As far as Buckner was concerned, that was all that mattered.

"All right," Shotwell said. "Things have been real quiet around here lately. There shouldn't be any problems."

"Fine," Buckner said. "Finish up that report you were working on. I'm going to find Peck and head on up to Taylor. I'll be back home for supper and then back up there tomorrow, most likely. Everybody else, go back to work."

When they were alone, Buckner asked Mullen, "What was Dutton all steamed up about?"

"All he said to me was something about somebody trying to run him out of business. When I told him you weren't here, he stormed out, like he does."

"That's just Dutton. He'll calm down after a while."

"I think it's pretty serious this time, Buck," Mullen insisted.

"What's serious about it? Dutton can usually take care of himself, and if he can't, Buster can."

"That's just it. Buster can't."

"Why not?"

"Buster can't take care of anything because Buster can't get out of bed."

"What? What are you talking about?"

"Buster's laid up in bed because somebody beat him half to death."

"How come I'm just hearing about it?"

"Because it just happened," Mullen said. He showed Buckner a report form filled in with Durand's bad typing. "It was last night, after closing," Mullen went on. "I was going to tell you about it first thing, but you were already after Amos."

Buster was Elroy Dutton's constant companion. He was big and strong and intimidating. His job was to make sure everybody drinking and dancing at Elroy Dutton's establishment had a good time without getting overly exuberant. Buckner, who sometimes liked to stop in for a drink, had more than once seen Buster quiet a rowdy customer with a single blow and had once seen him take two men by the collar, one in each hand, and hurl them bodily through the door and down the stairs. The idea of somebody beating Buster half to death was startling.

"Where is he? At home?"

"At his sister's. This was all just last night, but you and Carter were out chasing Amos first thing."

"All right," Buckner said. "That is serious, but I can't do anything about it right now. I'll go talk to him first chance I get, but you tell Shotwell I said he was to start poking around, find out what's going on at Dutton's. Oh, and shift Carter to that side of town for a while too. See what he can pick up."

"And if Dutton comes back, I'll just tell him we're looking into it, right?"

"Right."

 **2**

Buckner left the building and crossed the town square, passing the artifacts that celebrated the town's version of history. The cannon was a relic of the War for Southern Independence; the statue represented a soldier in the War to End All Wars. The former had been his father's war, the latter his own. Thinking about either—or both—made Buckner angry in ways he still could not articulate and for reasons he could not fathom. The fact that neither had lived up to its name, and that neither had achieved the goal set by the men in charge, probably had a lot to do with it. Anyway, he generally tried to avoid thinking about it, but there those things always were, the cannon and the statue, and he saw them every time he entered or left his place of work. And there they would stay, lest anybody forget the honored dead and the noble cause.

Buckner sometimes wondered if maybe he'd gone over with the American army in 1917 instead of the Canadians in 1915 he'd feel differently. And maybe if his father had worn blue instead of gray. Would any of that have made a difference? Would that statue bother him less if he didn't have the constant pain in his leg? Somehow he doubted it.

Coy's Drug Store sat prominently on the town square facing the town hall. Inside, there were sundries and a long lunch counter behind the big front window; the dining room was behind a curtained archway off to the side. Buckner didn't go inside; instead he kept going around to the back. A rickety wooden staircase slanted up the blank back wall to the second floor. He climbed and knocked on the door at the top. Nobody answered, but he knew that didn't necessarily mean anything, so he pushed in. The office and the examination room off to the left were both empty. Buckner turned and walked out. Back at the bottom of the stairs, he thought a moment. There was one other place to try. He headed across town. The new sign over the door said Corinth Café, and the place was under new management since he had cancelled out the former owners in a prolonged and deadly encounter several years ago. Now it was run by the same folks who operated the Corinthian Hotel. They were locals, interested in peace and quiet along with profit. And they knew Jeff Peck's habits and preferences.

A bright and sunny restaurant occupied the front of the building. A perky young waitress was moving among the clean checkered tablecloths as Buckner walked in. She welcomed him with a bright, questioning smile. He smiled back and kept walking, barely attracting the notice of the few diners enjoying an early lunch. He pushed on through a door at the back.

In the gloomy little room, several pairs of blurred and bloodshot eyes contemplated Buckner briefly before dropping to concentrate on glasses of pale amber liquid. The one drinker who did not look at him was the one he wanted. Buckner shook the man's shoulder roughly, and the gray head came up suddenly from folded arms. Empty eyes contemplated him, tiny sparks glowing from somewhere deep down in darkness. Thomas Jefferson Peck, MD, had slid into a pit while working miracles in an aid station a few yards behind the front lines on the Western Front. He had saved the lives and limbs of a lot of Second Division marines, but he had lost himself along the way. Now he drank whatever it took to put him under, saw a handful of patients, and occasionally looked at dead bodies for the Corinth police department.

"Who is it this time?" His voice was rough and harsh. He didn't try to smooth it. "And where?"

"Don't know who, for sure, but it's up in Taylor." Buckner glanced at the other drinkers. They were looking elsewhere—anywhere—trying hard not to notice … not to know what was going on. After all, that was why they were there. Buckner knew them all and was embarrassed by that.

"Well, I haven't been to Taylor in a while." Peck shook off Buckner's helping hand and got to his feet.

Buckner led the doctor out the back door. After a quick stop to pick up the doctor's medical bag, they headed across to the lot behind the town hall, where the police department parked its two Model T Fords. Buckner had been pestering the town to provide a shed—or at least a roof over their heads—so he wouldn't have to waste time brushing off snow in winter, but they still sat in the open. The economy had slid into a sharp downturn after the war, and if everybody else was recovering nicely, farming and mining were still in trouble, and towns like Corinth, which served farmers and miners, suffered with them.

Buckner had heard Ford was about to come out with a new auto, the Model A, sometime before the end of the year. It was supposed to be able to hit speeds of 65 miles per hour, maybe more, which seemed pretty fast to Buckner. The flivvers could hit 45 going downhill with a tailwind, and that was about as fast as he ever wanted to go. Anyway, they were expected to cost $400 and more, so he didn't expect the town would be coming up with that kind of money any time soon.

Peck got in on the passenger side while Buckner set the spark and throttle and cranked up the flivver. The new models were supposed to have electric starters, like most autos. Buckner would believe that when he saw it.

As he drove out of town, he explained the situation.

Peck laughed harshly. "So Josiah Powers persuaded our mayor to let the Company borrow Corinth's very own Sherlock Holmes to solve their problem for them, because the last thing Corinth wants is for the Company to have a problem. It might pack up and leave, and then where would we be?"

new Studebaker. As the Ford lurched to a shuddering halt, Jeff Peck suddenly sat bolt upright, staring around wild eyed for an instant before he realized where he was. He slumped back into his seat. Buckner ignored him and stepped down from the auto. Even here, well away from the remains of the fire, the mixed odors of burnt wood and corpse flesh stung his nostrils.

He went up to the porch and through the office screen door. Peck got out and trailed along, bag in hand. Powers' secretary, a bright, smiling young man with slicked down hair neatly parted in the middle, rose to greet them. He wore a high, stiff collar and a black suit and was sweating in the still office air. He knocked once on an interior door, opened it, and gestured grandly. Buckner and Peck walked through.

Powers was also on his feet. He had cleaned up and looked his usual self. Apparently the black suit and high collar were the uniform of the day. No fan in here either. Powers, the cool man, could have used it.

"Buck, thanks for coming so quickly," Powers said. "Welcome, Dr. Peck. I really appreciate this."

"Wait till you get my bill," Peck muttered.

"Doctor," Powers said, undeterred, "if you can clear this up quickly and quietly, I'll pay whatever you charge without a word of complaint. This is very serious business."

"Then we ought to go take a look," Buckner said.

"Right. Get right to it. That's the spirit." Powers led them out. "No calls, Tom. And have Will Big Foot meet us there."

The town looked deserted. From up the hill came the sounds of the smelter and the sharp burnt-metal odors. Women's faces peered from behind curtains. And if the streets were empty, Buckner knew that deep in the ground under their feet, gangs of men labored at the rock face. "Still working twelve-hour shifts?" he asked.

"Of course. Company policy. All that nonsense about the eight-hour day was so much socialist claptrap. Immigrants or Americans, most workers wouldn't know what to do with all that free time, and they'd just end up wasting their pay checks on cheap booze and cheaper women."

"So you're really doing them a favor," Peck said.

Buckner just shook his head. Peck actually had been a member of the Socialist Party of America and, as far as Buckner knew, still was, though since the arrests and deportations during the Wilson administration, the Party scarcely existed anymore. He suspected Powers was unaware of that fact.

"That's one way to look at it," Powers agreed. "Of course, that doesn't keep them from complaining. And trying to bring in the unions." He smiled in satisfaction. "We kept the Western Federation of Miners out, and the Industrial Workers of the World—the Wobblies—so I don't expect any trouble from the United Mine Workers. With Coolidge in the White House, we haven't had to worry about any so-called reformers from Washington giving us trouble. I expect that state of affairs will continue when Hoover wins next month." He chuckled. "No, gentlemen, things are going about as well as they could go."

"Except for this dead body," Peck said.

Powers frowned and said nothing.

They stopped at the boarding house site. All that was left of the building were the cellar walls, standing between a company storage shed on one side and a standard company house on the other. Both of these buildings showed signs of scorching and were dripping water. The firefighters had cleared the cellar. Blackened and soaked rubble lay piled around the edges, and workers were adding more as they continued to clear the cellar. Buckner nodded to the two company guards and spoke quietly. "How you doing?" Kelson and Garber were old acquaintances.

"Just fine, Buck. How's being chief of police?" said Garber. He was missing part of one ear. According to information Buckner had picked up several years back, he had left Pinkerton's under a cloud. He looked as if he had helped put out the fire. His clothes were rumpled and soot smeared, his sleeves were rolled up, and his jacket was slung over one shoulder.

"It has its moments."

"I'll bet it does," offered Garber, "and I'll bet this ain't one of 'em."

"No," Buckner agreed. "Not right now it isn't."

"I didn't know you fellows knew each other," Powers said.

"Oh, yes, sir," said the other man, Kelson. His hands were shoved in his pockets, and his black alpaca suit looked as if it had been cleaned and pressed at least once this year. All Buckner knew about him was that he had been a policeman in Memphis and Little Rock. "We knew Buck here way back when he was a shiny new deputy sheriff and we cleaned out that nest of Wobblies back in nineteen, ain't that right, Buck?"

"Pretty much."

"I remember reading the report about that," Powers said. "The one left by my ... ah, predecessor."

"You ain't got nothin' to worry 'bout, Mister Powers," Kelson was saying. "If Buck here can't figure this one out, ain't nobody can."

Buckner gave Kelson a quick nod and made his way carefully around the piles of sodden lumber and down the sodden stone steps to the cellar floor. He hesitated at the last step. The dirt floor had absorbed most of the water from the fire hoses, but several inches of muddy water remained. The company firefighters all wore high rubber boots. Buckner looked at his shoes, sighed, and stepped into the cellar. Peck followed. Powers nodded, and the firefighters stood to one side. He and the two guards looked on.

The cellar occupied only a portion of the ground under the house. It was about twelve feet square. The charred remains of wooden stairs led up to what must have been the kitchen above. The walls were barely five feet high, so anyone working down there would have had to stoop over. The walls themselves were made of large, river-smoothed stones held in place by mortar. Some of the mortar had crumbled, and several of the stones had cracked in the heat of the blaze. About a foot and a half above the packed earth floor, three had fallen out, releasing their hold on a pale arm and causing it to flop into view. Buckner felt dizzy ... closed his eyes for a moment. The arm hung suspended, palm up, a supplicating gesture to which nobody responded. He knelt and breathed slowly through his mouth until the dizziness passed. He glanced up. Nobody seemed to have noticed.

"Shouldn't we take it out of there?" Powers asked.

"Not just yet," Buckner said. He gestured at the watery floor. "No place to put it."

Another man joined them to watch. He was bandy legged and barrel chested, with dark copper skin and thick, straight black hair. His face, hands, and clothing were smeared with soot.

"Will Big Foot's fire chief up here," Josiah Powers said. Buckner nodded and pulled himself up. He did not offer a grimy hand to shake.

"Chief Chief, we call him" Garber said, and laughed. Nobody joined him.

"The place was gone by the time we got here," Big Foot explained. "We mostly worked on saving the buildings around it—you know, keeping the roofs wet so's the fire wouldn't spread. Then, when the building collapsed, we put the hoses on what was left. That's when it happened … a little after. The fire was out, everything was cooling down, and my men were pulling the wreckage out, cleaning up … anything that would burn, you know. And some of them stones had cracked and fell out like you can see there, and that arm just plopped out." Big Foot shuddered visibly, blinking away the memory. "The fire was out and we were just wetting everthing down, but I made sure they kept the hoses away from that arm and that section of the wall, you know, so's they wouldn't make things worse, and then they cleared out most of the mess. So it's pretty much like we found it."

"All right," Buckner said. "Thanks."

"That all?" Big Foot glanced at Powers.

"I think so, for now," Buckner answered. "I'm going to have more questions, though. You gonna be around?'

"Oh, yeah." Big Foot aimed a thumb over his shoulder. "Up the hill there." But he stayed to watch.

Buckner turned to examine the wall. Peck was waiting impatiently, his hands in his jacket pockets. Buckner pulled at the stones, and they came away easily until he had enlarged the hole enough to see the entire body. He took out his notebook and began jotting things down, making sketches. After several minutes, he went to the Ford and returned with his camera. He shot up an entire roll of film.

Peck had stepped back and was standing with the firefighters, smoking a cigarette and staring into space. Buckner looked at him, eyebrows raised. Peck ignored him and continued smoking, so Buckner went back to work. While he worked, Peck finished his cigarette, stubbed it out, and then crumbled the remains, letting the tobacco fall away as he rolled the paper into a tiny ball and put it in his pocket. "I can't do anything here. I'm going to have to take the body back into town for a real examination," he said. He looked up at Powers. "You got a flatbed truck, or a wagon big enough to handle this? And blankets. Several blankets."

Powers nodded, sent Garber to the office with a gesture, and then turned back.

Buckner turned to Peck. "What can you tell me at this stage?"

"Next to nothing, like I said," Peck said. "Well, one thing, it's a woman. And judging by what I can see on the hand and arm, I think the body has been immersed in acid for a bit, just can't tell how long."

"Acid?" Buckner said.

"Yes, I think so. Just a guess, of course, until I can get a closer look," Peck replied. He said to Powers, "Do you have acid around here in large quantities?"

"Of course. It's a by-product of the smelting process. But we usually put it in containers—big steel drums—and resell it when we've accumulated a certain amount."

"Do you keep track?" Buckner asked.

"Not very close track. Just that when we get enough drums of the stuff to fill a freight car, we ship it out. We just count the drums."

"Where do you ship it?" Buckner continued.

"The Company maintains a transshipment station in St. Louis. I honestly don't know where it goes after that, since the Company sends it wherever it can get the best price for it. I can put you in touch with the man who runs the station, if you like."

"No point," Buckner said. "It's the acid that didn't get that far that I'm interested in." He said to Peck, "Can you tell how long it's been in there?"

"No. I told you. I need to take it to town."

"And you're sure it's acid?"

"No," Peck snapped.

"All right," Buckner said. "I'm going to want to have a look at where you store the stuff before you send it to St. Louis, Mr. Powers."

"Certainly. Talk to Tom. He'll tell you."

"We'll take the body back to town," Buckner said. "I'll get my photos developed and put my notes together. But right now, I need some more information."

"All right," Powers said.

"Has anybody reported a woman missing?"

Powers turned to Kelson and Garber. They just shook their heads.

"Nobody's said anything to me," Kelson said.

"Me neither," said Garber.

"All right," Buckner said. He had not expected much from them. They knew their job was to protect Company property, keep an eye peeled for union agitators, and not much else.

"I'm going to have to talk to the people who were living here," Buckner said. "Do you know who they were?"

"Not personally," Powers said. "The Company didn't own the land or the building. It belongs to Bob Charboneau. His family's lived around here for years. Everybody who lived here was here only temporarily, waiting for regular company accommodations to become available. There're always transients here ... natural in a place like this. We try to keep it to a minimum, but you can't really stop it completely. My wife and I actually stayed here for a few days when I first came here, while my wife was supervising the preparations of our new home. That was nineteen twenty. In any case, I believe most of the people who lived in the building had some connection with the Company. Tom will have their names."

"Do you know were Mr. Charboneau is now?"

Powers shook his head. Buckner turned to the two policemen.

"I don't know for sure," Kelson said. "His wife's sister lives down the street in a company house."

Powers said, "I've got you set up in an unoccupied office down the hall from me. I'll have Kelson go get Charboneau and bring him in."

"No need," Buckner said. "I'll go down there and talk to him."

"All right, if that's the way you want to do it."

Kelson pointed. "On the left about fifty yards down. Number twenty-six."

"Thanks."

As Buckner turned to leave, a dusty Ford truck rumbled stiffly down from behind the office building and stopped in the street. People had drifted out of the houses and stood watching now, curious but not too curious, keeping well back, talking softly to each other, nodding and frowning. Garber got out of the truck with a pile of blankets. Buckner recognized them immediately. They were olive drab wool with *US* stenciled on them.

"Government's unloading them cheap," Powers explained as Garber dumped them in front of Dr. Peck. Then everyone stepped back and turned to him expectantly.

"I can't do this alone," Peck said.

Buckner moved over to where Peck stood. Kelson and Garber looked hopelessly at Powers. He shrugged and gestured for them to follow; then he folded his arms and stayed where he was.

It was crowded in the remains of the cellar, and Peck demanded great care. They pulled out more stones, enlarging the hole. The body lay flat on its back. They brought it out—the body of a woman, barely covered with ragged shreds of a dress, exposed skin coated with what looked like wax, facial features blurred, traces of long blond hair sparse on the pale skull. They wrapped it in a blanket. Buckner remained in the cellar as the others carried the body out into the sunshine and put it on the bed of the truck. Everybody was breathing carefully and trying not to stare. Powers and the fire chief moved away and got into a close, quiet conversation. As Buckner returned his attention to the hole in the wall, he noticed a single high-heeled shoe wedged between a couple of rocks. He pulled it out and put it to one side and then walked up the short flight of stairs to the truck. When he was sure everything was secure, he closed the truck's tailgate.

The others were still gathered around the truck. Kelson was staring at his hands with a kind of disgusted horror. Peck took one of them, turned it over, and peered closely at it. Startled, Kelson snatched it back.

"You might want to have somebody take a look at that," Peck said. "You might have a cancer there. You keep on worrying it, it won't get any better."

"Mind your own damned business," Kelson growled. He made a move to shove his hands into his pockets, thought better of it, and walked away.

"Use the washroom inside," Powers said softly, and the doctor and the two policemen went up the steps and into the office building. Buckner continued to poke through the charred rubble. After a while, the three men returned. Peck opened his bag and took out a large brown bottle. He removed the glass stopper and poured clear liquid onto his hands. The liquid bubbled and hissed on his skin. He rubbed his hands together briskly and shook them dry. He corked the bottle and replaced it in the bag. Then he got into the truck on the passenger side, leaned against the door, and went to sleep with his bag on his lap.

"Garber, you drive," Powers said. "And come straight back."

"Right." Garber sketched a brief salute and climbed into the cab. The truck rolled slowly down the road to Corinth.

"Am I still on guard duty?" Kelson asked. He was watching the truck, his hands back in his pockets.

CHRISTOPHER C. GIBBS

"Yes," Powers said. "Answer any questions Chief Buckner has and keep people away from here." He gestured at the onlookers. "I don't want anybody poking around in there."

"I don't think you've got anything to worry 'bout on that score," said Kelson.

Powers nodded curtly and turned to Buckner. "You need anything, just tell Kelson here, or see Tom in the office." He walked away. The fire chief headed back up the hill. Buckner looked at Kelson and shrugged. Kelson gazed off down the street and then took the makings from his pocket and built a smoke.

"Can you get me a flashlight?" Buckner asked.

"Got a penlight," Kelson said, reaching for a pocket.

"Something bigger, I think," Buckner said.

Kelson slowly lit his cigarette and walked up to the office. He returned shortly with a foot-long light.

"That ought to do the trick," Buckner said. "Thanks." He knelt carefully and began examining the hole that had held the body. He removed some more of the big, round, river-smooth stones. The soil behind the stones had been dug out to make room for the body. It had probably been scattered across the cellar's dirt floor. The body had then been put inside and the stones replaced. They had been cemented in. Buckner looked around the cellar. In a far corner lay a half-empty sack of cement.

How long would a job like that take? Buckner wondered. *Could you do it in the hours of darkness? And wouldn't somebody have noticed?*

Buckner was in the hole up to his shoulders. He found traces of white powder and sniffed at them. Lye. Probably to mask the smell. Buckner knew it was commonly used in out houses for the same purpose. He also knew its effect lasted only for a while. Buckner remembered something else—the insects that feasted on, nested in, reproduced in corpses—millions of them, or so it had always seemed to him, swarming in and out of wounds, eyes, gaping mouths. He stopped for a minute, pulled himself out of the hole, and sat on an overturned box with his back against the stone wall, resting, trying to clear his mind of those images. Kelson

| 36 |

looked at him curiously but got no response. Finally Buckner got up and went back into the hole. No insects here. Was that because of the lye? Because the body might have been covered with acid? Maybe Peck would know. He wasn't even sure whether it mattered. It was just odd.

He found an earbob lying in the dirt at the back of the hole. It was made of cheap wire and set with a fake pearl. He put it in his pocket and went back into the hole. He found a second shoe to match the first, and nothing else … no other clothing. That seemed odd too. He pulled himself to his feet and sat on the remains of the stairs to examine the shoes. They were cheaply made. The thin leather was dry and peeling, probably from the heat of the fire, but the soles showed almost no wear at all.

He put them aside and prowled through the rubble that remained in the cellar. There wasn't much to find. Big Foot's men had removed most of the mess. But he did find the remains of several pieces of luggage, including a large steamer trunk, plus a set of golf clubs reduced to their metal heads, and the metal frame of the bag that held them. There were several badly charred barrels, a set of old horseshoes, a gas-powered concrete mixer, and the gaunt, twisted skeletons of several umbrellas. A pair of heavy rubber gloves lay partially melted in a lump by one of the barrels, any one of which was big enough to hold a body. He also found three large demijohns, their basket coverings burnt black, the glass cloudy and cracked. He sniffed at them and detected a burnt metal odor.

Junk—all of it—and none of it reveled to him anything about the corpse that had similarly been discarded. *Did somebody think that woman was junk, too?* Buckner thought. *Something to be used and thrown away? The steamer trunk could have held a body too.* It was charred and smelled of smoke and that was all.

Buckner recorded everything in his notebook, just as Elmer Aubuchon had taught him to do on his very first day as deputy. Even though he hadn't been a policeman very long, he knew enough to know that he couldn't tell at this stage what was important and what wasn't. And there had been plenty of times during other cases when he'd had to retrace his steps to pick up something left lying around that hadn't seemed to matter at the time. So now he recorded everything.

Buckner put the shoes in the Ford and gave Kelson back the flashlight before going into the office. Tom directed him to the washroom. Hard scrubbing removed most of the soot from his hands and face, but his shirt and trousers would never be completely clean again. And he knew they would always smell of dead body. To him, anyway. But he wanted to interview the residents of the boarding house before they started sharing—and embroidering—their stories about the fire. They would have to put up with the smell.

Still, Buckner wondered, *wouldn't somebody notice a person trundling a steamer trunk or carrying big demijohns around town? Maybe not if it was all done in the middle of the night shift, when things were dead quiet.*

He headed down the street.

The village of Taylor spread across the hillside below the mine and smelter works. Homes the Company had built for its workers before the turn of the century lined both sides of the single street like uniformed soldiers. Each house was four rooms on the one floor with outhouse behind and tiny yard in front. Some of the residents had put up picket fences and planted flowers or vegetables; other had simply let the grass grow thick and the leaves and trash pile up. The dust and soot generated by the Company's operations colored everything in the same gray tone.

Worn paths led off both sides of the main street to other buildings, some little more than empty halls where gangs of unmarried miners slept in shifts. Here and there was a ramshackle building out of which men sold liquor or women's bodies, sometimes both. Farther along, the chat piles marked the boundaries of Taylor. These immense piles of dead rock had always seemed to Buckner to symbolize the town they loomed over. They were what was left after the Company had squeezed all the wealth out of the earth ... the residue heaped uselessly on any patch of bare ground. The people had always seemed to him the same, squeezed of anything that could be turned into money. Taylor was, in short, a grim, nasty little place at the end of a dirt road, a community that existed for no other reason than service to corporate profit. If the lead played out, would Taylor survive? Buckner had seen similar places in Arizona and New Mexico—abandoned copper or silver mining towns that were little more than collapsing houses lining a single dirt road, crumbling skeletons of machinery. He suspected a similar fate awaited Taylor.

Beyond the village rose the rocky, brush-choked hills in whose folds lay scattered farms, isolated homes, and the tough, hard, isolated people who lived and worked there ... remnants of a migration that reached back to the Celtic sanctuaries at the fringes of the British Isles long before our Revolution. Some of those people, Buckner knew, were his kin. They would remain in these hills long after the mine and the village of Taylor had sunk back into the earth.

Buckner stopped at the Charboneau house and climbed the stoop to knock on the door. A heavy, middle-aged woman in black answered. She must have recognized him, because she frowned slightly, opened the door wider, and stepped back, pointing.

"He's in there, Deputy."

Buckner smiled and entered, hat in hand. He always tried to smile when talking to people about crimes they might have been involved in, or might know something important about. He believed he had a warm, pleasant smile that put people at their ease. He was wrong about this, but no one ever corrected him.

He followed the pointing finger into the parlor. A man sat rocking slowly, glaring up at him. He wore a long coat over a nightshirt, which was stuffed into baggy trousers. With him was another heavy woman in black, looking so much like the first that Buckner turned to stare.

"Yeah," said the man. "Twins." He had bedroom slippers on his feet. "Bob Charboneau." He held out a hand. "I'm married to this one here, name of Joan. That one's Jean."

"How do. I'm not a deputy anymore. I'm chief of police down in Corinth. I need to talk to you about the fire."

"All the same to me," Charboneau said.

"Fire nuthin'," said Joan. "I hear they found a whole passel of dead people down in the cellar. That's what ye'r here about."

Jean nodded and left the room. In a moment, Buckner could hear kitchen sounds.

"Just one body," Buckner said. "And we'll get to that. Right now I want to start with the fire."

"Well, yo're wastin' yer time, 'cause we don't know nuthin' 'bout that fire," said Joan.

"Don't know nuthin' 'bout no dead people neither," said Charboneau.

"Do you have any idea how the fire got started?"

"No! I jus' tole you," Joan insisted. "We don't know nuthin' 'bout it."

Buckner turned to the man. "She smelt somethin' burnin'," Charboneau said. "Woke me up, and by the time I got my pants on, the place was fillin' up with smoke."

"What did you do?"

"Started yellin' loud as I could."

"Damned silly old fool run upstairs and started poundin' on doors! Coulda got hisself all burnt up, and serve him right, too." The woman cackled merrily.

"Well, I couldn't let those folks burn up, could I? They was our tenants. They trusted us."

"They didn't do nuthin' of the sort. They paid us rent, that's all, and we didn't owe them nuthin'."

"So you got outside, ma'am?" Buckner sought to regain control of the conversation.

"Course I did. I'm here, ain't I?" snarled Joan.

"Did you see anybody? Was there anybody around?"

"You mean did I see somebody come sneakin' outa the cellar with a empty coal oil can, then no, I did not." She gestured. "Just Widow Janeworthy that was already out in the yard, and then everybody else, runnin' out in their nightshirts."

"You mentioned the cellar. Could you tell where the fire was coming from?"

"Well, no, it looked like it was comin' from the main floor somewheres."

"All right." Buckner had taken out his notebook and was writing in it. "Were the cellar doors open?"

"You know, I b'lieve they was."

"Thank you. Now, you said everybody else came running out. Can you tell me the names of your tenants?"

"We on the ground floor," Charboneau said. "Was, anyway."

"Anybody else on that floor?"

"The dinin' room and the kitchen and the parlor," said Joan. "Ain't no room for nuthin' else. Anyway, they's Mr. And Miz Moon, and Lester Stratton, and William Thrasher."

"They's up on the second floor," said Charboneau. "And they's only Widow Janeworthy on the third."

"No," his wife corrected. "They's that dago, whasisname, Peralta, up there too, and that tramp he says is his wife." She sniffed. "Course she ain't."

"I don't b'lieve they was there," said Charboneau. "I didn't see 'em come out anyways."

"No other bodies were found," Buckner said. "Do you know where Mr. Peralta was? Do you know his wife's name?"

"I tell you, she ain't his wife," Mrs. Charboneau insisted. "Pretty little thing, though. Couldn't be but sixteen, seventeen. And I'll tell you somethin' else fer free, she ain't no Eyetalian, neither."

"Sure she is," her husband said. He turned to Buckner. "Real pretty, dark eyes, dark hair, pale skin, like milk." He thought a minute. "All the same, she don't have no accent when she talks to me. Maybe she—"

"When was you talkin' to that cheap—"

"When she pays the rent, dear. Once a month, when she pays the rent. That's the only time I ever talk to her, and she talks English good as you or me."

"Well, anyway, you're wrong about her, she has yaller hair."

"Yaller? No she don't. You sure?"

"Yes, I am sure."

"Oh." Charboneau shook his head, puzzled.

"All right," Buckner intervened. "As far as you know, all your tenants are accounted for, correct? Except for Mr. Peralta and his, uh … female friend." Buckner thought of the corpse they had taken from the cellar wall, and its strands of yellow hair.

They nodded.

"The folks living there now," Buckner said. "I understand they're all transients—folks waiting for the Company to provide housing. Is that right?"

"Yes, it is."

"The Moons and Old Man Stratton been there longest," Charboneau said. "Year or more each. The dago and his woman … oh, couple years, but they ain't in line for no Company housing. Thrasher's in and out, either stayin' with us or back up in the woods. Miz Janeworthy's the newest."

"Anybody just up and disappear on you?"

"You mean just move out? Oh, hell yes. Happens all the time. Town like this, there's always a fair number of floaters, you know, show up here, get whatever work they can, and then move on. Ain't my job to keep track of folks. Long as they pay the rent, I leave folks alone."

"All right," Buckner said. "There was, like I said, a body in the cellar. A woman. Do you have any idea who that might be?"

More shrugs, blank looks.

"Or how it came to be in the cellar of your boarding house?"

"No idea atall."

"What did you use the cellar for, Mr. Charboneau?"

"Nuthin'," he said. "Well, 'cept junk that piled up down there, stuff folks didn't want no more."

"Was it locked?"

"Oh, heck no."

"So anybody could go down there."

"Sure."

"From the outside, too?"

"Sure. They's doors from the outside. Was, anyway." Charboneau looked puzzled. "Wasn't nuthin' down there worth stealin', and everbody's got good locks on their rooms. Far as I know nobody ever goes down there."

"It was where that Eyetalian makes his wine, too, don't forget," said Mrs. Charboneau.

"Wine?" Buckner was curious.

"Yeah, he used to make wine down there." Charboneau shrugged. "Got him some barrels to make it in and the demijohns to keep it in, and he sold it. Ain't done much of it lately, though. I didn't care … wasn't usin' the cellar fer nuthin' else."

"Was there light enough down there?" Buckner asked. "How did he see what he was doing?"

"Oh, I had some wires runnin' down there and it was light enough, I guess. Anyway, he never complained 'bout it."

Or noticed a body rotting in the cellar wall a few feet away, Buckner thought.

"So he wouldn't've been using a candle down there, or a lantern … something that might start a fire?"

"Oh, no. But, anyway, he ain't been down there in six months or more, I'd say. See, he makes his money playin' cards with the miners now, and if he's doin' all right at that, he don't worry about havin' to sell wine."

"Nor his wife," snapped Joan.

"That's God's own truth," Jean called from the kitchen.

"And neither of you ever smelled anything down in the cellar?"

"I told you. Didn't hardly ever go down there," the man said.

His wife shook her head in agreement. "Course, I go down there time to time to lay traps for rats. We get 'em pretty bad, time to time, 'specially in the rainy season. They come in to stay dry, you know, and they sure get to smellin' if'n the traps get 'em an' I don't get right to 'em. And there's always kind of a sour smell on account of the dago's wine makin'. Anyway, round here, ever'thing smells pretty bad pretty much all the time. You just get used to it."

"All right. Now there was also a large steamer trunk down there. Do you know who that belonged to?"

"Nope," Charboneau said.

"I b'lieve it was Miz Janeworthy's," said his wife.

"You say so."

Buckner nodded and looked up from his notes. "One more thing, if you don't mind. Mr. Powers said the boarding house belongs to you. Is that correct?"

"Yes, sir, it is," Charboneau answered. "My family owned that ground from way back, and a lot more besides." He waved a hand. "All this we're settin' on right now. Used to farm it way back 'fore the War Between the States. When the Company come in back forty years ago now, they tried for years to force my grandaddy to sell it, but he never would. This is my grandaddy Taylor, not my grandaddy Charboneau. They was one of the first settlers in these hills. Anyway, the Company bought up all the land around, and he had to sell off most of his just to make ends meet. Wasn't left with nuthin' but that little patch of ground with the house on it—house I was born in—and he made a deal with the Company to fix the place up and turn it into a boarding house, and the way they worked it out, he'd make room for a certain number of company people and the Company'd pay their rent at a fixed rate and they'd stop tryin' to buy him out. Guess they finally figured it'd be a good idea to have someplace to put a few of their people, but he fooled 'em, my grandaddy did, put a extra floor on the house and rented out those rooms up on the third floor and made some decent money that way, since the third floor wasn't part of the original deal." He shrugged. "Anyways, they named the town after him."

"It's where we put the dago and his woman," his wife said, "Then they got them a fancy lawyer here 'bout a year ago, Company did, and he convinced Judge Dunstan up to the county seat that the third floor was still part of the original agreement and so we had to cut the rate down to what the Company said."

"So the place was yours, but you were prevented from getting as much profit out of it as you believed you could get on the open market?"

"You're damned right," Charboneau said. "Course, it's gone now." He settled back in his chair and glared at the far wall.

"Was it insured?"

"Oncet," he said.

"Humph," said his wife furiously, glaring at him.

"Do you have any idea where Peralta and his woman might be?"

"No," she answered

"All right. Now, can you tell me where I can find the others—Stratton and Thrasher and the Moons?"

"Don't know where none of 'em are." She smiled grimly.

"I think Stratton's got a brother lives here in town," said her husband. "That's probably where he is. But I don't know 'bout the others. And don't forget about Widow Janeworthy."

"One last thing. I don't suppose you kept a list of the people who have stayed with you over the years?"

The two of them just stared at him, open mouthed.

"I see. Well, thanks," Buckner said. He jotted a note to himself to check that out with Tom. If the Company way paying their rent, there should be a record.

He put away his notebook and stood up. "I may have some more questions after I talk to the others. Will you folks be staying here?"

"No place else to go," Charboneau said.

"Right. Well, thanks for your help."

Buckner was headed up the street when Charboneau's voice stopped him. He turned and waited as the man shuffled toward him in his slippers.

"One thing, Chief," said the old man, puffing to a stop and glancing over his shoulder. His wife and her sister were watching from the doorway, hovering, identical in black. "About Widow Janeworthy."

"Yes? Do you know where I can find her?"

"Not for sure, but I got a idea."

"All right." Buckner waited. The man seemed reluctant to continue.

"See, she's my sister," he said finally. "Janeworthy's her married name. Bill Janeworthy was her husband, and he was a engineer … run all the machines up at the mine—donkey engines, elevator engines, you name it. He could build 'em and he could take 'em apart with his eyes closed. Took sick here three, four years ago, coughing up blood and everthing. Him dyin' was a mercy."

"That's when your sister came to live with you?"

"Yeah. Well, not right at first. Bill and her had a pretty nice place up the street there, but it was company, like all these along here, just a bit nicer, you know, on account of he wasn't just no miner, but, anyway, when he died, the Company turned her out, and I had a room and told 'em I'd take her. Powers said that was all right, he did, but only for a while, till she could find someplace to settle."

"And where do you think she's gone now? Does she have friends here in town who might have taken her in?"

"Uh, well, see, that's just it. I mean, no, I don't think so. I hate to say it, but my sister ain't a very nice person. Puts on airs. Thinks she's better'n everbody else. Everbody says that's just on account of Bill havin' graduated high school and havin' him a good job at the mine—big salary, nice house, all the rest—but she was always kind of snooty and hard to get along with." He laughed grimly. "I'm tellin' you, she made life pretty rough for me when we was kids, that's fer damn sure."

"So you don't think anybody around here would be inclined to take her in?"

"No, I don't. But the point is, I don't think she'd be inclined to ask."

"Oh, yes. I see."

"Fact is, if she's anyplace, she's down in Corinth."

"Why Corinth?"

"See, her and Bill had a daughter, Beatrice, and Beatrice married Ostell Mouser, and he works down there in the cement plant, in the office there—bookkeeper or something—and they got them a house down there, so if I had to guess, that's where I'd guess she is." He paused a moment. "Why do you have to talk to her anyway? I doubt she'd be able to tell you anything about the fire. Or that dead body."

"You may be right, Mr. Charboneau, but I have to talk to her anyway."

"Well, I think that's where you'll find her."

"Thanks."

Charboneau returned to the house, and Buckner walked back up the road. He could see Kelson, strangely natty-looking in his suit, standing at the edge of the burnt-out cellar, lighting another cigarette. As Buckner approached, he tossed the match into the rubble and nodded a greeting.

"I need some help," Buckner said.

"Sure," Kelson replied.

"I need to find Lester Stratton and William Thrasher and the Moons. And somebody named Peralta, who might be Italian, and his wife, who also may be Italian."

"Eyetalian? I thought he was Mex."

"I don't know what he is. Charboneau said he might've been Italian. And he had a woman with him, maybe his wife, maybe not."

"Sure." Kelson was nodding. "I know who you're talking about. He looks foreign, right enough, but as for being Eyetalian, hell, Bob Charboneau wouldn't know an Eyetalian if one jumped up and bit him on the ass. Looked more like a Mexican to me, anyway."

"Uh-huh. Do you know where I could find them?"

"Nope. But they can't've got far. He never had no regular job around here, just livin' off what he made playin' cards, and one thing and another. Plus whatever wine he could sell."

"Yes, Charboneau said he made wine."

"Yeah. Made it in them barrels there, and kept it in them demijohns." Kelson puffed on his cigarette. "I never drunk none of it. Fit for damned foreigners, far as I'm concerned. Americans drink whiskey. Anyway, it's just what somebody told me one time, about him making wine. I never seen him do it."

"All right. How about the others?"

"I'm pretty sure Stratton's got a brother works underground, lives down yonder." Kelson pointed down the hill. "The Moons got kinfolk down that way too. Thrasher lives up in the hills when he ain't workin'."

"Anybody been nosing around here?"

"Nah. Some kids lookin' for souvenirs, I s'pect, but I run 'em off."

"The Company provide you with housing?"

"Hell, yes, they do," Kelson said.

"So you never stayed with Charboneau?"

"Might've, couple of days, back when I first started here."

"How about Garber?"

"Yeah, him, too, now I think about it. Quite a while though, as I recall. Durin' the build-up for the war, you know, and the town was brim full."

"Right. Thanks." Buckner headed for the office, leaving Kelson, hands shoved deep in his pockets, rocking on his heels, gazing into the middle distance with that look of watchful cop boredom Buckner now recognized. In the office, the reliable Tom sped expertly through a card file and located an address for Chester Stratton, currently working nights underground as a gang boss. Tom said the man did indeed have a brother named Lester, also a gang boss, whose address was the boarding house that had just burned down. "Say, Chief, you think Lester's staying over at Chester's place?" he asked.

"Maybe. What about the others?"

"Sure." Tom checked his files and scribbled on a piece of paper, which he handed to Buckner. "This is the Moons and Stratton. Miz Janeworthy's husband used to work for the Company, but he died. There's a daughter lives down in town. Maybe Miz Janeworthy's gone to stay with her. Here's the address. Thrasher was a local, one of the old timers. Kind of like Charboneau except that he comes from farther back up in the hills." He peered at a card. "It just says Ratliff's Fork here on the card. That mean anything to you?"

"Yes," Buckner said. "It's up by Flint Hill, where the Indians used to make their arrowheads. What about this Peralta?"

"I've got nothing on him, Chief. I mean, I know about him, because he's kind of famous."

"For making wine?"

"Well, no." To Buckner's surprise, Tom leered at him. The expression was so alien to his bland young face that Buckner almost laughed out loud. "Mostly for his wife."

"Uh-huh. What about her?"

"Well, according to what I hear, if he needs some cash, he'll let you go with her for five dollars." Tom held up a hand. "That's just what I hear. I don't know anything about it personally." He was suddenly very busy once more, shuffling papers and ignoring Buckner.

"Uh-huh." Buckner went on. "Does the Company keep records on the people it put up at the Charboneau place over the years?"

"Sure. Why?"

"I'd just like to know who was staying there recently."

"Oh, you mean somebody lived there might've done for that woman?"

"Maybe."

"Well, I'm not sure I can help you there, Chief. You see, the Company keeps a record of the money, but not the people, if you see what I mean. Just how much was paid out to Charboneau, listed under rentals." Tom grinned. "And of course the Company subtracted the rental money from the individual's paycheck."

"Of course," Buckner said. He realized that pressing Tom to dig deeper would be a waste of time and effort, so he went out.

"Tell you the truth, I never seen no fire, not till I got outside. All I ever seen was lots of smoke, and it was comin' from everwhere. But I got downstairs and outside, and Miz Janeworthy and Miz Charboneau was already there. That's when I could see flames in through the window, into the dining room where we et supper. Then the Moons come out, and we just stood there and watched Will Big Foot's men workin'." He smiled. "They's good, them fellers. Company hired 'em outa St. Louis, Kansas City, professionals. They don't do much else 'cept set around waitin' for somethin' to catch fire."

"Really?" Buckner asked. "It happen often?"

"Now and again. Not much, though."

"All right. One more thing. I heard this Peralta didn't mind if his wife went with other fellows, as long as they paid him."

"Sure, I heard that." He chuckled merrily. "Don't know nuthin' 'bout it personally, a course. Just heard."

Buckner closed his notebook and returned it to his pocket.

"Can you tell me where I can find Mr. and Mrs. Moon? They're supposed to be staying with relatives around here somewhere." Buckner looked around. "The Company sure didn't go bankrupt putting up street signs!"

"I reckon they figger if you don't know where you're goin', you don't have no business goin' there in the first place." Stratton pointed. "The place you're lookin' for's right back there."

"Thanks." Buckner walked in the direction indicated. He found another company house, only children were exploding from every opening in this one. Buckner counted over a half dozen, but they kept appearing and disappearing, and they were similarly dressed in raggedy clothing, so the total could have been higher or lower. They ranged in age from barely able to walk without falling down to surly adolescence. A baseball with a peeling cover flew back and forth; one of the adolescents was punching a smaller child without seeming to take much pleasure from it. Buckner noticed one child, perhaps six years old, wearing only a filthy undershirt. For the moment, he was the only child who was motionless.

"Moon residence?" He asked the child.

After a long, empty stare, the child shrugged and then turned and walked away. Buckner went up onto the porch and knocked on the moth-eaten screen door. Shrill screaming came from somewhere inside. He knocked again, louder this time. The door rattled loosely in its frame. An adult male came and peered at him through the screen. He wore denim overalls, no shirt, no shoes. His heavy, pale, speckled flesh sagged from his bones, and dark hairs sprouted, random and lonely.

"Yeah?"

"Mr. Moon?"

"Who wants to know?" His expression managed to be blank and belligerent at the same time.

A child wearing a miniature version of the man's overalls thundered down the hall and stopped behind him. The man turned suddenly and knocked the child to the floor with a quick swipe of one hand. Then he turned back to Buckner, a satisfied smile on his face. "Well?"

"I'm looking into the fire at the boarding house, and—"

"That's my brother and his wife."

"Are they here? Could I talk to them?"

The child on the floor was curled into a ball and sobbing. Another child came down the hall and stood and watched impassively. The children in the yard continued throwing and catching and punching.

"She is. He's up at the works."

"He works at the smelter?"

"Why else would he be there?"

"Fine. Could I talk with Miz Moon then?"

"Round back." The man turned away. He stepped over the sobbing child, shoved aside the other, and disappeared down the hall.

Buckner went around back.

A small shack, twelve by twelve, built of framing and rough pine boards and covered with tarpaper, stood in the middle of the bare, hardpan yard. The tarpaper was faded and curling, and the building leaned like a drunk. A woman in calico and a sunbonnet sat in a chair by the door. She was peeling potatoes into a bucket of water that sat on the ground beneath her feet.

"Miz Moon?"

"Yes."

"My name's Buckner, I'm—"

"Chief of police down to Corinth. I know. You used to be that fat sheriff's deputy. What can I do for you?"

"I'm trying to find out about the fire in the boarding house where you used to live, and about the dead body the firemen found in the cellar."

"Heard about that." On her lap the woman held an enameled bowl full of peelings. She dropped her knife into it and set the bowl on the ground by the large gunny sack of potatoes. She seemed anxious to talk, or at least to stop peeling potatoes. "What can I tell you?"

"How long have you and your husband lived there?"

"Near two year."

"Well, let's start with the fire first. Where was the room you and your husband occupied?"

"We're on the second floor ... were, that is." She shook her head sadly. "All gone now, I guess."

"Yes, ma'am. I'm sorry." Buckner had been talking to people to whom bad things had happened for as long as he'd been a policeman and he still did not know the right way to do it. Or even if there was a right way. Saying he was sorry never seemed like enough, but it was the best he could come up with.

"We heard everbody shoutin' 'fire!' Or I did anyway, and I woke up the old man and we got out of there fast as we could. Didn't have time to take nuthin' with us."

"Were you the last ones out?"

"I don't know. I don't think so. Widow Janeworthy was there, and Miz Charboneau was comin' down the stairs. And Mr. Stratton too."

"And your husband is employed by the Company?"

"Yes. He's a foreman at the smelter works. Supervises the day shift in the stamping mill."

"Important position."

"Yeah, and lucky to have it too. After the war, the Company didn't need so many workers, what with the price of lead comin' down—didn't need so many bullets, I reckon. He'd just been promoted to foreman, and they was all talkin' 'bout movin' him up some more. Now, though, it looks like that ain't gonna happen after all, but he's keepin' the foreman job, so we'll make out all right. And we're in line for one of the nicer houses ... soon as the folks that's in it get moved out." She gestured at the bare yard and the feral children. "We ain't gonna be here long. Still, I hated to lose everthing in that fire—pictures, mementos, all our clothes 'cept what we had on our backs."

"Yes, ma'am. Could you tell where the fire was coming from?"

"Oh, no. It was dark and there was smoke everwhere, and we just got out in time." She thought a minute. "Seemed like it mighta been comin' from downstairs—maybe on the first floor—but I can't really say for sure."

"Can you remember if the cellar doors were open or closed?"

"No. I didn't notice, I guess."

"Any strangers around? Anybody acting suspicious? Anybody you didn't recognize?"

"No."

"Did you ever notice any strange smells coming out of the cellar?"

"No. Never went down there. And as for smells around here, well, folks around here hunt, and when they dress out their kill, they just leave the mess lying on the ground. I know old Mr. Charboneau puts rat traps around down there, and when he got any, he'd just toss 'em out the back. 'Sides, if'n you'd ever drunk the water around here, you'd know it smells funny too. So you just take a deep breath, an' you'll get all the strange smells you want."

"Right. If you think of anything, or remember anything, just tell Tom. He works—"

"I know him. Works for Powers. He's that clerk with the patent-leather hair."

"Yes, ma'am. He'll know how to get in touch with me. Can you tell me where I can find William Thrasher or Mister or Miz Peralta?"

"No. I never knew any of 'em 'cept to say good mornin' to," said Mrs. Moon. "But I'll tell you this, that little slut wasn't his wife."

"This is Miz Peralta?"

"Yes."

"How can you be sure?"

"Take my word for it. A woman knows these things. She's nuthin' but a no-good tramp, but he's worser 'cause he's makin' money off her."

"Uh-huh. Well, thanks for you time."

"No trouble." She picked up her bowl and resumed peeling potatoes. "Looks like I'll be workin' here without no pay for a while, though, peelin' spuds for my brother-in-law and his kids now his wife's run off again." She pointed her knife at the main house. "He says we can stay long as I cook and clean, so maybe there's just different kinds of whorin'."

"Yes, ma'am. What about the Company?'

Mrs. Moon spat once on the ground. "No different from my brother-in-law. Work you twenty-four hours a day for nuthin' if'n they could."

Buckner thanked her and went back up the hill.

"How much longer am I gonna have to stand here?" Kelson sounded bored and cranky.

"You got someplace more important you have to be?"

"No, I reckon not."

"Well, then," Buckner said, pointing at the cellar, "I'm not through looking around in there, and I don't want anybody taking any souvenirs."

"So when do you think you'll be through?"

"I just need to talk to Peralta. Any idea where I can find him?"

"This time of day, no idea," Kelson said. "I don't believe I've ever seen him out and about before sunset—him or his woman neither."

"All right. When you do see them, where do you see them?"

"Most of the blind pigs around here got a table in the back, or a wheel, or a craps game going on."

"What's Peralta's game?"

"Poker, far as I know. Used to shoot craps, but a couple of the boys figured he was using shaved dice and they warned him off."

"High stakes or penny-ante?"

"Depends." Kelson shrugged. "If he's in the money, he'll play for pretty high stakes—two-bit ante, even higher around payday."

"What about the woman?"

"Near as I can tell, that's how he supports himself. Whenever he gets a little low on cash, or needs a stake, he puts the word around that she's available."

"And when she's not available?"

"Word I hear is he used to keep her locked up in that room they had here. Dunno what he's gonna do now."

"He sounds like a charming fellow."

"Just trying to make a living, like the rest of us," Kelson said.

"Any ideas where I ought to start looking for him?"

"Well, you might try that place down the road there." Kelson pointed. "Doesn't have a name, really, but everbody calls it Shorty's. Mick named Donahue runs it. Got a bar in front and a table in back, and there's a poker game going pretty much round the clock. I wanted to find Peralta, that's where I'd start."

"Thanks." Buckner turned to go, but Kelson stopped him.

"They don't care much for no laws at Shorty's."

"I'll keep that in mind."

"You carrying?"

"No."

"You want to borrow mine?" Kelson took a Smith & Wesson .38 from under his coat and held it out. "I wouldn't go into Shorty's less I was carrying."

"I'm not going to arrest anybody," Buckner said. "I just want to talk to Peralta about the body and the fire. Nobody else seems to know anything about them. Maybe he will."

"You might not get a chance to explain yourself," Kelson warned. "Folks around here know who you are, and they remember what you done back in nineteen. You pretty much cleaned out the Wobblies when you killed those fellers back then. I ain't sayin' they didn't deserve it—buncha Commies—but they still got friends around here."

"Thanks for the warning," Buckner said, and trudged back down the hill.

He remembered Shorty's only vaguely. The trouble was, he'd been in so many places like it over the years, here in the Lead Belt as a deputy sheriff, along the Border during his cavalry years, in the back alleys of London and Paris during the war, and they ran together in his mind—the same smoke-clouded darkness, the same smells of stale liquor and stale tobacco and stale sweat, and the same hard, grim faces that looked up at him coldly, briefly, before returning to stare at the drinks on the table. There was always considerable drinking going on in these places, but nobody seemed to be having much fun.

As he entered and crossed the room, somebody muttered, "Black and Tan," and he smiled. That was a new one.

The bartender, balding and emaciated, a dirty apron over dirty work clothes, was devoting his fullest attention to an invisible spot on the zinc surface of the bar, rubbing industriously with a dirty rag.

"Is there a game in back?" Buckner asked him.

The bartender continued rubbing and did not look up.

"Excuse me." Buckner tried again.

No response. He turned and headed for the narrow door at the far end of the room. At once, an enormous figure rose through the layers of smoke to block his path.

"You got no jurisdiction here." Tall as Buckner was, the figure towered over him.

"Mr. Donahue, isn't it?" Buckner said, smiling. Then he added, "You're right. No jurisdiction at all. Good thing I'm not here to arrest anybody then. I just need to talk to Mr. Peralta for a minute. Is he back there?"

"Peralta? Hmm."

"Italian-looking fellow? And his wife, if she's with him."

"Wife?" said Donahue. "Don't know about no wife." He turned aside like a huge gate swinging open. "You're just here to ask?"

"Yes."

"I wouldn't like to have my customers disturbed."

"I doubt they'll even notice I'm here."

"Be my guest then."

"Thank you." Buckner opened the door and went through.

The room was tiny and even darker than the bar, and oven hot. A single kerosene lantern hung from the low ceiling and illuminated the cards on the table while leaving the faces of the players in shadow. Five men were playing. Except for a few murmured words and the click of chips on the green baize tabletop, there was no sound. Buckner could see other figures sitting or standing beyond the reach of the lamp's soft yellow glow.

"Mr. Peralta?" Buckner said, his voice loud in the hushed gloom.

Everyone turned to look, and one man said, "Pretty busy right now."

He could have been Italian—or Greek or Syrian or Spanish for that matter.

"Moment of your time, Mr. Peralta."

"I'm in the middle of a hand," the man said. "In the middle of a run of luck, if you want to know. I'd hate to jinx it."

"He's not leaving till I get a chance to win my money back," said a tall, thin man in a black suit with frayed cuffs. He had a pencil-thin mustache, and his jaw was clamped on a cigar; in fact, it looked as if the cigar was growing out of the side of his face. Buckner turned to the figures in the dark. "Which one of you is Miz Peralta? I'll talk to you while your husband plays."

One of the figures got up and came toward the light. Buckner thought at first it was a child. Barely five feet high, the woman had a pale, delicate beauty. A cascade of dark hair tumbled loosely to her shoulders. But her body, if small, was lush and rounded and set off by the thin material of her lemon-yellow dress. It was very short, the hem just brushing her knees. Her eyes were a watery brown and looked at him from a depth of hopelessness that doubled her age.

Buckner smiled. "Why don't we go outside, ma'am," he said, and offered his arm.

"Whoa, whoa. Hold everything, folks," said the man, suddenly rising to his feet. He tossed his cards onto the table. "I fold. Cash me in, Phil. You boys can have my share of the kick." He pushed a considerable stack of ships in the direction of the thin man. In response to the looks he was getting from the thin man and the others around the table as they leaned into the light to reach for chips, he smiled. "You fellows know me. I ain't going nowhere. You'll have another crack at me, I promise, but right now I gotta go talk to this policeman." He grabbed the wad of cash thrust at him by the thin man and hurried to join Buckner and the woman.

"Let's go, folks," he said brightly, and led the way through the door, on through the barroom, and into the slanting late afternoon light.

"I don't know what to tell you, Officer," Peralta said. The door banged shut behind them. He shaded his eyes with his hand as he looked up at Buckner. "We was headed home, and just about the time we got there, we heard all the shouting and seen that old lady come running out—that widow lady—and pretty soon we saw all the smoke and such. We lost everything we had."

"Any idea how it started?"

"No. None at all."

"Ma'am?" Buckner turned to the woman.

"Huh?" She was standing hipshot, head down, waiting patiently. Now she raised her head and turned her watery eyes on Buckner. She had a blue bandanna in her hand and she dabbed at her nose with it. "What?"

"Do you have any idea how the fire might have started?"

"No," she said. Her voice was flat and dull; the fire didn't interest her. Her glance slid off Buckner and passed on to some vague middle distance beyond his right shoulder. He waited, and her eyes came back to him. He thought he saw something out of that depth, something pleading. She opened her mouth to speak.

"Neither of us saw anything, Officer," Peralta cut in. He put an arm around the woman and held her close. She did not resist ... did not respond at all. "Don't know what we're gonna do now. No place to live."

"Did you know the firemen found a body in the cellar?"

"I heard that, but I figured it was just talk," Peralta said. The woman was once again gazing blankly down the street.

"It's true. Do either of you know anything about that?"

"Not a thing."

"You used to make wine down there. Did you ever notice a smell?"

"'Course I did. Place stunk. That's one of the reasons why I stopped making my wine down there. I figured it was going to make it taste funny."

"Where are you staying?"

"Here." Peralta nodded in the direction of the door they had just come through. "Donahue's got a shed out back. Not much, but it'll do till we can get back on our feet." He tapped his pocket and grinned. "And that ought to be pretty soon, the way the cards've been running."

"All right, then," Buckner said. "If you think of anything, just talk to Kelson or Garber, or to Tom at the Company office. They'll know how to get in touch with me. And don't wander off. I may have some more questions later."

"Right you are, Officer. Yes sir." Peralta turned the unresisting woman toward the door. "That be all?"

"Yes. Thank you." *And,* Buckner thought as he started back up the hill, *that's the last I'll ever hear from either of you.*

4

Buckner decided to deal with the acid next.

Tom's directions took him to a building next to the smelter works. Directly above the building, a conveyor moved ore up to the stamping mill. A small man stood by the door. His face and hands were darkened by fine grit that looked as though it was permanently embedded in his pores. He nodded a greeting and beckoned Buckner inside. Buckner asked about acid, and the man pointed to half a dozen steel drums. "There it is," he shouted over the rumbling of the conveyor. "When I get a full dozen, I take the drums down to the siding and load 'em onto a box car. They run the car down to Corinth, 'long with whatever else we're shippin' out, hook it onto the next eastbound Iron Mountain freight train, and it goes on up to St. Louis."

"How do you move the drums around?" Buckner shouted back.

The man had adapted to his workplace, where speaking was usually pointless: he aimed a thumb at a hand truck leaning against one wall.

Just then, another man appeared in the doorway wheeling another drum on an identical hand truck. He carefully lowered the drum into place next to the others, leaned the hand truck against the wall, nodded at the small man and at Buckner, and went wordlessly out.

"What happens if you get any of this on you?" Buckner asked, resigned to carrying on the conversation at the top of his voice.

"Burns like hell," the man shouted. He pointed to a standing hat rack in the corner. A long rubber apron hung from one hook. Buckner nodded. Then the man pulled a pair of heavy rubber gloves from his hip pocket. "These help some." He pointed to his sleeves and shirtfront, which were spotted with several small holes. It looked as though moths had been at the fabric.

"Just how strong is this stuff?" Buckner asked. He leaned in close to hear the answer.

"Well, when it comes out of the smelter, it's got a lot of other stuff mixed in. They treat it in St. Louis—purify it, I guess is what they do—and that'd be pretty strong."

"Strong enough to dissolve a human body?"

"An entire one?" The man paused, frowning. "I reckon, but not till it'd been purified. And then only if you had enough of it. See, while it's dissolvin' stuff, it kinda loses its strength. It changes. But if you had a big old vat of the stuff, then, yeah, I s'pect it would. Is this about that body in Charboneau's cellar?"

"Yes," Buckner admitted.

"In one of the dago's wine barrels?"

"Yes." Buckner had learned long ago that information traveled fast in small communities—like Taylor, like Corinth, like the army—where a lot of people lived shoved together in a small space.

"Wouldn't do it," the man said confidently. "Not completely. Not unless you had another barrel full of the stuff."

"How do you secure this place?" Buckner said.

Again the man just pointed, this time at a cheap padlock hanging open from its hasp above the doorknob.

"That's it?"

The man shrugged and shouted, "Kelson and Garber keep an eye out."

"Are you here all day?"

The man nodded.

"What about at night? What's to prevent anybody from just walking in here and stealing a barrel of the stuff? That lock wouldn't stop a kid."

The man looked surprised and shook his head. "Who's gonna steal sulfuric acid?"

Buckner opened his mouth to speak, closed it, nodded his thanks, and left.

There were the remains of that steamer trunk in the cellar. A body in a steamer trunk would be hard to move unless you had something like a hand truck designed for moving drums of acid. That would make it easy, assuming of course that the woman was killed elsewhere and moved to the cellar, rather than being enticed or forced into the cellar and killed there. Anyway, whoever did the killing had the equipment available to deal with things like that. You could fill demijohns here and carry them to the cellar and fill the barrel there. And he remembered the half-melted rubber gloves on the cellar floor. Then just empty the acid onto the dirt floor when you're finished.

The Company's fire truck shared a large garage with several other company vehicles, including a heavy, horse-drawn ore wagon that looked as if it hadn't been used in fifty years. Buckner found Will Big Foot drinking coffee with two men in overalls.

"Want some?" Big Foot asked, raising his cup slightly.

"I believe I will have a cup," Buckner said. One of the men handed him a chipped china mug filled to the brim. He sipped carefully at it.

"You need to talk to me?" Big Foot asked.

"Just a quick question or two," Buckner answered.

"Sure." Big Foot turned to the others. "Be right with you." He walked with Buckner out into the doorway of the garage. "What can I tell you?"

"The main thing I want to know is, could you tell how the fire started? And where?"

"Can't say for certain, and I sure as hell couldn't testify to it, you know, under oath or anything like that."

"I doubt you'll ever have to."

"All right, long as you don't hold me to it. I'd say it started in the parlor on the ground floor. Somebody put a candle too close to a curtain in the front window, the curtain caught fire, and the whole place went up. I got no proof of that, of course, but I did find the brass candlestick."

"I understand the house was on the electricity."

"Sure. The Company's run wires to the whole town—runs 'em off the same generators it uses for down underground and in the smelter works."

"So if somebody wanted light in the parlor, they could just turn the switch."

"Well, yeah, sure."

"They wouldn't really need a candle."

"No, not really." Big Foot looked at Buckner. "That don't necessarily mean anything, you know."

"No, it doesn't."

"Some folks're just used to candles."

"True enough. So, no way to tell if it was arson or accident?"

"Not really. Anything else?"

"No," Buckner said. "I think that's it for today—anyway, until I can think of some more questions. Thank you."

"Sure. Any time. Just remember what I said. And I'd appreciate it if you wouldn't mention this little conversation to Mr. Powers."

"All right, if that's what you want. But why not? Powers asked for my help on this thing, and your helping me ought to go down pretty good with your boss."

"I don't think so," Big Foot said. "What Powers really wants is for this whole thing to go away. The fact that the fire took place on private land is just fine with him, and he'd be happy as could be if that dead body was just some stranger that wandered into town and didn't have nothing to do with Taylor or the Company at all. The less the Company is involved in it, the less chance there is of it getting back to the home office. I guess things ain't been too good for the lead mining business lately. It looks like the troubles in Mexico're over, for a while anyway, so the mines down there're back in operation, which means more lead coming onto the market when there's already too much. And the Company's under real pressure from the unions too. Plus, this operation's got a poor reputation with folks back east on account of that trouble back in nineteen."

"So it'll just be a fire of mysterious origins."

"Yep."

"All right. I'll keep this conversation under my hat. One thing, though."

"Sure."

"You still got that candlestick?"

"Yeah, got it someplace." He led Buckner back into the garage and began pawing through a box of junk on top of a desk. "Here 'tis." He held up a short brass candlestick, twisted slightly and blackened with soot.

Buckner wrapped it in his bandana. "Thanks," he said. He left his empty coffee cup on the desk and went out to the Ford. He dropped the candlestick on the seat and went into the office. Tom showed him straight in. Powers looked up from a column of figures on the desk before him and frowned at the interruption. Tom hovered at Buckner's shoulder until a glance from Powers sent him out.

"I've talked to all the residents of the boarding house except Mr. Thrasher, Mr. Moon, and Widow Janeworthy. I think Thrasher has gone back to his place up in the hills, and the widow's likely staying with her daughter down in town. Moon's at work, but I talked to his wife, and I doubt he'll have much to add to her story. I'm going to head on back to Corinth and talk to Widow Janeworthy now, and I'll find Thrasher tomorrow, and talk to Mr. Moon as well, just to make sure."

"Do you want me to have Moon brought up? It'll take a while."

"No. Tomorrow will do. I'm going to have to get up into the hills and find Thrasher too. And when I find out from Doctor Peck about the dead woman, I'll probably have to come back and talk to everybody again."

"You think Thrasher might have killed that woman and set that fire before he took off?" Powers put down his pen. "I wouldn't put it past him. He is a troublemaker and no two ways about it. Absolutely refuses to adjust to modern business practices—thinks he can work like he did back in the old days. He comes down here, digs twice as much ore in half the time as any man working, draws his pay, and heads back up in the woods."

"Why don't you fire him?"

"I'd love to. Unfortunately, he is good at his work—when he does it—and a lot better than most of the illiterate ridge-runners and wool-hats that come in here looking for a job. Plus, he's got a lot of friends in the area. A lot of people look to him as some kind of leader, so in the long run it's just a lot easier to put up with him and avoid all the trouble."

"He a union man?"

"No," Powers said with a satisfied smile. "That's another thing. Like a lot of the old timers, he's not interested in the union. Thinks it's a foreign plot to take his money." Powers chuckled. "So you could almost say he's worth the trouble—unless he started this fire, or killed that woman. Do you think it was him?"

"Can't say at this point. I just want to talk to him. I also asked people about the dead woman, but nobody seems to have known anything about her. Anybody gone missing around her lately?"

"Good grief, Chief Buckner," Powers said. "I hardly have time to keep track of the Company employees working here. I certainly can't concern myself with any riffraff that might wander through. Kelson and Garber are under strict orders to hurry such people along."

"You don't know she was a transient," Buckner said.

"No company employee has spoken to me or anyone else about anybody being missing, family member or friend. Beyond that ..." Powers shrugged.

"There are plenty of women in this town who aren't related to your employees, Mr. Powers."

"Yes, prostitutes … others. They are hardly my concern, though. Nor the Company's."

"All right. Gonna make it harder to find out who she was, and how she got in the cellar wall."

"Just keep me informed every step of the way. I want this wrapped up as quickly as possible." Powers retrieved his pen from the desk set, dipped the tip, and bent again to his work.

Buckner figured he had been dismissed and went back outside. While Kelson waited outside, Buckner got back down into the cellar. He picked through the rubble and found nothing that looked important. He peered back into the hole and again found nothing. He knew he'd be back here soon, so he gave up and climbed out.

"No more clues, Chief?" Kelson asked. He was grinning around another cigarette.

"Nope. Nothing."

"Bad luck."

"Yes." Buckner returned to his Ford, cranked it up, got in, and sat for a minute. His eyes were full of grit, and his hands and clothing were filthy. He felt as if he'd been up for a week. He let off the brake and drove back down the hill.

The Mouser family lived on Elm Street, west of the town square. On a street of nice houses, the Mouser home stood out—three stories, bright white clapboard with fresh green trim, carefully tended lawn, and a broad gallery running the width of the house. A maid answered his knock at the door, took his hat, and showed him into a cool parlor shaded against the setting sun. An extremely pretty young woman with honey blonde curls smiled up at him from a magazine.

"Hello, Chief Buckner. How are you?"

"Just fine, Miz Mouser, thank you. How are you?"

"Fine, thank you. Won't you sit down?"

"I don't want to take up too much of your time, ma'am. I just need to talk with your mother, if she's available."

"Of course." She turned to the maid, who stood in the doorway. "Elsie, go see if Mrs. Janeworthy is free."

Elsie dropped a quick curtsey and went out.

"May I ask what you want to talk to my mother about, Chief?"

"Yes, ma'am. I'm looking into the fire at the boarding house."

"Of course. My mother tells me a dead body was discovered in the cellar, but nobody knows who it is ... or was."

"Yes, ma'am, that's right."

She looked at him, plainly expecting more. He smiled and said nothing. They stood in awkward silence for a while.

"She won't come down, ma'am." Elsie had returned.

Mrs. Mouser frowned. "My mother was very upset, Chief Buckner, as I am sure you can imagine. She telephoned from the company office very early this morning, and my husband had to motor up to Taylor before dawn to get her and bring her here. She has no place else to stay, and all her belongings were destroyed in the fire. Could you perhaps come back another day?"

"I'd like to talk to her while the experience is still fresh in her mind, ma'am." Buckner returned her smile, but his voice had an unmistakable firmness to it.

"Well, I suppose ... all right. Elsie, take Chief Buckner to the guest room."

"Yes, ma'am."

The guest room was the entire third floor of the house. From the hallway at the top of the stairs, Buckner could see a bedroom, a small sitting room, and a bathroom. He thanked Elsie and went along the hallway to the door of the sitting room, where a woman in a dark robe sat looking out the window into the front yard. "Miz Janeworthy?"

She turned to look at him. Buckner guessed her age at fifty, but her hard, angular face and iron-gray hair and angry scowl added ten years.

"What do you want?"

"I'm Chief—"

"I know who you are. What do you want?" The robe was obviously not hers. The sleeves reached beyond her fingertips as she pulled its folds tightly about her small frame and glared up at him.

"I'd like to talk to you about the fire, ma'am, if I may."

"You want to chat about the fire? What for? The place burned down, and now I have to live up here in the attic in my son-in-law's fancy house." She snorted. "Thinks he's so high and mighty, but he's just a low, dirty immigrant. Changed his name during the war. Used to be Mauzer, now its Mouser. As though that would fool anybody. And it's ridiculous besides." She looked around and shook her head in disgust. "The attic."

Pretty nice for an attic, Buckner thought. Nice carpeting, flowered wall paper, all the comforts of home, and it certainly seemed that it would be an improvement over a single, small room in that boarding house, however big it might have been, and a shared bathroom at the end of the hall. Did she really mind the change that much?

"I need to ask you if you know anything about the dead body in the cellar. And I'm trying to find out if you know anything about how the fire started."

"Well, I don't know how it started, so that's that, and you can go on your way."

"Just a couple more questions, ma'am, if you please. Did you see anybody snooping around the place? Any strangers?"

She gave him a disgusted look. "Is that the best you can do? Mysterious strangers? What business is this of yours anyway? Taylor has nothing to do with Corinth. You have no authority whatsoever to be sticking your nose into fires up in Taylor."

"Folks in Corinth," Buckner said patiently, "think what happens in Taylor is important to folks who live in Corinth, so they—we—think it's a good idea to help out when we can, like good neighbors." Buckner knew how feeble this sounded even as he said it. He knew he was working as a stooge for the Company that helped rich men in Corinth, and elsewhere, stay rich. "Mr.

Powers asked for our help, and we're glad to give it. As for my questions, I have to start somewhere, ma'am."

"No, Chief Buckner, no mysterious strangers, no cloaked anarchists, no Black Handers skulking in the shadows ... nobody."

"Did you notice anybody in the parlor? Any of the residents using a candle?"

"A candle? No. Did my brother put you up to this? Is he trying to lay the blame on me?"

"No, ma'am. He said your family used to own a lot of land up there."

"Yes, we did. Our mother's side of the family this was, until the Company came in and took it away ... stole it right out from under us."

"Stole—"

"Oh, those carpetbaggers in Jefferson City, call themselves the state legislature. They made it all legal and everything, and they got their share of the loot, too, you better believe it. But, in the end, the folks that lived there ended up having to rent their own homes from the damned Company."

"And your husband, he worked for the Company, didn't he?"

"Yes. He was an engineer. Worked as an engineer and safety inspector, supposed to make sure working conditions were safe. Got sick himself, of course. So sick he couldn't go to work anymore. So sick he was coughing up blood. And the company doctor said there was nothing they could do for him, so he died."

"And you were living in company housing at that time?"

"Yes. They put me out of that house the day I put my husband in the ground."

"And your brother then gave you a place to live, is that right?"

"No, it is not."

"But, I thought—"

"He didn't give me a thing. He rented me a room—rented, you understand—in that house that used to be our home. That house we were born in and grew up in. And I had to take it because my son-in-law wouldn't take me."

"I thought the Company paid the rent for its own people," Buckner said.

"It's not the money," she answered sharply. "It's the principle of the thing."

Buckner remembered an earlier investigation. "Haven't you got other kinfolk here in town? I believe there's a Mr. Taylor—"

"That's my cousin's boy," she snapped. "We haven't spoken in years. They never cared anything about the family property except how much money they could get out of it."

"I understand." And he did. St. Louis was littered with his relatives—second and third cousins. They saw each other only at weddings and funerals when they were all on their best behavior, and by common, if unspoken, consent, nobody discussed religion or politics. "All right, then. All you know about the fire—"

"All I know about the fire is somebody yelling to get out, so I got out, and now what little was left of my home is completely gone."

"Yes," Buckner said. He was getting tired of having her interrupt him. "When you got out of the house, where did you go?"

"Go? I didn't go anyplace. I just stood there."

"Who else was there with you?"

"With me? What are you talking about? Nobody was with me." She stopped and dropped her eyes to her hands and then, after a moment, raised them again. "That's not right. Charboneau's wife was there, and the Moons, and Stratton, and that horrible man, Thrasher."

"They were all there?"

"Yes," she insisted.

"They were already there when you came out?"

She thought a moment more, eyes on her hands, and then nodded with certainty and said, "Yes. They were all there when I came out."

"All right. And can you tell me anything about the body found in the cellar?"

She looked at him suspiciously. "Don't you go thinking you can hang that on us, just because we owned the building and the land. I don't know a thing about that. And neither does my brother."

"Yes, ma'am. He told me. All right. Did you know the other tenants? The Peraltas, or the Moons?"

"The Peraltas," she sneered. "They're no more married than you are to me."

Buckner nodded. She seemed just as appalled at that thought as he was. She kept right on. "But he's a handsome devil, I'll give him that. And obviously has his way with the kind of foolish young girls that wind up with him."

"Yes, I met—"

"A cheap piece of goods, you can count on it." She spoke with the first sign of pleasure Buckner had seen, her eyes glittering fiercely. "Just like that other one he had."

"Other one?"

"Oh, yes. And you can be sure she wasn't the first either."

"No, I'm sure you're right. What other one are you talking about?"

"Oh, this was quite some time ago—two years or so. He brought this one with him when he first came to town."

"Do you remember her name? How long was she with him? What happened to her?"

"No, I don't remember her name." She sniffed, disgusted. "I do not consort with low people. But I did notice she wasn't with him any more, and he said she'd gone back to her family. At least that was one story. But my brother told me he'd told him she'd gone off with some fellow she'd met who had more money than he did."

"When was this?"

"I don't remember. A year ago, perhaps."

"Did he say where she was from? Who her people were?"

"I think someone said St. Louis."

"And this one that's with him now?"

"Oh, she's only been with him for about a year, if that. But I will say one thing, he sticks to the same type. This one's practically a carbon copy of the other one."

"Short, dark, with … ah … a well-developed figure?"

"Yes, exactly. Blond, though. The first one was just the same except for that. Same figure, same cheap clothes, same trashy look. Painted their faces, wore lots of jewelry. Obviously some men like that sort of thing, and not just the sort of men who work down in the mines, either, I can tell you that."

"Who do you mean, ma'am?"

"Just never you mind who I mean," she said, laying a finger aside her nose and winking grotesquely at him. "I know what I saw. Over a year ago, this was. You ask around. You'll find out that some folks that are all high and mighty about other folks ought to tend to their own affairs and not be casting stones."

Buckner nodded. "But you can't tell me any names."

"Course I can," she replied smugly. "But I won't." She smiled her thin, mean smile. "You won't catch me carrying tales. I mind my own business. Digging into decent folks' lives is your line, not mine."

"I see," Buckner said. "Can you tell me her name? Peralta's woman?"

"Which one? This one or the other one?"

"Either one?"

"No, I told you. I don't have anything to do with people like that."

"What do you think happened to her?"

"I haven't any idea. Probably got tired of him and went home to her mother. I will say, he was not too happy about it, whatever the reason. She was his bank account. She hadn't been gone but a month or so when he went off somewhere and came back with another one in no time at all. That's the one that's with him now."

"Do you know where she was from? Anything at all?"

"I never spoke two words to her, Chief, but the talk was she was from St. Louis too."

"All right." Buckner pocketed his notebook. "Thank you, ma'am. Uh, will you be here for a while, in case I have any more questions?"

"Of course I will. Where else would you expect me to be?"

"Yes, ma'am." Buckner went downstairs.

Mrs. Mouser had gone back to her magazine, but her smile was just as warm.

"I hope my mother was able to help with your investigation, Chief Buckner."

"Yes, ma'am. Thank you."

Elsie appeared and showed him out. As he went down the walk, he glanced at his watch. Nearly six. He hadn't eaten since breakfast—twelve hours ago. He crossed the town square, turned north, and spotted Durand on the other side of the street.

"Hang on a minute," he called. Durand waited while he crossed. "I need you to check into something for me. Ask around about Robert Charboneau, up in Taylor. Find out if he had that boarding house of his insured against fire. You might start with Walter Carroll. He sells a lot of insurance around here, and maybe up in Taylor too. Or knows somebody that does."

"Right, Buck. Anything else?"

"Not for right now."

"How deep should I dig on this? There's nobody up in Taylor selling insurance, I know that for a fact. But there's Bonne Terre, Steelville, Ironton. You want me to check that far away?"

"Start here in town first and let me know what you find out."

"Right."

Durand resumed his patrol, and Buckner headed for home.

 5

A short walk took Buckner to a small house in a tidy yard. A flagstone walk led to a porch just wide enough for a couple of wicker chairs. He went straight in and hung his hat on a rack in the short hallway. A dining room to the left led to a kitchen at the back. The tall woman with iron-gray hair standing at the stove turned to confront him. "What are you doing here?"

"I live here. Besides, I couldn't help myself. I could smell fried chicken all the way out on the sidewalk."

"Don't expect me to be flattered. I know Judith doesn't like to cook, but don't the two of you usually eat at that Chinese place?"

"Judith is up in Columbia."

"Oh? What's she doing there?"

"Taking classes so she can get another degree," Buckner said. He added, "She's tired of being assistant principal here in Corinth, but they won't promote her. She says having this other degree will improve her chances of getting hired as a school principal."

"Will the town be able to afford her once she gets this degree?"

"I don't know," Buckner admitted.

"And I don't suppose there's much chance of her settling down and marrying you."

"I've stopped asking," Buckner said.

"The two of you are in danger of becoming a subject of conversation."

"I've mentioned that a couple of times. Judith says she doesn't care. She regards marriage as an archaic … uh, vestige of the Middle Ages."

Buckner's mother snorted at that, but only asked, "When will she be back?"

"I don't know," Buckner said. "Anyway, nobody makes fried chicken the way you do."

"Don't be ridiculous," his mother said. She smiled and allowed him to change the topic. "Plenty of people make it this way. I learned it from Aunt Josie when I was a little girl."

"Sure. But Aunt Josie was born a slave on your grandfather's farm and she has been dead for twenty years and more, and I am starving half to death, so why don't I lay the table and we can just eat? I hope you made enough."

His mother merely snorted at that. She always made enough. Her husband had been dead for almost five years, and Buckner's sister had moved to St. Louis about the same time, but she still cooked for four, a fact that Buckner counted on whenever he tired of eating at Coy's or the Chinese restaurant.

Buckner and his mother ate at the small table in the kitchen. The large table and chairs that could seat twelve and filled the dining room had come down from the county seat when the family moved to Corinth before the war. They were for social events, but there had been no social events for many years. A stroke had crippled Buckner's father and ended his medical practice. That blow to the family's income had driven Buckner out of college and into the cavalry just as it had driven the family from the big house in the county seat to this much smaller house in Corinth. It had also somehow cast a mantle of shame over the family, as though the stroke were somehow an outward manifestation of their collective failing. And so now the unused table and chairs crowded the tiny dining room along with the matching sideboard and the tall china cabinet with its curved glass door and the glittering display of unused china.

The two of them ate in silence—chicken, boiled potatoes, greens. Buckner had two helpings of everything while his mother watched. "I've been on the run since early this morning and just never got a chance to eat anything."

"You don't eat more than a biscuit and coffee for breakfast, and usually nothing for lunch."

"Makes me sleepy."

"That is not a healthy way to live."

"I expect you're right. But I got into the habit in the cavalry and never got out of it." He finished and pushed back his plate. "I'll do the dishes."

She watched him as he worked. He pumped water into the large teakettle and set it on the stove to heat. He pumped more water into the enameled basin in the sink, added soap, and put the dinner dishes in to soak. When the teakettle was steaming, he added some of the hot water to the basin, topped off the kettle, and returned it to the stove. As he washed the dishes, his mother went to the dining room. When she returned, she was carrying a heavy crystal decanter and a tiny glass.

"Do you want sherry?"

"No, thanks. I've got to get back to the office and put together my notes from all the people in Taylor I talked to today."

"Taylor? What were you doing up there?"

"Job for Josiah Powers. Not exactly my bailiwick, but Powers needs help, and Stillson Foote's getting cranked up to run for state assembly and can't be bothered with law enforcement right now."

"He never did much along that line anyway."

"That's true."

"You worried Corinth will suffer a crime wave in your absence?"

"No. I put Shotwell in charge."

"You did? Hoping that would get you off the hook?"

"Yes, but it didn't work."

"Maybe this town's not as backward as you think."

"You may be right." He turned back to the sink. When the dishes were washed, he rinsed them in the boiling water from the kettle, putting them all to dry in the wooden rack next to the sink. As he finished, he told his mother about the dead body and the fire in Taylor.

"Why do you rely on Jeff Peck to provide you with medical information?" she asked. "His brain must be so pickled at this point that nothing he says can be credited as anything more than drunken rambling."

"Simple. I rely on Peck because nobody else in town will do the job. Big cities have medical examiners in their budgets—real physicians, some of them with real training in that sort of thing. But Corinth can't afford it, and the county won't help, so I'm left with Peck if I need that sort of information. I don't, usually. There aren't a lot of killings around here anyway, and when there is one, I can pretty well count on finding the killer standing over the corpse waving a knife or a baseball bat or a pistol still warm to the touch, and claiming it was all the dead fellow's fault. But if it's tricky, then I need Peck, and believe it or not, he does the job well. Or well enough."

Buckner emptied out the basin, dried the counter, and then dried his hands with the damp dishrag. Something Jeff Peck had said earlier made him stop. What was it? Something he'd said when they were up in Taylor. Whatever it was, it eluded his grasp. He hung the dishrag on the pump spout.

"I suppose you know best," his mother said.

"I'm not sure I do. I just know the way things are around here, and I've finally learned they aren't going to change any time soon."

"Are you talking about Jeff Peck, Judith, or the town of Corinth?"

Buckner ignored that.

After his mother had finished her sherry and disappeared upstairs, he went back to the police department. Bill Newland, who answered the phone at night, was snoring softly with his feet up on the desk. Michael Mullen would certainly disapprove, but Buckner walked quietly down to his office. Somewhere out there, Officer Carter, who seemed to prefer night duty, was probably enjoying a quiet cigarette in a dark corner. Corinth was a sleepy little town; commonly weeks went by with nothing more disturbing than a loud drunk on Saturday night. Which was exactly the way Buckner liked it. The quieter things were, the better for them all.

The cells were empty, and Mullen had left a neatly typed note on his desk: "Judge set bail at five dollars, and Amos's wife paid it. Trial next week." It was carefully signed and dated. Buckner guessed that somewhere in Mullen's files was a carbon copy. Amos Monroe's crime spree had not lasted long; neither had it caused much damage. The money and the auto he'd stolen had all been returned. Buckner expected the judge would give him sixty days on the county road gang and let it go at that.

It took Buckner only a few minutes to organize his notes from the day's round of questions. He still had to interview Moon and Thrasher. And he needed Peck's autopsy results before he could complete a report, but he read over what he had, hoping something would pop out at him … something that would clarify what had happened at the boarding house. A fire had begun. After they'd put it out, the firefighters had discovered a body concealed behind the cellar wall. Nobody so far could explain that; nobody so far knew of any missing women. The cellar was scarcely used, even less now that Peralta had stopped making wine down there. Everybody agreed it smelled bad, and nobody went down there if they could avoid it. None of the residents had been there for long, except the owner and his wife. The boarding house was used by the Company as a convenient place to put transients, but there was no record of who had stayed there over the years. Even Josiah Powers had been a tenant.

Buck turned his attention to the fire itself, and jotted names on a blank piece of paper along with random questions like "electricity?" and "wine barrels?" and "who came out first?"

but nothing popped up. He believed the origin of the fire was suspicious at best, and he had absolutely no solid reason for thinking that.

He caught himself falling asleep, so he put everything in a drawer and stared at the opposite wall and thought about it for a while. That didn't produce anything either, so he went home and went to bed.

Buckner got an early start the next morning, and was at the livery stable before six. Walter Greene, who had been mucking out stalls, leaned on his pitchfork and watched him coming. "Where you headed to this early, Buck?" he asked.

"I've got to go talk to a feller back in the hills." The sharp stable smells made Buckner's eyes water, and instantly he was back in a remote cavalry outpost doing his own tour of duty with a pitchfork and wheelbarrow. He smiled at the memory. He had joined the cavalry in 1907. He always said it was because the family couldn't afford to keep him in college, but the truth was he thought college was boring and couldn't wait to get away. When the Bankers' Panic that year combined with his father's stroke had cut deep into the family's finances, he'd made his escape. He had served along the Border, chasing Villistas and Apache reservation jumpers until the shooting started in Europe. Then he had gone north and joined the Canadian army. The experience of the trenches—all that went with that—had turned those dusty years patrolling the desert into a fond memory. He knew that was stupid. It had been hot, boring work that every now and then became extremely dangerous and absolutely terrifying. His smile broadened thinking about it.

"I can let you have that old roan horse you rode yesterday, Buck," Walter Greene said. "He's 'bout the only horse round here big enough for you ever since that bay you used to ride got kilt here couple years ago." He spat tobacco into the sodden mass of straw. "You been doin' a lot of ridin' lately," he added, openly hoping for news. "You after somebody up in the hills?"

"Fine, Walter," Buckner said. "The roan will do." He went into the corral. The horses shuffled suspiciously away to a far corner, watching him carefully. He took off his hat and bent and picked up several pebbles. He put them into his hat and shook it. The horses, having just eaten, weren't hungry, but they were curious, and they looked over and began edging his way. When they were close enough to stick their noses into his hat, he clipped a lead rope to the roan's Johnson halter and looped the other end through a ring on the barn wall. He got his saddle—a Modified McClellan—from the tack room. He preferred the 1885 model to the newer ones the army was experimenting with. Just why they were experimenting with saddles was not clear to him. If the war in Europe had proved anything, it had proved that the days of the horse cavalry were over—had been over for a long time, except that those cement-headed officers in their flared breeches and high-topped boots and spurs couldn't let it go. Still, he had to admit there was something about a horse, and though an hour in the saddle put fresh fire in his bad leg, he still used any excuse to get on one.

Walter Greene kept asking questions while Buckner worked, and Buckner kept parrying the questions. He finally went on the offensive. "How's that new gasoline pump working, Walter?"

"Oh, all right. Cost me plenty to have the tank put in, and the oil company leases me the pump, but lots of folks come here to get their machines gassed up. I expect I'll have the whole thing paid for by the end of next year. Maybe."

"Why maybe?" Greene owned the only remaining livery stable in Corinth, and the gasoline pump was a new addition.

"Cause it ain't a-gonna last," Greene answered. "Most folks can't afford them new autos, and you can't drive 'em anyplace 'cept around town, the roads is so bad. And if they break down somewhere out in the country, you can't fix 'em and you're stuck."

"A passing fad, you figure?"

"Yep. Not like horses. Folks been relyin' on horses since the beginning of time, and if they're smart, they'll go right on with it."

"That'd be all right with me, Walter." Buckner mounted and rode out of town.

The roan had a nice trot that ate up the ground without tiring him out—or rattling Buckner's teeth loose. Three hours later Buckner was in the hills above Taylor, following a faint track through scrub oak and pine. Here, out of the direct sunlight, the morning air was cool and still. The sound of the roan's hooves blended with the singing, chirping, buzzing, rustling sounds of the forest. Buckner relaxed and breathed easy and for a moment wondered why he didn't spend more time up here. The answer intruded at once. He wasn't here for pleasure, after all. He was hoping to find out why someone had killed a young woman and stuffed her in a barrel and poured acid on over her body. Then buried it in a cellar wall.

Ratliff's Fork was a narrow trickle of water flowing sluggishly below a hill of tumbled gray rock, working its way down to the St. Francois River and eventually to the Mississippi, many miles away. Buckner dismounted and let the roan drink while he pushed the toe of one boot through flint chips along the bank. He found a few worked flakes and one or two broken points, but nothing worth saving. He had known plenty of Indians during his cavalry days—scouts like Sergeant Riley, who worked for the army; the reservation Indians; and the ragged bands of renegades he had tracked and pursued. But the Indians who had made arrowheads out of this flint and hunted these hills were long gone, disappeared from the land long before his people had moved in. Had they been driven out or killed off by other Indians, or by the whites who took the land from them? Or maybe they had simply moved on, looking for better hunting grounds. He would never know, and all that was left of them was these stone chips and the arrowheads he sometimes collected and kept in a cigar box at home … his way of touching a bit of that unknowable past.

When the roan was finished drinking, Buckner bent down and scooped up a handful of water, drank some of it, and rubbed his face with what remained. Leading the roan, he turned downstream, and then northeast, following the base of the hill. He smelled wood smoke immediately … wood smoke with an undertone of bacon grease. He could see a thin line of smoke rising above the treetops. In a moment, he saw the house. It was a traditional dogtrot house—two totally separate rooms of squared-off logs fitted with wooden pegs and chinked with clay and gravel and then joined by a covered bay. The bays of some dogtrot houses were not walled; this one was. Some dogtrots had a covered gallery running across the front; this one did not—just a screen door that opened into a weed-choked yard. Buckner guessed the house had been built before the War Between the States. The heavy green shutters still had the original cruciform firing slits that were included routinely back then, even if they were never used in defense against those vanished Indians.

He stopped in the yard and waited for a moment in plain view, so that anybody inside could see him clearly. It did not pay to appear to be sneaking up on a house back in these hills. Finally, he called out. "Mr. Thrasher!" In a minute, a short, stocky, weathered man with a frying pan in one hand came to the screen door.

"Yeah? Who're you? Whaddya want?"

"I'm Chief Buckner from Corinth, Mr. Thrasher. I want to talk to you about the fire the other day at Bob Charboneau's boarding house."

"You mean about that dead body they found in the cellar, don't you?"

"That, too, Mr. Thrasher."

"Well, come on in. You can leave your horse over there." He gestured with the frying pan at a ring post by the corner of the house. Buckner tied the lead rope loosely, giving the horse enough slack to nibble at the sparse grass, and went inside. The smell of bacon frying was stronger in here, making his mouth water.

He must have looked hungry, because Thrasher said, "You want some?"

"No, thanks," Buckner said, following Thrasher into the right-hand cabin, which was furnished with a heavy iron cook stove, a table, and three mismatched chairs. "But your coffee smells fresh made, and I'll have some of that if it's all right."

"Help yourself." Thrasher set the frying pan down on a shelf next to the stove, took a plate from a lower shelf, forked the bacon onto it, added beans from a pot at the back of the stove, and sat down. Buckner got a tin mug from the shelf and filled it with coffee; then he refilled the cup sitting on the table in front of Thrasher. He sat in a chair opposite and blew carefully on the coffee before sipping. It didn't help; the hot tin burned his lip.

"I don't believe I can tell you a thing about the fire, nor about them bodies, neither," Thrasher said, chewing bacon and beans. His head was completely bald, and his eyebrows were so light colored they seemed to vanish as well, making him look surprised, with a forehead that began just above his nose and ran clear over the top of his head. His eyes were a washed-out blue. "I woke up when I heard everbody yellin' 'fire!' and I got out right smart, stood in the yard, and watched the place burn down. Then I borried me some clothes and shoes from a feller I know there in town and come on up here."

"Did you know any of the other tenants in the building?"

"Some. Mostly just to speak to. I only put up there when I'm workin', and when I'm workin', that's all I do … 'bout all I got time for."

"Then you'd come back here when you'd made your score?"

"Shore." He grinned. "Ain't many of us old-timers left. The Company broke the Western Federation and kept the Wobblies out, and now the United Mine Workers is trying to get in, but the Company's too damn strong." He paused a moment. "Fer one thing, they got all the cops on their side."

"Did you know Peralta and his wife?" Buckner asked. He did not want to discuss labor theory with Thrasher. He never had anything against the Wobblies—the Industrial Workers of the

World—only against its members who had been trying, at the time, to kill him.

"Well ..." Thrasher leered at him. "I knew better'n to play cards with that dago, so you'd have to say I knew the wife a lot better'n I knew him. If you get my meanin'."

"So you paid Mr. Peralta the five dollars to go with his woman?"

"Shore. Both of 'em."

"Both of them?" That other woman again.

"Yeah. There was that first one, the one come with him when he first come to town. Then she took off, and he got him the second one. He was what you might call a real businessman. Took it real serious. Gambling was his calling, but he needed a woman for backup."

"So he had two different women, and you went with both of them?"

"Hell yes. I ain't that old, and even a feller my age likes to get his ashes hauled once in a while."

"And you used their room in the boarding house?"

"Oh, hell no. Charboneau wouldn't've allowed that sort of thing."

"Where'd you go, then? Where did she conduct her business?"

"Oh, wherever. You know how it is. If the weather wasn't too bad, just off in the woods. But there's places, if'n you know where to look."

"The shed behind Shorty's?"

"That's one," Thrasher agreed.

"All right. Do you know either of their names?"

"No." Thrasher seemed surprised. "I wasn't lookin' to get to be friends with 'em."

"Other than yourself, then, did you see Peralta's woman—either of them—with anybody in particular? Did she spend extra time with any one man?"

"Not that I saw. The company cops kept both of them on the move, I know that."

"This was Kelson and Garber?"

"Yeah. They was always after the both of 'em ... kept 'em jumpin', that's fer sure. If ever that Kelson seen either one of 'em around, he'd move 'em on right smart."

"But they never ran either of them out of town, did they?"

"Well, no, I guess they didn't, now you mention it," Thrasher acknowledged. "Just wanted 'em to know who was boss, the way cops do."

"Did you ever see either of them with her? Kelson or Garber?"

"Huh. That's funny. Now you mention it, I don't believe I ever did. But that's no surprise, knowing how Old Lady Powers feels about that sort of thing."

"How does he feel?"

"Oh, you know how the Company's always been. They was always hell on booze and women, but they really just settled on a live-and-let-live policy. I guess they figgered they could tolerate the booze and gamblin' and the women so long as they could keep the unions out. That was their main concern. But Powers, he hates all that. He's got that wife and that little boy of his, prances around like Little Lord Fauntleroy in them fancy outfits. They figger they's better'n everbody else on earth. They's the first ones into the church come Sunday mornin', and they go to Wednesday prayer meetings, and she plays that new organ they got last year. Won't let nobody else touch it, even Reverend Scobby. Anyway, he can just barely tolerate the sight of folks like Peralta and his woman, but he knows company policy is to just leave it alone, even if it's never been written up anywheres. So he's always tryin' to get them fallen women to go to prayer meetings ... reform themselves ... save their souls." Thrasher shook his head. "Don't have much luck there, I s'pect. Anyway, he keeps a pretty close eye on his people, you can bet on that."

"Uh-huh. What about Powers himself?"

"What do you mean?" Thrasher looked at Buckner. "You mean him and one of them whores? Huh. That's interestin', is what that is."

"Why?"

"Oh, nuthin' really. Just what some folks said about him, that's all. His wife bein' poorly an' all."

"But nothing that you know of."

"No, not really." Thrasher leaned forward in his chair. "Looky here, I don't care much for Powers, but he lets me work the old way an' he leaves me alone. So I leave him alone. All right?"

"Sure. Now, about the fire. What happened that night?"

"Oh, hell, I don't know. I was asleep and I heard all that bangin' and yellin' and I got out."

"Who was out there when you came out?"

"What do you mean?"

"Were you the first one out of the building?"

"Oh, no, I wasn't. There was the Widow Janeworthy and Miz Charboneau already there when I come out; then the Moons followed after, and old Lester Stratton come last, best as I can recall."

"All right." Buckner made notes. He asked, "Did you ever have occasion to use a candle when you were living there?"

"What for? They was on the electric that the Company provided, like everbody else. Wasn't no need for candles."

"I see. Well, Mr. Thrasher, thanks for your time."

"Wait a minute, hold on there. What about them bodies in the cellar?"

"Just one body, Mr. Thrasher." Buckner smiled his friendliest smile. "You spend much time down in the cellar, Mr. Thrasher?"

"Me? Hell no! No, sir. I mind my own business."

"And you never went down there?"

"Nope. Not once. I know that dago used to go down there a lot, though." Thrasher leaned forward, eager to tell the story. "Said he was makin' wine down there, but, hell, you can't believe nuthin' he says. He coulda been doin' anything down there, you know what I mean? Not me, though. I come into town, make my score, come back up here, do some fishin'. I got trotlines set. Traps too. Eat the meat, sell the pelts. All I ever did was sleep in that room Charboneau rented me."

Buckner nodded. "Did you ever see anybody moving a steamer trunk in or out of the cellar?"

"Steamer trunk? No. Well, I b'lieve the Widow Janeworthy had one when she moved in, but that's all I know about it."

"What about sulfuric acid? Did anybody move sulfuric acid into the cellar?"

"Sulfuric acid? You mean like they keep up at the smelter? Hell no. Man, that stuff's dangerous—burn a hole right through you, you ain't careful. So, no, sir, I don't have nuthin' to do with no sulfuric acid."

"All right, then." Buckner got up. "This is a nice place you got up here, Mr. Thrasher."

"It'll do. My grandfather built it, way back. Built it to last. It'll be here long after we're gone, that's for sure."

"I expect you're right. Well, I'll be seeing you."

"Shore. Glad to help. Hey, you ain't finished yer coffee." Buckner ignored him and went outside. He untied the roan and waved good-bye to Mr. Thrasher.

The way back to Corinth took Buckner close enough to Taylor to stop at the company office. Tom was working at his desk. "Mr. Moon's the last occupant of the boarding house I need to talk to," Buckner said.

Tom grumbled but went out to get Mr. Moon. Buckner paced the silent, empty office for half an hour. Finally, he heard heavy boots coming up the steps. Tom entered followed by a powerfully built man wearing dusty work clothes and carrying a miner's hat. His face was also covered with dust, and his eyes were tired and red rimmed. He stopped and looked at Buckner. "You're the chief of police that talked to my wife," he said.

"Yes, sir, I am. I was hoping you might have some more information for me." Buckner was aware of Tom going to his desk and sitting. Moon's eyes also followed the secretary's movements.

"Could we just step outside a moment, Mr. Moon?" Buckner asked. "We want to let Tom here get back to work." And he smiled.

Moon just nodded and the two of them walked out.

"I'll just walk you back to work, Mr. Moon, if that's all right."

"I guess so."

The mine head, with the heavy steel structure that brought ore up and took men down, was a hundred yards up the hill. The two men moved slowly, crossing the tracks for the ore carts, passing men at work.

"I ain't sure I can tell you anything 'bout that fire that my wife didn't, Chief," Moon said.

"That'll be all right, too, Mr. Moon. I just need to get everybody's account of what happened."

Moon's story was an exact copy of his wife's, with one exception. "Your wife told me you lost everything, is that right?"

"Everthing but this." Moon took large wallet from his rear trouser pocket and opened it. He unfolded it and handed Buckner an oval-shaped photograph of himself and his wife in their wedding outfits. "I grabbed this," he said. "Didn't have time for nothin' else."

"I'm sorry," Buckner said.

"Oh, we'll do all right," Moon said. "Company's been real good to us right along. They'll have us in one of their places pretty quick, you can bet on that." He laughed. "'Course, we're runnin' short on clothes and such right now, but we're all paid up at the store, so we're all right on that account, too." He indicated the photograph. "This is the only thing mattered to me anyway."

"Did you know Mr. Peralta or his wife?"

"Not more'n just to speak to." Moon grinned. "My wife didn't think much of them two, and she sure wasn't about to put up with me talking to that woman, neither, so I just said howdy and let it go at that. And she won't have me gamblin', so there really ain't no reason for me to be doin' much more'n that."

Buckner asked about the cellar.

"Never went down there," Moon said. "Not once in the time we lived there. Wasn't no need."

Buckner thanked him and watched as he got into the elevator, waved, and descended into the ground. Back in the office, Buckner found Tom bent over pages filled with columns of figures. When Buckner requested an audience with Powers, Tom was reluctant to interrupt his boss.

"He's going to want to hear what I've got to say."

Tom frowned, but knocked on the door anyway, opened it, and stepped back. Through the doorway, Buckner saw Powers look up from a file thick with columns of numbers. He had a large calculating machine at hand and was in the process of punching keys and pulling the handle.

"I just wanted to let you know I talked to Thrasher, Mr. Moon, and Miz Janeworthy," Buckner said. "And none of them knows any more about the fire or the body than anybody else."

Powers leaned back in his chair and looked at Buckner for a long time before speaking. "So we're nowhere, really, is that right?"

"Yes, that's about right."

"All right. I'm glad you stopped in. I was going to telephone you anyway. I was finally able to track down the county sheriff. He's set up an office over in Jefferson City to coordinate his candidacy with the state party leadership. He as much as told me he wasn't interested. As far as he is concerned, the whole thing happened on company property and it's up to the Company to clean up its own mess."

"Even if part of that so-called mess is a dead woman?"

"He said as far as he is concerned, it's no different than some miner falling down a mine shaft or getting killed in a cave-in. Company business."

"Even though she wasn't a company employee, and the fire wasn't on company property?" Buckner sometimes wondered why Foote bothered calling himself a lawman.

"As far as Sheriff Foote is concerned, it's all company property."

"Are you familiar with this man Peralta and his wife?" Buckner asked. "They were residents in the boarding house."

"Peralta?" He frowned slightly. "Is he an employee? The name doesn't ring a bell. Tom could tell you for sure. Who is he?"

"He's a gambler who travels with a woman he claims is his wife, only when he runs short on cash, he lets other men go with her for five dollars."

"That's disgusting. They live here?"

"Yes. They lived in Charboneau's boarding house."

"And you say he's a gambler and, in effect, a pimp for his wife? Is she really his wife?"

"I don't know. I just wondered if you were aware of them."

"Honestly, Chief Buckner, I don't involve myself in the employees' private lives any more than I have to. I run a mining and smelting operation, and that consumes my full attention. The fact that the operation happens to have an entire town connected with it is a consequence of conditions beyond my control. I wish the situation were otherwise, but there you are. I leave things like that to the company police. Of course, I'm in charge." Powers smiled his thin smile. "I suppose that makes me chief of police of Taylor. But all of that is their job, and I try to stay out of it. Unfortunately, a place like Taylor attracts parasites … people who produce nothing themselves but suck the money out of people who do the way a tick sucks blood. The Company's policy is reluctant tolerance of such people, but I have strict orders for my people to move them along. Otherwise, I try to stay out of it."

"Until something unpleasant turns up, like a dead body," Buckner said. This was not exactly the picture Thrasher had painted of Josiah Powers.

"Yes. It has nothing directly to do with the operations of the Company—nothing whatever to do with my primary responsibilities—but the fact that it happened in the midst of company property complicates matters and in effect compels my involvement."

"One more thing. As near as I can tell, all the people living in that boarding house, except the Charboneaus, were temporary residents on their way to someplace else. Is that correct?"

"Yes, I believe it is," Powers said.

"All right. I'll have a preliminary report for you this afternoon, and by then Dr. Peck will be done with his work on the body, so we'll be back, either later today or first thing in the morning."

"The sooner the better." Powers went back to punching keys, and Buckner walked out. He stopped at Tom's desk.

"Kelson or Garber around?" he asked.

"They should be," Tom answered.

"Anyplace in particular?"

"They patrol the town, Chief Buckner. They could be anyplace."

"Thanks." Buckner went out onto the porch. People were at work or at home; the streets were empty. Buckner walked to the mine entrance, where he found Garber chatting with the man who operated the donkey engine that raised and lowered the elevator the miners took to get to work.

"Howdy, Chief," Garber said, grinning and winking at the engine operator.

"I just need to ask you a quick question," Buckner said.

"Well, I'm pretty busy," Garber replied, his grin broadening. "So make it quick."

"How long have you worked here in Taylor?"

"Oh, gosh, over ten … twelve years now," Garber said. "Back in nineteen fifteen it was when I started."

"The Company provide housing?"

"Not right away. They put me up at Charboneau's for about six months. That's the way they do it, you know. They got operations all over the place, and they move folks around a lot and they ain't always got places for 'em to stay in."

"How about Kelson?" Buckner asked. "Did he stay at Charboneau's too?"

"Couldn't say. He was working here when I started and had him a nice, cozy little place down the way there." Garber pointed down the street.

"Right. Thanks. Just out of curiosity, how was it? Staying at Charboneau's?"

"All right." Garber shrugged. "Nothing fancy. Food wasn't much neither."

"You ever go down in the cellar?"

"Never had no reason to."

"Did Charboneau keep it locked?"

"I don't believe so. Why would he?"

"No reason. Thanks."

Buckner went back to the office, retrieved his horse, and mounted. He rode slowly down the hill wondering why Josiah Powers hadn't mentioned his work saving the souls of fallen women. In his experience, people who did good works were seldom reluctant to talk about their efforts.

Walter Greene offered to take care of the roan when Buckner got back. "Part of what you're payin' for, Buck," he insisted.

"I know that, Walter, but I like to do it myself." So he unsaddled the roan, rubbed him down with a feed sack, brushed and curried him, and then turned him into the corral.

"Just like the old days, huh, Buck?" Walter said, watching from his seat on an empty molasses barrel.

"Only if you were wearing first sergeant's stripes and cussing a blue streak, Walter."

Greene laughed and agreed.

6

Buckner spent lunchtime in his office finishing his report. He had encountered typewriters in the army, where they were used for the morning report first and then for everything else. But he had never been able to do more than hunt and peck laboriously at the keys with two fingers. Recently, Judith Lee had given him the typing book students in the eighth grade used, but he still had not gone beyond the first lesson. Michael Mullen, of course, typed with machine-gun speed, and without looking at the keys at all. As a product of the local school system, he had got all the way through the lesson book and passed with flying colors. This opened up the chance for him to learn shorthand, and Mullen had effortlessly mastered that as well. Buckner often thought about having Mullen type up his reports, but decided since he was making all his officers type out their reports, he ought to face the same hazards. So it took him an hour to go over his notes, sketches, and photographs and then another hour to type up a summary and one-page report. It all looked so brief, containing little more than a list of occupants and length of occupation, plus their stories about the fire. He had included details about usage of the cellar and the dead rat smell that several tenants had noted. All of this he carefully folded into his pocket. After leaving carbon copies on Mullen's desk, he crossed to the back of Coy's Drug Store and climbed the stairs to Peck's office. He found the doctor sleeping on his examination table. The table was narrow and short, and Buckner wondered how he managed to avoid falling off—or, for that matter, how he got onto it in the first place, given his normal state.

He shook Peck gently by the shoulder.

"Leave me alone," he mumbled.

"Did you finish the autopsy?" Buckner said.

"What autopsy?"

"The one of the dead—"

"Of course I did. Go away."

"Do you have a report?" Buckner insisted.

Peck fumbled in a pocket and found a crumpled envelope, which he waved in the air.

"Fine," Buckner said. "Get up and we'll take it to Josiah Powers."

"Why do I have to go with you?"

"What else do you have to do today?"

"I was planning on drinking."

"You do that every day. You ought to take some time off every now and then. All work and no play, you know."

"What's the rush?"

"Powers promised to give you money. You don't want him to forget."

"Oh. Right." Peck struggled into a sitting position. His suit coat and vest and shirt collar lay in a pile on a chair in the corner. Buckner handed them over. While Peck got dressed, he scanned the envelope. Peck's scrawled notes were indecipherable. "Can you read this?" he asked, holding it out.

"Certainly." Peck put the envelope in a pocket of his coat. From the other pocket he extracted a tie and held it up. "Do you think I'll need to wear this?"

"Probably wouldn't hurt your professional standing with Powers."

"He is not qualified to evaluate my professional standing," Peck said. But he put on the tie.

"Sure," Buckner agreed. "He's just the one paying you. Let's go."

As they drove out of town, Buckner said, "Well, are you going to tell me what you found?"

"I'm going to tell you and Powers at the same time. Save my energy."

Peck slumped in the corner and slept all the way to Taylor. When they arrived, Buckner noticed that nobody was guarding the site of the fire. People walking past barely glanced at it. Were they avoiding knowing about it? Or had it already dropped out of their minds? Most of the debris had been cleared away, so there was little to look at in any case.

Tom ushered them in when they arrived.

"You're very prompt, Chief Buckner," Powers said, rising to greet them.

"You said the sooner the better. Besides, I want to get this over with as much as you do." Buckner turned to Peck. "You want to go first?"

Peck nodded. He took the folded envelope from his pocket. It slipped from his fingers and fluttered to the floor. As he bent to pick it up, Powers looked at Buckner with raised eyebrows. Buckner shrugged and returned what he hoped was a reassuring smile.

"All right," Peck said, standing and brushing imaginary dust from the envelope. He glanced at it and then up at Powers and began. "There were two corpses—"

"I was there, Doctor," Powers interrupted. "There was only one corpse."

"Really?" Peck said. "Were you standing next to me during the autopsy and somehow I missed seeing you because you're so self-effacing?" As Powers' face got bright red, Peck continued. "Then let me do what you're going to pay me money to do. The body we took out of the cellar wall," he said, ignoring his notes, "was that of a woman in her late teens, perhaps as old as twenty, and she was approximately ten weeks pregnant."

"Good God," Peck whispered.

"Probably no deity was involved," Peck said. "But that's just my medical opinion."

"How can you tell all that ... the woman's age, all that?" Peck said. "If you don't mind my asking."

"I do. Teeth, pelvis, bone development, other things. I've looked at a lot of human bodies, dead and otherwise, over the past twenty-odd years—more than you have, I expect—so you'll just have to take my word for it. And if you keep interrupting me, we'll be here all week, and since I charge by the hour, my bill will keep going up."

Powers, a vein pulsing in his crimson forehead, clamped his mouth shut. The muscles in his jaw writhed with the effort of holding the words in. He nodded for Peck to continue.

"The woman was strangled," he said. "Judging by the damage to the hyoid bone—that's a U-shaped bone down in your neck, kind of keeps your tongue from flopping around. You can feel it for yourself if you want, right above your Adam's apple. Strangulation was likely manual, but I won't swear to it. And the corpse had been subjected to an acid bath."

"So what did the acid do to the body?"

"Dissolved some of the flesh. In addition the flesh was saponified. Which all means that we couldn't identify the corpse by facial features or fingerprints. But the teeth are in pretty good shape, and I understand there has been some work lately on identifying corpses by dental records. Of course, that requires a dental record to compare her teeth with. Assuming she ever went to a dentist. There weren't any fillings, so there's no way to tell. Besides, which dentist where, if you see what I mean. Anyway, as nearly as I can determine, the body was subjected to the acid bath only briefly before it was taken out and immured."

Buckner glanced at Peck.

"Walled up."

"Oh, like 'The Cask of Amontillado.'"

"Yes, only our lady was dead at the time. The hole was reasonably air tight, cool and dry, and the soil must have been highly alkaline, all of which explains the saponification."

"Saponification?" Powers said.

"Conversion of fatty tissue into adipocere—grave wax—although I'm not really sure how the acid would affect that process. That goes beyond my experience."

"Oh, yes." Powers looked for a moment as though he might throw up. "Why only briefly, Doctor?" He continued swallowing hard. "In the acid bath, I mean."

Peck shrugged. "Couldn't say. Maybe the murderer ran out of time and couldn't leave it in the acid as long as he wanted. If you're going to dissolve something as big as a human body, you're going to need a lot of acid. Maybe he ran out. Maybe he just didn't care beyond erasing identifying characteristics. I haven't got much else to add, anyway. No other identifying marks, except that she had broken her arm at some point early in life. Left radius, if you're interested. And it wasn't properly set. You could feel it with your hand."

"And the ... the, uh ..." Powers stammered.

"The fetus died when the mother died, which was, by my estimation, about a year ago," Peck said. He reached out and took the pen from Powers' desk set, flipped open the ink well, and dipped the pen. He thought a moment and then scribbled something on the envelope, returned the pen, and handed the envelope to Powers. "That's it. Here's my bill."

Powers frowned at the envelope, but he nodded and opened a drawer low down in his desk. He took out a small metal box and then retrieved a small key from a pocket in his vest. When the box was opened, he counted out some bills behind the open lid of the box, and gave them to Peck. He then scribbled a note on a scrap of paper, tossed it into the box, shut and locked the box, and returned it to the drawer.

"Do you want a receipt?" Peck asked. He folded the bills without looking at them and stuffed them in a pocket.

"Not necessary," Powers said, tucking the key back into his pocket. He turned to Buckner. "What do you have for me?"

"Less than the doctor here.

"All right. We'll see. Go on."

"I talked to everybody who was living in the boarding house at the time. Nobody knows anything about the fire, and nobody knows anything about the body in the cellar. There is a general impression that the fire started on the ground floor, possibly in the parlor, but nobody knows for sure. Basically, nobody knows anything at all about anything."

"But ... well ... don't you have any leads, any clues ... anything?"

"I have all kinds of leads about all kinds of things. I really have no idea where she was killed. I think she was put in one of those barrels after she was dead. I think acid, carried to the cellar in those big demijohns, was poured over the corpse; then the acid was poured onto the dirt floor and the body walled up. But that's really just supposition. I know now, thanks to Doctor Peck, that she was about twenty and pregnant and that she was blonde. But none of that tells me who she was or how she got there. Or how the fire started. Or if there is any connection between the body and the fire, other than the one causing the discovery of the other."

"Not much," Powers agreed. "What other things?"

"I'm not sure they're relevant to the body in the cellar, Mr. Powers, although they might be relevant to the fire. In any case, they're just leads ... ideas ... possible areas to look into."

"But—"

"I will continue to look into them, but unless they lead me to identifying the body, or the cause of the fire, I'm not sure they're a company matter. In fact, I'm not really sure the body in the cellar is a company matter."

"Not a company matter?" Powers was muttering to himself. "As far as New York is concerned, everything that happens in this town is a company matter, and hence my responsibility. The Company and Sheriff Foote are in complete agreement on that." He laughed unhappily.

"The boarding house and the land it sat on were private property," Buckner said. "If it ever comes up, you can remind them of that. And as for the body, I really don't know at this point beyond what I've just told you. But, if I can turn up anything—

anything at all even remotely connecting the body in the cellar, or the fire, with the Company—I will inform you immediately."

"Well, Chief Buckner," Powers said in a calmer, satisfied tone, "you're really telling me you have no information at all for me, and I don't see how I can pay you for that."

"I don't either," Buckner said. "No information, no charge. Although, technically, no information is still information." He looked at Peck. "You ready to go?"

"Been ready." Peck tapped the pocket that held his money.

Buckner thanked Powers and they left. He spotted Garber, cloth cap pushed back on his head, jacket off, sleeves rolled up above his elbows, crossing the road toward them. The butt of a large revolver stuck ostentatiously from one pocket. *Probably carries brass knuckles and a sap somewhere as well*, Buckner thought. He held up a hand.

"Did you ever see Peralta hanging around the storage shed where they keep the sulfuric acid?"

"Nah. He never got up this way. He was always hanging around the blind pigs—Shorty's, places like that. That's where his money came from."

"And you and Kelson are in charge of keeping an eye on the acid once it's in drums?"

"Sure, along with every other damn thing in this town." Garber showed Buckner a large ring of keys hanging from his belt. "Keep the key right here. Kelson's got one, too. I guess that stuff's valuable, and the Company don't like to lose track of anything worth money."

"All right. Thanks."

"Sure." Garber continued up the office steps and through the door.

"One more stop," Buckner said to Peck. The doctor shrugged.

They went to Shorty's. Donahue was out. There were men drinking, but neither Peralta nor his woman was around.

"Haven't seen 'em since the other day," the barman said without looking up from his polishing.

Buckner ran his gaze over the handful of drinkers, but nobody looked back.

Buckner and Peck returned to the flivver. Buckner drove in silence while Peck muttered and glared out the window.

"You talking to me?"

"No, I'm not," Peck said.

"Who are you talking to?"

"Myself."

"What are you saying to yourself?"

"One thing I'm saying is that Josiah Powers had better watch his blood pressure. Did you see the way his face got red? He's heading for a stroke if he doesn't watch out."

"Anything else?"

"Are you calling it quits on this thing?"

"I thought you were talking to yourself."

"I was. Now I'm talking to you. Are you?"

"I don't know. I told Powers I'd keep looking into it. I'm curious about Peralta's first wife ... woman ... whatever she was."

"What first wife?"

Buckner told the doctor what he had learned from Mrs. Janeworthy and Thrasher.

"And she just disappeared one day?"

"That's what they told me."

"Any chance she disappeared into the cellar wall?"

"Yeah, that had occurred to me." Buckner drove a while in silence and then started again. "What if she got pregnant and Peralta decided to cut his losses and find himself another woman? After he'd given the first one a quick acid bath? Wouldn't be hard to pick up plenty of the stuff, since it looks like they don't keep very close track of it. He could put it in one of those barrels he was using for wine down there in the cellar. Take it over a bit at a time and pour it in one of those barrels. Nobody ever went down there, so nobody'd be the wiser. Then shove the body in." He thought some more. "How long would it take to dissolve a body in acid?"

"You mean completely? I couldn't say. A long time would be my guess, and you'd need plenty of the stuff, too. More than a barrel full, because as it dissolves something, it changes and loses its capacity for dissolving stuff. As I recall, anyway."

"But a barrel full would sure take care of fingerprints."

"Seems to have done in this case." Peck considered this. "It's not a bad idea."

"Of course, that's all it is, an idea. Finger prints are fine, but you have to have something to compare them with."

"Well, how does the body get into the cellar?" Peck asked.

"I don't know. I guess it depends."

"On what?"

"On where she was killed. You said she was strangled, so he doesn't have to worry about blood or noise."

"Not if he's quick, and whoever did it was quick. That's how you snap the hyoid bone."

"All right. If he does it in their room, he's got to get her to the cellar."

"He could just carry her."

"Kind of risky. Maybe he could use that steamer trunk that was down there. Haul it upstairs, put her in it, haul it back down."

"Even riskier, wouldn't you say?" Peck said. "Hauling a steamer up and down the stairs. Easier to get her down to the cellar, maybe to help with the wine making, strangle her there, dump her in the acid, pull her out after it's done its work, and put her in the cellar wall."

"There was a pair of rubber gloves down there. Would those protect his hands?"

"Yes. Then just dump the barrel out onto the dirt floor, where it'd be absorbed in time."

"But why use acid at all?" Buckner said. "Why not just dump the body in the woods?"

"And why kill her at all?" Peck asked.

"Because she was pregnant and was getting unpleasant about that? Or because pretty soon she wouldn't be able to work anymore and would just be dead weight?"

Buckner went silent, thinking and driving.

"So what are you going to do about it?" Peck demanded.

"I don't know. I'm going to keep checking, I guess. Trouble is, that girl, whoever she was, is not really my responsibility, but the town of Corinth is."

They were in town by now, and Peck subsided into silence. Buckner pulled the Ford into the empty lot behind the town hall, stopped next to its departmental twin, and shut off the engine.

"Was there anything you left out of that report you gave Powers?" Buckner asked.

"Of course not," Peck snapped. "What are you talking about?"

"I don't know," Buckner answered. He tried to explain. "There was something you said while we were up there that's been nagging at me, only I can't remember what it was."

"Well, let me know when you think of it," Peck said. "But I didn't leave anything out."

"All right."

"All right," Peck said. He got out and slammed the door. "Be seeing you."

Buckner sat for a moment alone in the Ford and then got out. He stopped and stood for a moment with one foot on the running board, watching Peck's receding back, trying to remember. After a bit, he realized that he was speaking to himself, so he went inside and down the stairs. Mullen looked up briefly, smiled and nodded.

"That back lot up there's full of broken glass and a lot of other trash," Buckner snapped. "I want it cleaned up by the end of the day. It looks like a junk heap, and I'm going to wind up with a flat tire one of these days."

"Uh, okay, Buck, but there's nobody around—"

"Just get it cleaned up. I don't care who does it—you, Willis, the man in the moon! Just get it cleaned up."

"Right, Buck."

Buckner shut the door of his office and sat at his desk. He heard the clock in the tower strike four. Footsteps, quick and sharp, came down the hall, and his sister walked in and sat down.

"What's this about a fire and dead bodies piled up in a cellar in Taylor?" she demanded.

"Hello, Marthy," Buckner said.

"Hello. About these bodies." She had a notebook and pencil in hand and looked at her brother expectantly. "Well?"

"Mother telephoned you?"

"No. Got a wire from George Ligget over at the *Democrat-Observer.*"

"How did he … Never mind. First of all, it's just one actual body, is that clear? One body, two corpses."

"What? Fine. One body, two corpses. Makes perfect sense. Who is it?"

"I don't know."

"Right." She scribbled. "Unknown body. Male or female?"

"Female. Peck says she was about ten weeks pregnant."

"Pregnant! Wow, this gets better and better." She scribbled some more and asked, without looking up, "Peck got the body?"

"Yes. It's at Murtaugh's. He's done his autopsy and the body's being held until we can identify it or somebody claims it."

"Anything else you can tell me?"

Buckner thought about it. His sister had moved to St. Louis in 1919 to work at *Reedy's Mirror,* a progressive journal, but Reedy had died soon after her arrival. She had managed to jump to the *Post-Dispatch,* but a couple of years covering garden parties and flower shows in St. Louis had demonstrated beyond any doubt her unfitness to cover St. Louis society. Coming as she did from a family of ancient lineage and eminent respectability, she naturally jeered at what she considered the nouveau riche shoe and beer barons and their pretensions, and this was reflected in the stories she wrote about their doings. A barrage of complaints to her editor led to her being quietly moved to a job her bosses probably hoped would lead to her sudden and unlamented end, that of crime reporter. It turned out that was the job she wanted in the first place. It immediately occurred to Buckner that a story in a big city paper like the *Post-Dispatch* might help identify the corpse in the boardinghouse cellar. So he told his sister everything he knew about it.

"And that's it?" she asked when he was finished. "That's all you've got?"

"Yes. Remember, I only started on this yesterday."

"Right." She jotted a quick note. "Police stymied." She grinned at him. "And Powers just wants the whole thing over and done with?"

"Yes. No question about that."

"Despite the fact that you still don't know how the fire started, or who the dead woman is?"

"The fire looks to be an accident at this point, and he's not particularly concerned about the dead body."

"Then why did he bring you it?"

"Because he wants to keep it local, keep New York out of it. And because he doesn't have much faith in the company policemen up there. I'm just cover for him, so that if New York does get word of it, he can show he had it taken care of." He watched her writing. "But I didn't say any of that, so don't you go quoting me."

"Um, right." Her pencil never stopped moving. "Maybe. And maybe they know—Powers ... his goons—way too much about what goes on up there, and you don't, so you really are just window dressing."

"Sure."

"So Powers gets your report, and thanks you very much, and there's the door."

"Yeah." Buckner admitted. "But I may not let it go at that."

"Really?"

"Yes. Look, somebody killed that woman—girl, really, just a kid. And her unborn baby. And I think I know who did it, and I'd like to nail him for it."

"Who?"

"I'm not going to tell you. You'll have to wait till after he's convicted. Or at least until I make an arrest."

His sister glared at him for a moment and then stood up. "All right. See you around."

"You're not heading back up to town?"

"I'll talk to Peck and then borrow one of your Fords and run up to Taylor. Talk to Powers. If that's all right."

"It's not. I can't let you go running around in a police car just so you can follow some leads. The St. Louis cops let you do that?"

"Usually they're happy to drive me anywhere I want to go," she said. "They just love to show off for a girl."

"And I'll bet you're happy to let them."

"So I'll just borrow Elroy's motor. He's got a new roadster, and it's a lot more fun to drive than your old flivver."

Buckner clamped his mouth shut tight. His sister and Elroy Dutton had been friends for several years now. Buckner didn't know how far that friendship went, but he was pretty sure he wouldn't like it if he knew. Dutton was a gambler and a saloon keeper. And a Negro. And Buckner wasn't sure which of those things bothered him the most where Martha Jane was concerned. But whatever was going on, he knew protesting to his sister was pointless.

"Then I'll type up my story on one of Michael's typewriters, and I'll have Young Clarence wire it in tonight. It should run tomorrow or the next day." She made a quick note and then packed the notebook and pencil into her shoulder bag. "After I'm done, maybe I'll hunt up Judith Lee and we can go drinking at Elroy's."

"Judith's out of town," Buckner said. He refused to rise to the bait.

"Oh," Martha Jane replied.

"You haven't heard from her?"

"No." She looked at him closely. "Have you, since she left?"

"No."

"Hm, all right, then." Martha Jane was carefully neutral.

"I guess she's been pretty busy," Buckner added lamely.

"Probably," Martha Jane agreed. "Well, anyway, I'll spend the night here and then catch the eastbound first thing in the morning. Oh, and I think Mother's coming with me. She wants to do some shopping, visit some of the cousins. She says. Mostly, I think she just wants to check up on me." She laughed at that and walked out before he could answer. Her sharp, pounding footsteps echoed down the hall.

That's Marthy, Buckner thought. And that was the end of Powers' hope of keeping the story local.

7

Buckner went home at seven. The house was empty. A note, in his mother's firm copperplate, said, "At the church." Underneath, Martha Jane had scrawled "Not me! I'm at Elroy's." Buckner wondered which church his mother might be visiting, since she filled her time doing good works at one church or another in Corinth, from the African Methodist Episcopal (Zion) to her own Presbyterian, and several in between. She had even paid a visit to the small Greek Orthodox chapel where some of the immigrants worshiped, but she soon stopped. She claimed she liked the music but couldn't get used to the different calendar.

Buckner ate cold ham, pie, and milk from the icebox, cleaned up, and went back to his office. He got out the paper bag with the items he'd found in the cellar—the pair of red shoes and the pearl earbob. He looked at them for a while and then put the shoes back in the bag. He tucked the earbob in his shirt pocket and went out.

A couple of years before the war, back when Buckner was still patrolling the Border with the US cavalry, the leading businessmen of Corinth decided they needed to give travelers a reason to get off the train in Corinth besides an opportunity to stretch their legs. After several months looking into the matter, they sent to New Orleans for Mrs. Belmont. She demanded a great deal of money to start, plus fifty percent of the gross, complete control over hiring and firing, and, most important, freedom from harassment by local law enforcement. Several of Corinth's leading businessmen traveled to New Orleans to look over her operation there and interview some of her staff. They returned completely satisfied after assuring Mrs. Belmont that the chief of police was perfectly in accord so long as his officers received the kind of special treatment due them as keepers of the peace.

The interested parties signed the necessary documents, and by the time Franz Ferdinand and poor Sophie were dying of gunshot wounds in Sarajevo, Mrs. Belmont was doing business out of a renovated three-story brick building conveniently located across from the train station. No sooner were the British in Room 40 decoding Zimmermann's telegram to von Ekhardt than Mrs. Belmont's reputation had spread across America's railroad network, and traveling men up and down the line were finding reasons to stop off in Corinth, Missouri. By the time James Buckner became chief of police, the woman and her business were an essential part of the town's economy and simply untouchable.

Buckner was not happy about that, but he had learned to live with it. He crossed the tracks and climbed the stairs to the door of the renovated red brick building, used the gleaming brass knocker, and waited. In a moment, the green door swung inward to reveal a large black man in a cutaway and striped trousers. His fierce, scarred face broke into a broad smile when he saw Buckner. "Howdy, Chief. How are you?"

"Fine, Isaac. Just fine. Is the boss in?"

"She is, she is." Isaac Joe stepped back into the red-carpeted hallway. "C'mon in. I'll tell her you're here."

The thick, wine-red carpeting and matching flocked red wallpaper muffled sounds as Isaac Joe closed the door carefully and walked back down the hall. Buckner put his hat next to the polished silver tray on the small table under the gilt mirror. *Do her customers leave their calling cards?* he wondered.

In the silence of the hallway, he could hear music coming from somewhere upstairs—someone playing hesitant arpeggios on a violin. A glance through the curtained archway to his left showed the parlor dark and empty. It was early yet, and the girls would not be down for a while.

Isaac Joe returned and beckoned. As he led Buckner down the hall, he said, "They showin' *Riders of the Purple Sage* over at the Ozark. Tom Mix. Pretty good movie, but I read the book, and the movie ain't nothin' like it atall. Can they do that?"

"Beats me, Isaac. I expect Zane Grey got paid for them using his book."

"I s'pect so. An' I s'pect if they paid him enough, he wouldn't mind what they done with it."

"I sure wouldn't."

"Is it true they gonna have talkin' pictures nex' year?"

"That's what I heard."

"Not sure as I care for that. Movin' pictures is supposed to be 'bout the pictures."

Isaac Joe had arrived in Corinth with Mrs. Belmont and served as her mayor of the palace, seneschal, doorkeeper, and enforcer. His size and his scarred face and battered knuckles were usually enough to quiet the most restless customer. He was also Corinth's most avid motion picture fan and had what amounted to a reserved seat in the front row of the "colored only" balcony in the town's new movie house. He would arrive for the first matinee showing of the latest film, a large sack of peanuts in his hand, regardless of the particular subject of the film. Romance, adventure, comedy—Isaac enjoyed them all, but he liked cowboy pictures the best.

He tapped on a door, opened it, and ushered Buckner in. Then he silently vanished.

Mrs. Belmont, born Sadie Munch in a sharecropper's shack somewhere between Baton Rouge and Memphis, was standing by her desk to welcome Buckner. She was tall and slim, elegant in her customary black silk pajamas. A pair of glasses sat perched atop her gleaming black helmet of hair. Buckner had begun to notice a few random silver strands there and wondered at her age. But when her bright red lips curled into a warm smile, the question of age slipped from his mind. "How are you, James?" She extended a hand. Her grip was firm, dry, and quick. She gestured Buckner to a chair and sat behind her desk. A ledger lay open on it, but she closed it and pushed it to one side. "Would you like some coffee?"

"No, thanks. I just need to ask a couple of questions."

"Of course you do." Her smile broadened. "You never come to see me otherwise."

Blood rushed to Buckner's face. She could always unbalance him with a word, and that bothered him. Despite her dirt-poor background, she now ran one of the town's most profitable establishments and had become one of the town's leading citizens. During the war, she had raised her fees and required her customers to give over half to the Red Cross or the YMCA. She made sure each of her girls had at least one war bond. During the influenza epidemic, she had shut down entirely and turned her place into the closest thing Corinth had by way of a hospital. She was one of the founders of the local chapter of the League of Women Voters. She ran a quiet, orderly business, and the fact that the chief of police disapproved seemed only to amuse her.

Of course, he had also informed his officers that the special arrangement enjoyed under his predecessor was no longer in effect. If they wanted to do business there, they would pay for it themselves.

"The reason I stopped in," he said, "is that I'm sort of looking for a girl, and I thought about your place, and something occurred to me. This girl was traveling with a man who claimed to be her husband but mostly was her pimp. He used to work up in Taylor, but I thought he might've tried to set himself up here in town before heading up that way. You know, being a stranger here and all, he might not have known you've got that sort of thing all sewed up. But, as you're in the same business, I wondered if you knew anything about him."

"We're not in the same business at all," Mrs. Belmont said coldly. "What was his name?"

"The name he goes by is Peralta. Claims to be Italian. Average height, black hair, black eyes. The girl was short, good figure, pretty, blonde hair."

Mrs. Belmont was nodding. "And a coke fiend."

"You've seen her, then?"

"Yes. A man fitting that description stopped here yesterday. He said his name was Pagano and he had a girl with him like the one you described. He said she was his sister and he was looking for a place for her to stay while he went out to try to earn enough money to take them both home."

"Did he say where home was?"

"He said St. Louis."

"You turned him down."

"Oh, yes. It was obvious he was going to dump her here."

"Do you know where they went after you turned them down?"

"No."

"All right." Buckner nodded. It was what he expected. He got to his feet. "Thanks."

"Not at all. But it wasn't the first time I'd met Mr. Pagano—or Peralta."

"It wasn't?"

"No. He was in here, oh, I'd say well over a year ago."

"Why?"

"Same reason. He wanted to leave a girl here." She shook her head. "He seemed to have forgotten. I suspect he is not very smart. Cunning, but not smart."

"Did you take him up on his offer?"

"No, and for the same reason." She looked closely at Buckner for a moment before going on. "I know you don't have a very high opinion of what I do for a living."

"With the kind of protection you've got, my opinion doesn't mean a thing."

"True. But you also know I run a clean house and I take care of my girls. I don't force anybody to come through that door out there, but if they do come in, I make sure they pay top dollar for the service we provide. My girls make good money, and they all have savings accounts with Fred Linderman's bank because I want them to have enough put by to get out of this business while they're still young enough to make a decent life for themselves."

"You're just engaged in community service, right?"

"No, I'm engaged in business for profit."

"And you seem to be doing all right."

"I am. But you're missing the point."

"Which is?"

"This Italian—or whatever he is—he's nothing but a parasite. He uses women, treats them like dirt, and then throws them away. That's not just bad business, that's … Well, it's disgusting." Her voice was low, harsh, and her face twisted with anger. She seemed almost to be speaking to herself. "It's everything I hate about men."

"I always thought you didn't particularly care for men at all."

She looked at him, her eyes hard and piercing, and did not contradict him.

"They're just profit to you," he went on. "Like hogs to a butcher. So you make them pay."

"Yes," she replied, her voice like a whip. "I make them pay."

"But you turned Peralta down."

"Yes. I don't need anybody at the moment, and, besides, she was a coke fiend, too, the first one. You could spot that a mile away."

"Yeah," Buckner agreed. "I noticed the one he's with now sure is. What do you think Peralta would do if his woman got pregnant? Do you think he'd kill her if he couldn't get rid of her some other way?"

"Oh, I don't …" Her eyebrows went up. "Oh, so that's what this is about, that dead body up in Taylor." Buckner nodded. "Yes, he might," she was saying. "You have to understand, James, the woman is just a convenience to him—a way for him to get what he needs."

"Like your customers."

"Yes, only for Pagano, it's money he needs, not sex."

Like you, Buckner thought.

Only she read his mind. "And no, not like me at all. Not at all." She pulled her glasses down onto her nose. "If there's nothing else, Chief Buckner, I have work to do."

"Just to make sure," Buckner said. "You know nothing at all about this man or either of his women."

"That is correct. Now, as I told you, I'm busy."

"Yes, ma'am. Thank you for your time." As Buckner turned to go, Isaac Joe magically appeared in the doorway. He had, as usual, taken the temperature in the room and said nothing as he showed Buckner out. Buckner walked home where he fired up the stove and filled the big kettle for coffee. He ground the beans while the water boiled. He put the coffee in the pot, crumbled and added a couple of eggshells, and waited. When the water was boiling, he took it off the heat, waited a minute, and then poured it into the pot. He waited some more. When it was ready, he poured himself a cup, but was interrupted when someone knocked on the porch screen door. A massive figure loomed in the darkness.

"I can't believe you could smell this coffee all the way from the county seat," Buckner said. "But come on in and have a cup."

"Thanks, I b'lieve I will," said former sheriff Elmer Aubuchon. The floorboards creaked and the chair groaned as he entered and sat and sighed heavily. He wore what he always wore—bib overalls and a chambray shirt starched to board-like rigidity and buttoned up to his many chins. A pale, sweat-stained Panama sat square on his massive head. Buckner guessed there was enough material in that outfit to make clothes for two—maybe three—normal-sized men. At four inches over six feet, Aubuchon had always carried his nearly 300 pounds with surprising grace, but it looked to Buckner as if age was finally beginning to catch up. Aubuchon had been born before the War Between the States and had first been elected Highland County sheriff in 1892, so Buckner guessed him to be around seventy-five. And it showed. His face was red, and his breathing labored, and for an instant Buckner caught himself worrying about the old man. And the old man caught him at it.

"Don't you fret about me, son." He laughed. "Just need a cup of that coffee to put me right."

"Coming up." Buckner poured and handed Aubuchon a cup. He took his own cup and sat down. "You here on account of you somehow heard what I've gotten myself into and figured I needed some advice?"

"I'm down here to pay a visit to Harold Vernon and play some checkers. He was supposed to come up to see me, but he fell and broke his hip, so I had to come down here for our regular game." He sipped carefully at the hot coffee. "That's the trouble with old folks, Buck. They break easy."

"I didn't know Judge Vernon had hurt himself."

"Accordin' to the sawbones over in Bonne Terre, he's gonna be laid up for about six months. His daughter's been keepin' a eye on him since his wife died, and she found him lyin' on the kitchen floor one afternoon, said he'd been there since the mornin'. Anyway, she's stickin' around now, makin' sure he eats the food she fixes for him, but she wired me how he was gettin' bored and fussy and would I come down for the game this time. So here I am."

"And you stopped by here for a free cup of coffee on your way."

"Yep. But what's this fix you've got yourself into? Doin' investigatin' for the Company accordin' to what I hear."

Buckner explained about the corpse in the cellar wall. Aubuchon nodded and drank coffee. When he had drained the cup, Buckner refilled it and continued his story, ending with his visit to Mrs. Belmont.

"Well, I can see you've got yourself a problem, all right," Aubuchon said. "Linderman and them have got you lookin' into this, but you've got no jurisdiction up there, which means no authority, only whatever Powers will let you have, so you won't be able to do more than scratch the surface."

"That's right."

"And he only brung you in so he didn't have to call on them private cops that handle that sort of thing for the Company—American Protective, I think it is."

"Yes."

"All right, then. You just write up something all nice and official lookin' like you used to do in the army and hand it over to Powers and you're done." Aubuchon looked at Buckner, who sat frowning into his empty coffee cup. "What's botherin' you?"

"I keep thinking about the girl ... the dead girl."

"What about her?"

"Well, maybe she's got family somewhere, and maybe they're missing her and would like to know what happened to her."

"Could be." Aubuchon nodded.

There was a long pause, and then Buckner said, "What do you think happens after we die?"

"What?" Aubuchon did not look surprised at this, just puzzled.

"You know, heaven and hell and all that."

"Don't know nuthin' 'bout it," Aubuchon said. "Never met anybody that was what you might call a reliable witness, so I don't worry none about it."

"What if it's like the Indians say—you know, that if I don't find out what happened to that girl, bring the killer to justice, her spirit or something will wander around homeless."

"Do you think that's what's gonna happen?"

"No, not really," Buckner admitted.

"Then what?"

"All right," Buckner said after a moment. "Couple of things. First, I'm just plain old curious, about who she was ... about why she died. Second, I think there's a murderer out wandering around, and I'm pretty sure who it is, and if I can work up some proof, I can arrest him and get him locked up, and maybe hung so he won't be murdering anybody else."

"Uh-huh. That it?"

"No. There's justice."

"Justice? You been a policeman long enough to know there's no such of a thing. Not in this world, anyway."

"I know, I know," Buckner insisted. "Some things don't bother me and some things do, and murder is one of the things that bother me, that's all."

"So you're going ahead on this."

"Somebody has to put her to rest, and it might as well be me."

"You got somebody can keep an eye on things around town while you're chasing after justice?"

"Yes. Shotwell."

"He's that … that colored officer I've heard about?"

"Yes."

"Well, I know his people—up in the county seat—and they're good people."

"He's a good officer, no question, but I'm not sure how folks'll take it, him being in charge. Plus, there's something brewing over on that side of town, and I've got him looking into it while I'm on this murder, but I don't want to be missing if whatever that is over there blows up."

Aubuchon sat for a moment, thinking, and then said, "You're gonna follow this thing to the end, right?"

"Pretty sure, yes."

"Just to satisfy yourself—your notion of justice." Aubuchon laughed. "This girl's murder has disturbed your notion of right and wrong, and you're going to restore things, put 'em back the way they should be by puttin' her killer in jail. I remember you was like that when I first hired you on, back during the war."

"Like what?"

"Things is out of order, and you have to put things right."

"Somebody's got to do it, and it looks like it's me. That's all."

"All right," Aubuchon said, heaving himself out of his chair. "Sounds like as good a reason as any. You let me know how it turns out."

Aubuchon put his empty cup on the counter and walked out, leaving Buckner sitting motionless at the kitchen table. Finally, he got up and went to his room. It contained the narrow cot, a small chest of drawers, a ladder-back chair, and a bedside table with a lamp on it. Buckner kept the floor swept, the bed made, and the surfaces free of dust. In the top drawer of the chest he found a cigar and matches. His mother didn't like him smoking in her house, so he went onto the front porch, sat in an old comfortable chair, and lighted up.

Was this going to work? Standing up for a dead girl whose name he didn't know? Poking around in Taylor, where he had no authority? Ignoring Corinth? And if he did find out who killed the girl, would that restore the balance? Would her spirit rest easy? He decided he didn't know the answers to any of those questions, but he was going to find out who killed the girl. That made him smile, and he blew a fat smoke ring that sailed lazily out in the heavy air, over the porch railing, and into the yard, where it seemed to hover forever before vanishing entirely in an instant.

"Pretty impressive," said Martha Jane as she came up the walk. "You must be pleased with yourself."

"I suppose." He smiled at her.

"Dutton asked after you."

"Huh."

"Don't be such a grouch." She came up onto the porch and leaned back against the railing.

After a long silence, Buckner said, "You know, I can't quite figure out what you see in him. He's a crook. He's a gambler."

"Hold it," she said, raising both hands. "I don't want to fight. You looked so peaceful, I just thought I'd join you for a bit before I went to bed."

"He must have half a dozen women on the line. Why do you want to spend time with him?"

"Well, first of all, how I spend my time is my business. And second of all, I don't care about the dozen women. But, mainly—and remember, you brought this up—I see the same things in him I see in you."

"Bullshit!" Buckner exploded.

"Oh, yes," Martha Jane insisted. "You two are practically carbon copies. It really is too funny."

Buckner got to his feet abruptly, threw his cigar into the street, and went inside without a word.

The next day was Sunday. Buckner slept late and didn't get into his office until seven.

"Dutton's waiting for you," Mullen said as he walked in.

"Must be serious." Buckner continued down the hallway.

Elroy Dutton, elegant in a lightweight, gray, vested suit, sat with his legs crossed, smiling easily.

"How've you been? You haven't stopped by for a while now."

"I've been busy." Buckner consulted his watch. "Kind of early for you. You going to church?"

"Not this morning." Dutton's smile broadened. "Going to be hot today," he said. "Strange weather for this time of year."

"Uh-huh." Buckner asked, "How's Buster getting along?"

"Oh, fine, fine. Be back on his feet in a day or so." Dutton waved it all away with one slim hand. "A couple of fellows who didn't like getting tossed out for causing trouble thought they ought to get something back. Nothing to worry about."

"Uh-huh," Buckner said again. Puzzled, he sat and looked at Dutton.

"Just a social call," Dutton said by way of a reply. He was still smiling. "I heard you were up in Taylor. I heard they've got a real who-dunnit on their hands up there and needed somebody a little smarter than company thugs to solve it for them."

"Only a little smarter?"

Dutton chuckled pleasantly. "Okay, a lot smarter. You got it figured out yet?"

"Not yet." Buckner found himself smiling as well. "I'm having Shotwell check around ... see if he can find those fellows that jumped Buster."

"Thanks, but no need. We're pretty sure who it was. No need for the police department to get involved."

Buckner, confusion deepening, only nodded.

"Just a misunderstanding is all."

"I hope you're not thinking about getting back at those two fellows, whoever they might be, for that little misunderstanding."

"No, no." Dutton was chuckling again. "Of course, they're not exactly welcome at my place anymore. They're going to have to do their drinking somewhere else. But that's really all there is to it. Nothing at all to be concerned about."

"That's good to hear. I've got plenty to be concerned about already." Buckner wanted to ask about Martha Jane, but he bit that back, since he was pretty sure he wouldn't like any answer he got.

Dutton got up and put out his hand. Buckner stood and shook it.

"Stop by some evening," Dutton said. "I've got some good Irish whiskey came in on a special shipment. You might like it."

"Maybe I will."

"Good. See you, then." He looked at his wristwatch. "Maybe I'll go to church after all." And the smiling Elroy Dutton strolled out and down the hall.

Buckner stood at his desk, waiting. He heard Dutton offer a cheerful good-bye to Michael Mullen, and then the double doors swung open and shut. He counted to ten, got his empty coffee cup, and went out front.

"Where's Shotwell?"

"He's going on nights this week. It'll be Carter over on the other side of the tracks this morning."

"All right. I'll pick him up and take him with me to see Buster."

"But, I thought Dutton said everything was all right." Buckner looked closely at Mullen, who blushed and said, "I didn't mean to be listening, Buck, honest, it's just that, well, when the door to your office is open, I really can't help hearing."

"That's why I leave the door open, Michael."

"Oh." Mullen looked surprised; then he suddenly grinned. "Oh. Right. But you're going to talk to Buster anyway."

"I am."

"Even though Dutton said you didn't have to."

"*Because* Dutton said I don't have to."

"Right." Mullen glanced at his watch. "Bit early yet. You might want to wait till after church."

"Good idea."

Buckner returned to his office and drank a second cup of coffee while he went over his notes from the interviews with the residents of the boarding house. He decided he did not have enough solid information to support any kind of possible explanation of how a woman's body ended up in the cellar of the boarding house. Finally, because he was at a dead end, he got his hat and went out.

He found Officer Carter leaning against the wall in front of the ice cream parlor just a dozen yards on the other side of the Iron Mountain train tracks. He was enjoying an ice cream cone. Next to him, also leaning against the wall, was a little boy, maybe eleven, also enjoying an ice cream cone.

"How come you fellows aren't in church?" Buckner asked.

"Oh, we been already, ain't that right, Eldon?"

The little boy nodded solemnly.

"You save the receipt on those?" Buckner indicated the ice cream cones.

"Nah," said Carter. "They ain't but a nickel apiece."

"You mean this isn't that high-price informer you've been keeping under wraps over here?"

"Oh, sure he is. He's one of my own Baker Street Irregulars. Knows more about what's going on over here than anybody else, him and his friends." Carter finished his ice cream with two quick bites. He looked down at his colleague and sketched a brief salute. "You git along now, Eldon. Me and the chief got business. But you keep your eyes open."

"Right." The little boy returned the salute with a wink and strolled away, his casual saunter suggesting a hint of arrogance, and a perfect imitation of Officer Carter.

"We going to see Buster?" Carter asked.

"Yes. I just had a visit from Elroy Dutton."

"So that's where he was comin' from when he passed by a while ago," Carter said.

"Yes. He wanted to make sure I understood everything is just fine at his place … no need to worry. Buster's fine, and it was all a misunderstanding."

"He said that?"

"Yep."

"That's … well, uh … I guess that's real interesting."

"That's what I thought too."

"And so now we're goin' to see Buster."

"We are. And you are going to tell me what this is all about along the way."

"Absolutely." They started walking. "According to Shotwell, this was three nights ago. Buster and Dutton closed up the place and walked home. You know Dutton lives just two doors down."

"Yes. When he's not living with some woman."

"Right. And Buster's got himself a little place 'bout a hunerd yards further on. He says he heard somebody hollerin' round back of one of them houses 'long the way, and he went to look, and that's when these two fellas jumped him. Next thing he knows, he's wakin' up in the mud, got blood all over him from where they dented his skull. He got up and made it to his sister's house. She told Shotwell she found him on the front stoop, and she and her husband practically had to carry him into the bedroom to get him undressed and cleaned up and into bed. Course, they had to wake up the kids, move them onto the sofa, and they was sleepy and grouchy, so the whole house was pretty much in a uproar. Shotwell says she still pretty upset about the whole thing."

They stopped before a small, tin-roofed house, deal covered with tarpaper, sitting in a small, tidy patch of grass. The stoop was too small to hold them both, so Buckner went up and knocked. In a moment, a tall, broad-shouldered young woman in a print dress and steel-rimmed spectacles opened the door and smiled. "Hello, Chief Buckner. Hello, Robert." She opened the door wide and stepped back. "I s'pect you're here to see Buster."

"Yes, ma'am," Buckner said, taking off his hat and entering, Carter following.

She showed them to a back room where Buster, enormous under a white chenille bedspread, propped up by several large pillows, looked like a whale in a snowdrift. The entire top of his head was expertly wrapped in gauze and adhesive tape. Two children, a boy about six and a girl perhaps two years older, were perched on the narrow space left on either side of Buster's bulk. The girl was pouring water from a toy teapot into a toy teacup that Buster's sausage-sized fingers could barely hold without crushing. The boy was showing Buster a large picture book.

"That's a pyramid, Uncle Buster," he said, pointing.

Buster nodded and tried to avoid spilling water as he sipped delicately. The woman hustled the children out of the room, and Buster, looking relieved, carefully set the teacup and saucer on the bedside table.

"I can tell you right now I don't know who done it, Chief," he said.

"I understand. Carter says it was two men. Is that right?"

"I reckon so. Two anyway. I know somebody jumped on my back and somebody grabbed me round the legs, and somebody started hittin' me on the head, and that could've been the one on my back, but I can't be sure, 'cause I think I remember him havin' his arms round my neck too."

"Could you tell if they was white or colored?" Carter asked.

"Nope. It was dark, and they jumped me from behind. That's all I know."

"Any idea why these men jumped you?"

"Nope. They's plenty of fellas round town might want to, on account of I has to get rough with some fellas sometimes, you know, at Mr. Dutton's. But they didn't rob me, I can tell you that."

"You been especially rough with anybody lately?" Carter asked.

Buster raised his eyes to the ceiling as he thought about it.

"Well," he said. "They was a couple fellas got into a fight the other night. It was over a gal."

"Serious?" Buckner asked.

"One of 'em pulled a knife. T'other pulled a razor."

"And you broke it up."

"Yep."

"Local boys?" Carter asked.

"Never seen 'em before."

"White boys?"

"Colored."

"And that's it?" Buckner asked. "No other little spats or quarrels with Dutton's customers?"

"That's all lately, yeah." Buster thought some more. "They was some complainin' 'bout the booze, but nobody got to fightin' over it."

"The booze? What's wrong with it?"

"Folks said it tasted soapy."

"Soapy?" Carter, who had been recording all this, looked up from his notebook. "What was that all about?"

"Dunno. This was the same night I got jumped. Some folks said what they was drinkin' tasted funny. Some of 'em said it tasted soapy."

"What was they drinkin'?"

"The ones doin' all the complainin' was drinkin' that stuff Mr. Dutton gets from Neb Healy."

"I thought Dutton only bought that fancy Canadian he gets from Kansas City and St. Louis bootleggers," Buckner said.

"Lately," Buster explained, "what with the govmint tryin' to patrol the Border more and stoppin' the trucks that's carryin' the stuff, their costs been goin' up, so Neb Healy can undercut 'em on the price."

"Only now folks are complaining about the quality of his booze?"

"Yep."

"What'd Dutton do?" Carter asked.

"Oh, he had plenty of stuff stored away, and he had Jackson check out the old stuff, and it was all right, so he served that. But that won't last forever, so he tryin' to decide what to do next."

"All right." Buckner turned to Carter. "Anything else?"

Carter put his notebook and pencil away and shook his head.

"When do you expect to be back at work?"

"Not for a week at least!" Buster's sister's voice came down the hall to them. She followed immediately after. "Those people that jumped him hit him at least three times on the head. He probably got a concussion, scrambled his brains. What there is of them. He go back to throwing folks outta Elroy Dutton's before he's all healed up, he might just fall over dead some night." She felt her brother's forehead with the back of one hand. "You tell Elroy Dutton I said he'll just have to do without Buster for a few more days."

Buster grinned and shrugged.

"You want me to send Jeff Peck around?" Buckner asked.

"That no-good drunk!" The sister scoffed. "You can just tell Jeff Peck I learned nursing at the Lincoln Institute, back before they got all high and mighty and changed the name to Lincoln University, and I can take care of my brother a lot better than he can, even if he was sober, which mostly he ain't."

"No point in arguin' with her, Chief," Buster said. "Never has been, not since we was kids, so I just don't bother." He smiled. "And you don't need to tell Mr. Dutton anything atall. He stop by here usually couple times a day."

Buckner, thinking of his own sister, just laughed.

"You're in charge, ma'am," he said. "Let's go, Carter."

The two men went out into the street and headed back across the tracks.

"So two strange Negroes get into a fight that Buster breaks up, and that same night he gets jumped."

"Yeah," Carter said. "Why don't I poke around, see if I can talk to anybody seen that knife fight … maybe find out who these two fellas were."

"Right. I'm still working on this Taylor thing, so I'll send Durand down to check with Healy … see if he's got him a serious problem."

"Isn't Healy as like to shoot him as talk to him?" Carter objected. "He didn't get to be the biggest operator in this part of the state by bein' careless 'bout his security."

"I think Durand'll be all right. Neb is pretty sure I like drinking his whiskey too much to cause him any trouble, so he might be willing to answer a couple of questions."

"What about Elroy Dutton?"

"Stay out of his way. A couple of days ago, he was all hot under the collar, demanding to see me about something that just couldn't wait. Now, all of a sudden, everything is fine, and he doesn't need our help looking into this."

"Which is a pretty good reason for us looking into it."

"It is. Just keep me posted."

"All right, but where'll you be? You still workin' up in Taylor?"

"Off and on. But I'm around town some of the time."

"All right." Carter sauntered off.

From behind, he looked so much like Eldon that Buckner almost laughed out loud.

8

Buckner found Durand on Sunday morning in the squad room, sweating over a report form. "Did you find out anything about Charboneau's insurance?" Buckner asked.

"This is it right here." Durand rolled the form out of the typewriter and handed it to Buckner.

"Thanks. I've got another job for you."

"Sure. Anything beats walking around town. I have to keep talking to folks just to stay awake."

"This will keep you awake," Buckner promised. He told Durand about Dutton's whiskey problem. "I don't know how important it is, but I'm curious about what's going on over there. And Dutton trying to warn me off makes me even more curious."

"And that's where you do your drinking," Durand said with a grin.

"That's right, it is." He went on, "Look, Elroy Dutton runs a gambling hell and violates federal law. But he does it out in the open, where I can keep an eye on him—out where I can make sure his table is honest and he isn't selling the kind of liquor that turns people blind when they drink it. So when he starts getting secretive, I worry."

"All right, Buck. But how am I supposed to get there?"

"There's a road into Neb's place, but you have to go way south, pretty far out of your way. Best to take a horse. You can ride, can't you?"

"Well, sure."

"And you know the way, don't you?"

"Yeah. But how am I supposed to keep from getting shot?"

"I don't think you'll get shot. Somebody with a rifle will meet you before you get too close. Probably one of Neb's sons. Just go along easy, make a lot of noise, don't look like you're trying to sneak up on anybody, and you'll be fine."

After Durand had gone, Buckner went to the lot behind the town hall, started up one of the Fords, and drove to Taylor. Tom was at his desk, but Mr. Powers was at home on this day of rest.

"Big house there on the right," Tom said, pointing. "But he doesn't like to be disturbed on Sundays unless it's important."

"Thanks."

The manager's home was the nicest in town, and as the boss he had the shortest walk to work. But, like everything else in Taylor, the house was coated with grit.

A red-faced girl with a Belfast accent told Buckner to wait while she fetched her employer. As he stood just inside the door, hat in hand, a tiny, pale woman with her brown hair in a bun stepped out of the parlor and smiled at him. She looked to Buckner as though a stiff breeze would knock her over. "Won't you come in, Chief Buckner?" She extended a blue-veined hand. "I'm Mary Powers. I don't believe we've met, but, of course, I know your mother. We're on several committees together."

Buckner carefully held the frail hand. It felt like fine silk over thin, delicate bones.

"How do, ma'am."

She led Buckner into the parlor. He had been there before, almost ten years gone, back when he was Aubuchon's deputy and he had to see the Company's man in charge on county business. It looked almost unchanged. The furniture was different, but in the same style—dark, overstuffed, and respectable. That was how

Buckner thought of the Victorians. Once something was decided on, in place, it would never be moved.

China figurines and framed photos crowded every level surface. All the photos, no matter who else was in them, included a little boy with pale hair and serious eyes, but there was no other sign of a child in the room—no toys left lying around … no books, games.

Every corner held a potted plant or sculpture, and the walls seemed to sag with the weight of paintings of dramatic seascapes and landscapes. A small upright piano stood just inside the door. The rifle rack still hung on the wall, but now it held figurines. Buckner noticed that most of them were religious, and the hymnal on the piano was open to "What a Friend We Have in Jesus." Immediately, the tune started up in his mind. Sunlight, softened by the drapes, filled the room as a subdued glow in which fine particles of dust floated.

Just as Mrs. Powers was gesturing for Buckner to sit down, her husband walked in. He was in his vest and shirtsleeves, no tie, no collar, and not looking happy to see Buckner.

"Come to my office," he said sharply. He glanced at his wife. "Thank you, my dear. I'll take care of this."

"Of course, dear. I can send Alice with tea if you'd like."

"That won't be necessary, my dear," Powers said, herding Buckner out and down a short hallway. "Chief Buckner won't be staying long enough for tea."

They entered a small office at the back of the house, and Powers closed the door. Buckner could hear the faint sound of running water and clattering dishes. Powers squared round to face him, anger hunching his shoulders and balling up his fists. "What do you think you are doing, coming to my home on a Sunday? What is this about?"

"I just had a couple of questions about the dead woman in the cellar."

"And as I have already informed you, I am satisfied with the results of your investigation. Your services will no longer be required."

"I know, I know," Buckner said, nodding agreement. "There's just a couple of things I need to ask. I know you've decided this matter is concluded, but I'm worried there might be a murderer loose here in your town, and that would be a problem, don't you think? Even one that deserves attention on a Sunday?'

Powers seemed satisfied with that and nodded. "You've got about two minutes. But don't expect a lot of answers. We haven't had a killing here since I took over—no deaths of any kind. The sorts of problems you had to deal with as a deputy sheriff no longer trouble us. In any event, I want to get this thing behind us as quickly as possible."

"All right. I just wanted to know about Peralta and the woman he claimed was his wife. Mostly about the woman. What was your relationship with the woman?"

"My relationship!" Powers' voice rose sharply. He clamped his mouth shut, his jaw muscles working. Buckner noticed the vein in his forehead pulsing brightly. Powers then said, much more quietly, "This is that gambler and his whore?"

Buckner nodded.

"I had no relationship at all with those people. I told you, I never had anything to do with them. Someone killed a woman and buried her in the cellar of a private house on private property. None of that touches the Company or its operations here. You yourself have proven that. There is nothing in this matter that concerns me or the Company. And now I'd appreciate it if you'd leave."

"I understand you feel that way," Buckner said without moving. "When you first asked me to look into this, you said everything that happens here concerns the Company and you. Now it doesn't. But I know someone who saw you with Peralta's woman, and my guess is, if I ask around, I'll be able to find some others."

"Leave now," Powers said. "Leave now, or Mayor Allgoode will hear of this."

"Mr. Powers, it's all right with me if you want to discuss your relationship with Peralta's woman in the mayor's office, but are you really sure you want to?"

Powers didn't move for a full minute. Finally, he seemed to relax slightly. "All right," he said. "This is really none of your business, but I may have spoken with the woman on one or two occasions. What of it? If I did, it was certainly to suggest that she attend church."

"Church," Buckner repeated. "All right. Were you trying to boost membership?"

"I was trying to save her soul, Chief Buckner."

"Just hers?"

"What?"

"Was she the only person in town you made that suggestion to?"

"Oh, I see. No, she wasn't. I have, in fact, encouraged others to attend. People I thought would benefit from it. You surely understand what I'm talking about. Your mother, I know, is often engaged in similar work."

"Mm. How was it working out? Did she show up? Did any of them?"

"Well, no." Powers sighed. "It really is more trouble than it is worth to try to drive out all the gamblers, the bootleggers, the prostitutes. Company policy is to tolerate that sort of thing, but those people are just like any kind of pest; they just keep coming back. So I try, in my small way, to approach the problem from, let's say, a different angle."

"Uh-huh. All right." Buckner started to go and then turned back. "Just a couple more questions. These folks you were trying to save, were they all young women?"

Powers looked outraged, his lips a thin, tight line, his eyes glaring. But he said nothing.

"Never mind. Thanks for your time. Tell your wife I'm sorry I couldn't have tea."

Powers stood motionless in the hallway. Still, he said nothing. Buckner went out the front door, walked across the porch, and stepped into the street. As he was crossing to the Ford, Kelson came from the office. He wore is wool cap, and Buckner could see the obvious bulge of his pistol under his buttoned-up suit coat.

He shoved his hand in his coat pockets and grinned at Buckner. "Been over to see the boss?"

"Just a courtesy call. Nothing important." He paused, his hand on the Ford's crank. "Where would I go if I wanted some female companionship?"

If Kelson was surprised at the question, he hid it behind a sly smile. "At this hour on a Sunday, I expect they're all resting up from a busy Saturday night," he said. "Why?"

"Just tell me," Buckner said.

"All right." Kelson shrugged and then pointed. "House down there on the right, just under that chat pile. Sally Little's place."

"Sally Little," Buckner repeated. "Don't tell me—she's big."

Kelson laughed. "No, not really."

"All right. Thanks. Shall I say you sent me?"

"Do whatever the hell you want, Chief." Kelson walked away.

Sally Little's place looked like all the other houses on the street: foursquare, company built, coated with grime. A woman stood on the small stoop. With one hand she managed a small, folding fan and a cigarette; in the other, she held a delicately painted coffee cup. She was wearing a flowered housecoat, and she squinted against the smoke as she watched Buckner walk toward her.

"Good morning," Buckner said from the bottom step.

"I think it's past twelve," the woman said. She had high cheekbones, a generous mouth, and pale blue eyes tilted slightly up at the corners. She might have been forty years old, but it was a well-preserved forty.

"I'm Chief Buckner, from down—"

"In Corinth. I know. We're closed. I seen you talking to Kelson, that company cop. He must've told you that." She tucked a thick coil of dark red hair behind one ear.

"He did. I'm here on my business, not yours."

"And your business is that dead girl, right?"

"Yes."

"Well I sure as hell don't know who did it," the woman said. She took a final deep puff on her cigarette and tossed it into the street. The smoke sent her into a spasm of coughing, which she quelled with the dregs of her coffee. Buckner waited. "All right," she said when she had caught her breath. "C'mon in."

Buckner went up the steps and followed her into the house. It was the usual company house inside as well, only all four rooms were used as bedrooms, and the kitchen was in a shed patched on at the back. The hallway was dark and silent. Sally Little showed Buckner into one of the rooms and sat on the bed. Buckner sat on the only chair, a low, armless Eastlake-style affair covered in coral fabric. The wearing and stains suggested to Buckner that it was not used solely for sitting.

Someone had tried to make to room look inviting, hanging drapes and pictures, papering the walls. The effort had failed. The woman was attractive enough, but the room was dark, stuffy, and oppressive. Whatever went on in it, Buckner suspected it was cheerless, perfunctory, and cheap. Though the specific furnishings were different, the general atmosphere was so reminiscent of similar rooms Buckner had been in—in Paris, in London … elsewhere—that for a moment, he lost himself in memory.

"So what do you want to know?" she prompted after a moment.

"Uh … well, I was wondering about your customers," Buckner said, collecting his thoughts.

"Miners," Little said. "What about 'em?"

"Does Josiah Powers ever come here?"

"Holy Joe? Are you joking? He's never a customer of mine." She was laughing now and lighting another cigarette. "He does come here, though, from time to time."

"What for, if he's not a customer?"

"Why, to talk to the girls, of course. To show them the error of their ways, and to try to turn them to the paths of righteousness, what else?"

"And you let him?"

"Well, can't stop him, really, now can I?" She laughed some more. "But that seems to be the deal."

"What do you mean?"

"I mean, he doesn't like the kind of business I run, but he knows I provide a service that his employees want and will pay for. Now, company policy is opposed to all sorts of sin, but they know there's a market for it. In the past, when different fellers was running things here, they'd mostly turn a blind eye as long as we paid a certain percentage of profits back to the Company—sort of a tax, you know. And it's the way things are done in other towns around, according to what I hear."

"But not in Taylor," Buckner said.

"Not in Taylor," Little said. "Here it's a different kind of tax."

"Regular visits from Josiah Powers bearing a message of salvation."

"Exactly," Little said. "He comes around here maybe half a dozen times a year, and gathers all the girls together and preaches them a little sermon, and then he goes away." She shrugged. "And that's it."

"Does it ever work?" Buckner asked.

"If you mean, does he ever convert anybody, then no, not very well. I did lose one girl here a couple years back, but that was all."

"And that's all he ever wants to do? Preach?" Buckner asked.

"That's all," Little said. She read Buckner's expression. "Honest, that's absolutely all."

"There a lot of other ... ah, establishments like yours here in Taylor?"

"Nope. One or two, maybe. And a couple of independents."

"Powers visit them too?"

"According to what I hear, yeah."

"For the same reason?"

"Yeah. He's like one of them missionaries that's always going off to places like Africa to convert the natives, only he does it here."

"All right," Buckner said. He got up. "Thanks."

"My pleasure," Little said. She smiled at him. It was a nice smile. "What about your pleasure? We open for business in about a hour, but I'm always willing to make an exception for officers of the law."

"Officers of the law? Like Kelson and Garber?"

"Sure, if they're interested. Which they sometimes are. Kelson anyways. Garber's married, and I guess his wife keeps him on a short rein."

"All right," Buckner said. "And thanks, but no thanks. Like I said, I'm only here on business—my business. And I have to get to it."

"Suit yourself," Little said. "Way I hear things, you got yourself your own little arrangement with the high and mighty Mrs. Belmont down in town."

"Uh-huh," Buckner said. "Don't believe everything you hear along that line."

"Doesn't matter to me what you do in your spare time, Chief," Little said with a smirk.

Buckner turned abruptly and walked out.

Kelson was back on guard as Buckner went up the hill. Buckner shot the man a question: "Say, you ever spend any time with Peralta's woman?"

Kelson, momentarily caught off guard, looked confused. "Might've." Kelson got a smug look on his face. "Mr. Peralta was pretty careful, liked to stay on the right side of the folks that run this town. So that means there's certain advantages to bein' a cop, wouldn't you say?"

"I suppose," Buckner said.

"Way I hear it, you get on pretty good with that Miz Belmont down in town," Kelson said, still grinning. "So you know what I'm talking about. What the hell, it just goes with the job."

Does everybody in the county think that? Buckner wondered, his jaw clamping down tight. He looked at Kelson for a minute and then said, "So I can take it as a yes?"

"Take it any damn way you want to, Chief," Kelson said. His smile seemed permanently fixed to his face. Buckner gritted his teeth and returned it.

"Right. I will. What about Sally Little down the way there? Do business with her?"

"Might've. What do you care anyway?"

"Just trying to get a picture of the way things work around here," Buckner said. Kelson was getting angry, and Buckner didn't want to make him angrier. "Be seeing you."

As Buckner cranked up the Ford, he noticed Kelson staring at him and frowning slightly. Buckner released the brake and drove away. As the auto rattled through the dust, he thought about his conversation with Powers. Would a healthy, vigorous man like Powers really be interested in an available and attractive young woman simply out of a care for her soul? Especially if he had a frail and sickly wife at home? And was he in a position to enjoy that young woman's favors freely, without consequences? But according to Sally Little, all Powers was interested in was women's souls.

He shook his head. *Have I gotten that cynical?* he wondered. Then he thought about Kelson and Garber, and what Kelson had said. Buckner certainly understood that being a police officer presented lots of opportunities to a man interested in opportunities. And that wasn't cynicism, either. It was the way things had been in Corinth before he took over, and apparently the way things worked in Taylor right now, where law enforcement was the private property of a private corporation concerned with generating profits for shareholders, and where law enforcement officers were its employees, presumably working toward the same goal. And as near as Buckner could tell, nobody in Highland County or the State of Missouri was particularly interested in disrupting this situation. The police had the authority and the firearms to back it up, and all the power the community could give them; how they used it all was mostly left up to them so long as decent people were left in peace.

Buckner thought about Kelson's remark, the one about him and Mrs. Belmont. Obviously, in Kelson's mind, there was little difference between Buckner and himself. *So, Buckner thought, how much difference is there?* Plenty, he finally decided, since he'd never accepted any of the offers Mrs. Belmont had thrown his way. Anyway, with her protection, it hardly mattered what he thought about her, and that wouldn't change until things in Corinth changed.

He pushed that thought firmly to one side and drove the rest of the way into town singing the old hymn, surprised—and pleased—that he still knew all the words.

Late that afternoon, Buckner was going over his photographs of the boarding house cellar when Durand limped in. His shirt was sweat stained and covered with dust, and his face, under the dust, was burnt bright red. He looked exhausted.

"How's Neb Healy?" Buckner asked.

"He's fine. Sends his regards."

"What'd you find out? You want to sit down? You look worn out."

"I am worn out, yes, but no, I do not want to sit down. I have done my sitting for today. Maybe for tomorrow too. How did you take it?"

"Take what?"

"Sitting. In a saddle, I mean. All day … when you were in the cavalry?"

"You get used to it. Besides, we used to spend plenty of time walking, so as not to wear out the horses."

"Right," Durand said, nodding. "Wouldn't want to wear out the horses by actually riding them."

"If you have to move fast all of a sudden, you sure don't want a worn-out horse under you," Buckner said.

"I suppose," Durand conceded grumpily.

"Neb treat you all right?"

"Oh, sure. Some kid—looked about twelve—with a bolt-action rifle bigger than he was stopped me on the trail and escorted me at gunpoint to the house. Then the kid took care of my horse, and Healy's wife fed me the best chicken dinner I've had since I left home, plus coffee, peach pie, and cigars after, like I was President Coolidge himself come to visit. He's a strange one, all right, Healy is. And does that wife of his ever smile?"

"Not that I've seen. Did you find out anything about the soap in Elroy Dutton's whiskey?"

"No. Healy sends the stuff to him in the barrels he makes it in and he checks every one personally on account of Dutton's such a good customer. The barrels—usually three or four a month—travel in Healy's wagon driven by one or another of his boys with another two or three riding shotgun, and they go straight to Dutton's where the stuff is off-loaded and stored by Dutton's people, with Buster watching, sometimes helping. After we ate supper, he showed me around the operation a little, and it seems pretty obvious to me there ain't nothing happening there that he don't know about."

"No, he's too careful by half," Buckner agreed.

"And he swore up and down that none of his boys would put anything in the whiskey, on account of Dutton's too important to Healy's profits."

"So whoever's putting the soap in the whiskey is doing it at Dutton's place and is after Dutton only, and not aiming to hit Neb Healy at the same time." Buckner said this mostly to himself. To Durand he said, "That means, what ever is going on, it's aimed at Dutton."

"And he's not the sort to take something like that lying down," Durand said.

"No, he's not," Buckner agreed.

"Can I ask you something, Buck?"

"Sure."

"How come you let him get away with it? Healy, I mean."

"Well, chasing moonshiners isn't my job, the way I see it. If the federal government wants to get involved, that's all right with me. But Healy's family has been making whiskey down there for a hundred years now, and they make good stuff and they charge a fair price. Anyway, some folks want to drink, amendment or no amendment, and if Healy wasn't there, somebody else would be, and they might be making the kind of stuff that turns folks blind, or kills them, so, in the long run, I'd just as soon have Neb down there, if you see what I mean."

"I guess so," Durand said. "Still, it don't seem right to me." He frowned. "And then there's Dutton, operating just over the way there."

"My problem," Buckner said.

"I reckon," Durand replied. "Anyway, I'm just glad I ain't in charge."

"Well, you did just fine today, so go take a hot bath. You look like you could use one. Oh, did you get a receipt for the horse from Walter Greene?"

Durand retrieved a rumpled paper from his shirt pocket, handed it over, and hobbled out.

That night, Buckner decided to go check on Elroy Dutton for himself. He put on a suit and walked across town, past the train station, and over the Iron Mountain tracks. The air was still unusually warm for October—warm and heavy—and Buckner wondered when it was going to break.

The entrance to Elroy Dutton's place was through a barbershop and was overseen by an elderly man who could, in fact, give you a shave and a haircut if that was what you wanted. Mostly he just nodded regular customers up the stairs and pushed a button that rang a little bell at the top, after which the massive door would either swing open or not, depending on how many times he had pushed the button. If he didn't like your look at all, or suspected your intentions, the old man had the use of a shotgun leaning against the wall next to the button.

"Howdy, Chief."

Buckner said, "Evening," and went up. The door swung open.

"You standing in for Buster this evening, Jackson?" he asked the slight young man holding the door open for him.

The young man, in carefully pressed black trousers, crisp white shirt and collar, and short starched waiter's jacket, smiled and said, "Yeah."

"And you're just hoping there's no trouble, right?"

"Oh, I don't expect there'll be much of that tonight," Jackson said. "It's been pretty quiet since we opened."

Buckner scanned the room. A handful of drinkers sat scattered at different tables across the large room.

"I guess so," Buckner said. "Where's the band? I thought there'd be dancing tonight."

"Afraid there won't be any dancing, maybe not for a while," Jackson said. "You'd better talk to Mister Elroy about that." He closed the door and resumed his station.

Elroy Dutton, elegant in evening clothes, was at his usual table against the far wall. Jeff Peck sat at the same table, holding on tight to a tumbler full of whiskey as though it were the only thing keeping him upright. He ignored Buckner.

"Evening," Dutton said. "Bourbon?"

"Yes." Buckner sat and gestured in the direction of the nearly empty room. "Doesn't seem to be much going on tonight."

"Business has been a little slow," Dutton admitted. A new waiter, Jackson's replacement, similarly dressed, brought Buckner's whiskey and refilled Dutton's crystal flute from the magnum in the ice bucket at Dutton's elbow. "It'll pick up, though. Always does."

They sat in silence for several minutes, sipping their drinks while Dutton subtly tried to watch for Buckner's reaction.

"Pretty good," Buckner said. "This Neb Healy's?"

Dutton nodded, looking relieved.

"Well," Buckner said. "Now that I'm here, is there anything we need to talk about?"

Dutton shook his head, frowning slightly at the room. "Nothing at all. I told you."

"I know what you told me. And I was glad to hear everything's been going so well for you lately." Buckner glanced at the room and continued. "I just wanted to tell you I stopped by to see how Buster was doing."

Dutton said, "I heard about that from his sister. I was over there myself."

"Buster did mention something about the whiskey tasting funny," Buckner continued. "So I sent Durand down to have a talk with Neb Healy."

Dutton, still frowning, said, "I know that too."

"Neb showed him around. You know how he likes to show off, especially if it's the law. And he explained how the whole operation works, and he said it'd be next to impossible for anybody to interfere with the making of the stuff or to tamper with it while it was on its way up here to you."

Dutton said nothing. He seemed to Buckner to be thinking of something else altogether. "So that means your problem is a little closer to home, doesn't it?" Dutton smiled faintly. Buckner shifted gears. "Where's the band tonight?" he asked.

"No band," was all Dutton would say.

"So no dancing."

"What do you care? You never dance anyway."

"Hurts my bum leg."

"Sure."

"But I like to listen to the music."

"I guess you'll have to buy yourself a Victrola."

The conversation lagged, and everybody stewed in silence. The few people scattered at the surrounding tables seemed equally unhappy, glaring at their drinks or into space without the usual chatter and laughter. Finally Buckner tossed off the last of his drink. "All right, then." He picked up his hat and stood.

Dutton was instantly on his feet as well. "Sorry," he said. "I'm not worth being around tonight."

"That's the truth," Buckner said. "And this place is as dead as Murtaugh's Funeral Parlor."

"Come back next week," Dutton said grimly. "I have to take care of a few things, but the place should be jumping by then."

Buckner looked closely at him, but Dutton merely smiled blandly and gave a slight shrug. "Whatever your problem turns out to be," Buckner said softly, "be careful how you go about solving it."

"What does that mean?"

"It means you always walk a pretty thin line. You seem to enjoy it. And I don't mind watching you walk it, that's for sure. Best balancing act I've seen since I went to the circus. But if you step wrong, you might bump into me, and that would be too bad."

"I run a business here, Chief," Dutton said, his voice hard and sharp. "If I have a business problem, I take care of it. Now, if you're not interested in purchasing any more of what I sell, then I'll say good evening." He sat back down and scanned the room, frowning heavily.

Peck, who had not said a word, or acknowledged Buckner's presence, glanced up, his face expressionless, his eyes empty. Buckner ignored him, turned, and walked toward the door. Jackson had it open by the time he got there. The old man at the bottom of the stairs seemed sorry to see him go. "Leavin' so early?"

"Might as well," Buckner said. He paused and lowered his voice. "Do you know what's going on around here?"

The old man glanced up the stairs and then at Buckner. "Might not be a good idee to say right now," he whispered.

"On account of what happened to Buster?"

The old man just nodded and shrugged helplessly and muttered something under his breath. "Big city niggers movin' in."

Buckner thanked him and left. As he crossed the tracks, he thought about what the old man had muttered there at the end. *What*, Buckner wondered, *did he mean?* Whatever it was, he was going to have to find out, and quickly. He couldn't let what was going on in Taylor distract him from his primary concern—the town of Corinth.

 **9**

Buckner was at the train station early Monday morning. The sun shone with a metallic brightness, and the air was still and heavy with moisture. The few people on the street moved slowly through it. The westbound had stopped, and a handful of passengers were getting off. Buckner stood with one foot on the running board of the Model T. The train chuffed noisily. As he watched his mother walk toward him across the platform, he saw another familiar face. A heavy-set man in a cheap, too-tight brown suit grinned at him from under a plug hat, a cigar thrust jauntily from one corner of his mouth.

Buckner's mother and the man reached him at about the same time. "Say," said the man to Buckner, "this is mighty nice of you, coming down to welcome me back to town." He lifted his hat an inch off his balding, sweating head, and his smile broadened as he turned to Buckner's mother. "Miz Buckner, lovely day, ain't it."

"Harris," Buckner said, his tone flat and uninviting. He took his mother's battered gladstone and put it in the Ford. His mother was smiling her cool, polite, remote smile and nodded so forbiddingly that Harris actually lost his smile and took a step backward. Buckner demanded, "Have they run you out of St. Louis?"

"Aw, shucks no, Chief Buckner," Harris replied, his smile returning, warm and cheerful. "They gonna vote me in for Veiled Prophet this year."

"Actually, I'm not surprised to hear that," Buckner said as he got his mother settled in the Ford. Harris stayed close.

"Believe it or not, Chief, I'm here to talk to you," he said quietly. "Business."

"You know where my office is. I'll be there shortly."

"Yeah, I think I remember the way." And with another tip of his hat, Harris sauntered off.

Buckner had left the Ford running. He got in and drove away.

"Is that that awful man who used to work as a detective for Baxter Bushyhead?" his mother asked.

"Yes. But even he found Bushyhead a little too strong for his stomach. He quit before I ... ah ... replaced Bushyhead as chief of police."

"I suppose that shows a certain amount of good judgment on his part. But surely he was joking about being picked as Veiled Prophet. They call it the social event of the season, but it's nothing more than a chance for the city's idle rich to show off each other's marriageable daughters to their layabout sons for breeding purposes. It's a stock show. But the important word there is 'rich,' and he doesn't look as though he could meet that standard."

"No, he can't. But, Mother, you mustn't make fun of the Veiled Prophet Ball. Only folks who can't get in do that. It's an old St. Louis tradition."

"It's not all that old. We never paid a bit of attention to it, our side of the family, so you don't know. It started out as an anti-labor, anti-Negro demonstration by the nouveau riche—the immigrants who'd made their fortunes in beer and shoes—to show they wouldn't allow any foolishness in their city. Why, the first prophet rode in the parade dressed just like a member of the Ku Klux Klan. And carried a shotgun in case anybody missed the point."

"I guess I didn't know that part," Buckner said.

"Well, he was, and he did."

"Didn't you ever go? Wasn't that how proper young ladies like you were introduced into society?"

"I went once," his mother said, her voice tight and thin. "With Harold Taussig. That was the last time. I met your father the next year."

"Yes." Buckner laughed. "And he took you away from all that. Down here to Highland County."

"Mmph," his mother said. After a little, "Your great-uncle Roane was one of the early prophets, although I believe they'd given up carrying the shotgun by then."

"Ah. I always wondered why you never had a kind word to say about poor old Uncle Roane."

"Let's just say it's one of the reasons. One of many."

"Any chance you'll tell me the other reasons?"

"None at all." She pointed. "Drop me at the church," she said, changing the subject with her usual sledgehammer subtlety.

"Which church? I can never keep straight which one you're working at on any given day."

"Our church, of course. The one we've been going to since we moved here. It's just up ahead on the left. The red brick building with the cross on top."

"I remember."

"Oh, good. I wasn't sure, since you haven't been near the place in years. Not any house of worship, as far as I can tell."

"Didn't you go to church with Marthy yesterday?"

"I walked up to Westminster Presbyterian. I haven't been there in a while. Your sister practically lives in the shadow of the place, but she admits she never goes. I honestly thought I'd raised you both better."

Buckner clamped his mouth shut and brought the Ford to a stop at the curb in front of Corinth's Presbyterian Church. It was rather less grand than the one in St. Louis, but it served the same respectable portion of the population. As Buckner opened his door to get out, his mother said, "Don't bother. Just drop my bag off at the house." She paused. "Are you planning on coming home tonight?"

"Yes."

"Invite Judith."

"Can't," Buckner said. "She's still in Columbia."

"Fine, then. Pork and greens and the last of the late sweet corn Miz Longstreth brought me." She closed the door, and he pulled away.

He left the Ford in the lot behind the town hall and went downstairs to find Harris drinking coffee and watching Mullen make entries in one of his ledgers. "You sure have made some changes around here, Chief." He indicated Mullen. "We never had nothing like all these reports and facts and figures."

"The only things Bushyhead ever kept close track of were the payoffs."

"Yeah, well, that's true enough. The old boy kept his eye on what was important all right." Harris shook his head with something that looked like sadness. "I guess that's why he missed that fast freight train coming down the tracks at him." Harris chuckled. "You bein' that freight train and all."

"You said you wanted to talk to me about something," Buckner said.

"I do, yeah. In your office, if that's all right."

"Sure. Soon as I get some coffee."

In Buckner's office, they both settled into their chairs and sipped coffee and watched each other for a minute before Harris finally spoke. "I'm looking for a girl," he said. "St. Louis girl. Been missing for a while now, about a year, and I think she might be down this way."

"That long? What kept you? Is there that much work for a private detective up in the big city?"

"I only just got hired to look for her a couple of weeks ago. Her family got tired of waiting for the police to do anything about it."

"All right. That's very interesting. Explain to me why you're here talking to me about it."

Harris took a photograph from his pocket and handed it to Buckner. "That's her," he said.

Buckner looked at the picture. It showed a pretty girl with a headed-for-hell smile and eyes that dared you to go with her. Dark hair tumbled around her face.

"And who is she?"

"Rachael Binkley. Her father's in business in the city. Come over from some *shtetl* in Poland or somewheres over there when he was a kid. His old man was a tailor in the old country, but nobody could pronounce the name over here, you know, so he changed it from whatever it was to Binkley on account of that's more American, and he set up as a tailor over here. Anyway, the son took over the business, and he started working for the right guys in the city, and all of a sudden he's got more work than he knows what to do with and more money too."

"He makes a lot of money as a tailor?"

"Oh, yeah. 'Cause, see, the guys he's doing all that work for—turns out they're Italian." Here Harris winked. "If you know what I mean."

"Italian," Buckner said. "I'm guessing you mean like those Italians that Bushyhead was in business with back a couple of years ago … back when they were trying to take over the liquor business down here."

"That's the ones."

"And this Jewish tailor works for them."

"Got an exclusive contract. The Italians like nice clothes, and they like them made to order."

"So he hires a top operative like you to look for his daughter."

"Sure." Harris smiled. "But I'm charging him double on account of he's a Jew and can afford it."

"Why doesn't he just ask some of his Italian friends to come down here and find his daughter and take her home?"

"Well, I'm not too sure about that," Harris admitted. "But, the way I hear it, they remember what happened last time they sent some of their rough boys down this way. Seems they ran into a hard-case ex-deputy sheriff and they got all shot to pieces and so they thought it might be a good idea to go legit on this, maybe keep the body count to a minimum. Especially since they're busy up in town, fighting it out with the Irish gangs."

"And you're the family's idea of going legit?" Buckner had no intention of discussing that day with Harris. He'd almost died himself, and the scars still twinged with pain.

"Yeah. Pretty funny, ain't it? And this'll get you—I convinced them I was good friends with that ex-deputy sheriff, now that he's chief of police and all."

"Uh-huh. All right. Tell me what you've got on this girl."

"You think you can help?"

"Maybe. Just tell me."

"Right." Harris put his empty cup on the corner of Buckner's desk and took out a notebook. He thumbed through several pages, nodded, and returned it to his pocket. "All right, here's what I've got. It's actually an old story … so old you're gonna laugh. The girl's parents are still real old-country, real traditional, so they think the thing to do is keep the kid locked up at home until some old lady in the village back in the old country can pick a husband for her. But the girl's not having any of that, right? She's American, a real hundred-percenter, and that's not the way American girls do it. She's pretty, she's high spirited, she wants to have some fun before she has to settle down and start cranking out babies. So she gets to know this fellow Perino—"

"Italian," Buckner said.

"I guess so, by the name, but I asked around, and none of Mr. Binkley's, ah … clients will admit to knowing anything about him, except they're sure he ain't one of theirs."

"But maybe he doesn't let on to that, and if the girl jumps to a conclusion, this Perino might just let her."

"I don't know that for sure," Harris replied, "But, yeah, that might work. Anyway, this fellow, he's glamorous, dangerous, good looking, and she falls hard for that."

"Uh-huh. Nothing new there."

"Nope. So, anyway, they meet, as near as I can tell, at some gathering at this fancy girl's school she goes to, and this Perino starts romancing her, taking her around town … all the best places. Only along the way, he gets her hooked on cocaine. And that means she's willing to do just about anything he wants her to do so long as he keeps supplying her with the stuff."

"And it turns out," Buckner interrupted, "that he's a gambler, and whenever he needs a stake, he arranges for her to be nice to some rich guy. For a fee."

"Uh … yeah." Harris gave Buckner a sidelong look. "I told you it was an old story, but you sound like you know it pretty good."

"Finish your version of it."

"Well, there ain't much more to it. By the time her parents figure out what's going on, they've skipped—Perino and the girl. The father tries the police first, but he also goes to the people he makes all them fancy suits for and tells them his story on account of he thinks maybe this Perino is one of theirs. They swear he ain't, and they promise to help out, and so they start looking around, and they find out that a while back, this Perino told some people he knew up there about this town down in the Lead Belt where there was a lot of lonely miners with more money than they could spend and nobody to spend it on."

"Where law enforcement is, let's say, kinda loose," Buckner added. "As opposed to a place like Corinth, where that line of business is all sewed up."

"Exactly," Harris said. "Just the place for a fellow who plays cards for a living and sells his woman to keep him in chips."

"Just the place."

"Which is where you come in."

"Yeah. 'Cause some of the boys in St. Louis remember doing business with me back in the old days … back when Bushyhead was sitting in this office and I was working as a detective."

"And they know what a straight shooter you are."

"Sure. Anyway, they know I can find a trail, and once I find it, I keep following it till I get to the end."

"So the girl's father hires you with their approval. But you figure you better check in with your old pal the chief of police first."

"Just being polite," Harris said.

"Hogwash. You know better than to come snooping around here without checking in."

"Damn right, I do." Harris grinned. "Besides, I'm hoping you'll led a hand here."

"I might."

"So tell me what your take on this is. Since you been hinting around you know something about it."

"Right," Buckner said. "Well, first off, I think I've seen the girl you're after."

"Swell. Where?"

"Up in Taylor. She's keeping company with a man named Peralta."

"Italian-looking fellow?"

"I guess so," Buckner said. "Anyway, he definitely plays cards up in Taylor, and pimps his wife. If she really is."

"It might make sense if she was. He stays on the high side of the Mann Act that way."

"And she can't testify against him in court."

"Sure."

"He showed up in Taylor a couple of years ago with a woman, and they were living in a boarding house up there—Charboneau's." Harris nodded. "Only the woman left him ... ran out on him according to what I heard, and he went back to St. Louis and came back in no time with another one that sounds like the one you're after. I've met her—the new one—and she's a ringer for the one in that picture, if you count a year on cocaine and turning tricks for Peralta. That kind of life will age a girl pretty quick. Anyway, the boarding house burned down, so when I talked to them, they were looking for someplace to stay."

"And what's keeping us from heading up there right now?" Harris asked.

"Not a thing, except I haven't finished my part of the story."

"Fine." Harris leaned back and crossed his arms across his chest. "Go ahead."

"Won't be but a minute. The boarding house burned down, like I said, and the firemen found a dead body—a woman, blond hair—in the cellar while they were putting out the fire, so Powers, the man who runs things up there for the mining company, he asked the town fathers here in Corinth if he could borrow me to find out who the dead body is and how it got there."

"That's why you were up there snooping around outside your jurisdiction."

"Yes. And that's how I met Peralta—Perino—and the woman he's with now. And I'd bet money she's the one you're looking for."

"All right." Harris stood. "Can we go up there and get her then?"

"Yes, we can."

"What about company cops? Kelson and Garber still strutting around up there?"

"They are, but I doubt they'll be any trouble."

"Since we're doing their job. Is Peralta likely to cause us any trouble? If he tries anything, I'm ready." Harris patted his hip.

"I don't think you'll be needing that. He seemed more like the kind of fellow who gets by on his looks and what he thinks is his brains."

"All right. I recollect you don't like carryin' guns."

"Got my fill of it, is all."

"It's gonna get you in trouble one of these days."

"Maybe." Buckner led the way down the hall.

Harris spent the drive to Taylor looking at the countryside, saying nothing. Buckner decided to head for Shorty's first, without bothering Mr. Powers. He parked the Ford, and they went in. The place was full, the air thick with smoke and the smell of corn mash. Seeing the two of them, Donahue was all smiles. "Jaysus, must be pretty serious if you're bringing help along, Chief. And how are you this fine day, Mr. Harris? How are things up in the big city?"

"Just fine, Mr. Donahue. I don't suppose you could sell me a little eye opener?"

"I could, indeed, sir."

"Maybe later," Buckner said, nodding in the direction of the back room. "Is Peralta in there?"

"He is not, I'm glad to say. I have been forced to warn him off."

"Have you now? I'd've thought he'd be good for business—or she would, anyway."

"And I thought the very same thing, Chief Buckner, I surely did. But it turns out, he cheated at cards."

"You're surprised?"

"Not at all. Only he got caught, and that led to trouble, and he threw down on a couple of fellas that caught him at it, and it looked for a while I was gonna have a shootin' on me hands. But I was able to prevent the tragedy."

"Because you're a brave and noble fellow yourself?" Buckner asked.

"Never," said Donahue. He turned to the bartender. "Mickey?" And the bartender reached under the bar and came up with a double-barrel sawed-off that looked to Buckner like a ten gauge. "Mickey persuaded him to put away his weapon, and I persuaded him to leave."

"Good thing," Harris said. "An item like that'd clear the room in a hurry, take half your clientele with it."

"It would, it would … no doubt about that. But it cleared Mr. Peralta without any further trouble, and that was all I was interested in at the time."

"And his wife went with him?" Buckner asked.

"She did, and I was that sorry to see her go. So sorry, in fact, that I almost offered her a job."

"But they left together," Buckner said.

"They did."

"Do you know where they went?" Harris asked.

"I do not, nor do I care."

"Fine. Thanks for the help," Harris said.

"Maybe next time, Mr. Harris," Donahue said.

"Now what?" Harris said when they were outside.

"Now we try the company office."

The office was dark and stuffy, and the slowly rotating fan did little to stir the air. Tom, jacket off and sleeves rolled up, barely glanced at them. "I've no idea where they might have gone," he replied to Buckner's question. "And Mr. Powers isn't in today. He had to run over to Potosi for a meeting."

"All right. Can you tell me where Kelson or Garber are right now?"

"Garber's up at the smelter," Tom said after consulting a clipboarded sheet hung on the wall behind him. "Supposed to be, anyway. And Kelson's around town somewhere."

"All right. We'll find him." And they did. He was chatting with two women over a washtub of bed linens. As a concession to the oppressive air, he had taken off his jacket and hooked it with one finger over a shoulder. He recognized Harris immediately. He was not cheered by the fact. "What the hell are you doing here?"

"Working," Harris said. "What are you doing?"

"Same as you." Kelson slipped his jacket on, but left it unbuttoned, the butt of his pistol peeking ostentatiously out. "And this is my patch," he continued. "What're you doing on it?"

"We're just looking for Peralta," Buckner said quietly. "We'd like to talk to him."

"Yeah," added Harris. "Donahue says they've left town."

"And good riddance," Kelson said.

"Do you know where they went?" Buckner asked.

"I know they're not in town because I drove them down into Corinth late yesterday and left them at the train station."

"But you don't know where they went?" Harris said.

"No. I just told them to stay out of Taylor. Him anyway. She could've stayed. For all I know, they're still in Corinth, which makes them your problem now, Chief." He smiled happily.

"Right. Thanks for the favor." Buckner thought a minute. "Who's idea was this, then—them leaving?"

"Well, as a matter of fact, it was Peralta's. Come to me yesterday and asked if I'd drive the two of them to the station. Said him and the missus was striking out for greener pastures. I told him it was a good thing, too, on account of I was just about to ask him to move along anyway."

"Pretty convenient," Buckner said.

"I thought so. And I'm glad he's gone."

"Her too?" Harris asked.

Kelson grinned. "Naw, hell, I'm gonna miss her. She was as fine a piece as we've seen around here in a while."

"Since the other one—the blond—took off," Buckner said.

Kelson shrugged. "Dime a dozen."

"Right. Thanks."

Harris and Buckner returned to the Ford and drove back to town. Buckner parked at the train station and the two went inside. Young Clarence, at the Iron Mountain ticket window, remembered the couple buying tickets.

"When?" Buckner said. Young Clarence was sixty-five at least, and was Young Clarence because his father, still living but long retired, had been the original Clarence, and since they had both worked for the Iron Mountain for decades, the name helped people keep them straight. The Iron Mountain might now be part of the Missouri Pacific, but it was still the Iron Mountain to people in Corinth, and Young Clarence was forever young.

"Yesterday afternoon about four thirty."

"Where to?" Buckner continued.

"Headed south," Young Clarence said.

"There's a lot of south down there, Clarence," Harris said. "Can you pinpoint it for me?"

Young Clarence, who remembered Harris from his days as a Corinth police detective, consulted his records diligently. "Little Rock," he announced triumphantly.

"Fine," Harris said. "Gimme a ticket on the next westbound for Little Rock." He turned to Buckner. "You wanna come along?"

"Not a chance." Buckner smiled. "I've got my hands full here."

"Your loss." Harris collected his ticket and they walked away. "Looks like I might be able to clear up your mystery woman problem. I'd bet you money this Peralta's your man, and that blond was his woman before this one."

"I expect you're right, but I can't prove it."

Harris laughed. "Yeah, your hands are kinda tied in that way. Me, I don't have to worry about that."

Buckner left Harris smoking a cigar and staring patiently into space, a man practiced in waiting.

James Shotwell was sitting in Buckner's office when he got back.

"You look like you've been up all night," Buckner said.

"I have. But I found out what's going on with Buster and Dutton and all that."

"Good. I was over at his place last night, and you'd think the Spanish influenza had come back. I doubt there was more than half a dozen folks there, and Dutton looked like he'd lost his best friend. Of course, you can't blame folks for staying away, what with those stories about soap in the whiskey. And I'll tell you another thing, there wasn't any music." Buckner looked at Shotwell. "Why are you nodding your head at me like that? Stop doing that. You've never been inside Dutton's in your life."

"No, I haven't, that's true." Shotwell was smiling confidently. "But I have been to where his customers are. And where his band is too."

"You have? All right, where's everybody gone?"

"Brand new place, just opened the other night. They had a big celebration and invited everybody."

"Everybody? Both sides of the tracks?"

"I don't think so. Not exactly. What I mean is, technically they're on this side—the white side—but up north a ways, just outside town limits. So maybe not on any side. But we also didn't see any white folks there, so they look to be aiming at Dutton all right, because a lot of the folks we saw there last night are folks that I know used to go to Dutton's regularly."

"And this place just opened?"

"Yes. Ever since you told me to start investigating, I've been hearing word around, you know, and wondered if there was any connection with what happened to Buster, and with Dutton's problems, so I thought I'd better take a look. I asked my wife to come with me."

"You did? What did Augusta say about that?"

"Well, I told her it was work, and I was investigating, and I couldn't go to a place like that by myself—I'd stick out like a sore thumb." Shotwell laughed. "She just gave me one of those looks—you know the one."

"The one that says 'I don't believe a word of it.'"

"That's the one. But then I explained it might be connected with what happened to Buster, so she said all right."

"Really?"

"Yeah. I almost fell outa my chair when she said that, but thinking back on it, I suspect she just wanted to keep an eye on me."

"So you went. What'd you find?"

"Dutton's customers, like I said, and Dutton's band."

"Uh-huh. Any chance you ran across the fellows that jumped Buster?"

"Maybe so. Anyway, there was a bunch of big fellas kind of standing around, you know, keeping an eye on things, and they looked like they might've been able to handle Buster, if they all jumped him at once."

"So who's running this operation?"

"Not real sure yet."

"Negroes?"

"Oh, yeah, that I am sure about. At least that's who was there last night, and that's who the big bruisers were, and there was one fellow who was going around chatting folks up, making sure everybody was having a good time. Looked like he was in charge. And these weren't country Negroes, either, none of 'em. Everybody talked nice ... acted nice. Served good liquor, too ... very smooth sipping whiskey." Shotwell frowned. "Whoever this is, they're spending a lot of money on it."

"Oh, boy." Buckner leaned back and looked at the ceiling. "So that's what the old man was muttering about."

"Huh?"

Buckner told Shotwell about his conversation at the barber shop."

"Yes, sir," Shotwell agreed. "Big city ... ah ... Negroes is right. Dutton's pretty much had things his way around here since he came home from the war, and now it looks like somebody's challenging him."

"And I don't think a town this size can support two fancy drinking establishments." Buckner laughed grimly. "Hell, we've only got enough musicians for one dance band."

"Yes, sir," Shotwell agreed, nodding seriously. "Not enough customers, not enough money, even with white folks coming in, which is the only way Dutton's been able to make it pay, far as I can see. But, other than Dutton's, and now this new place, there's only a couple of blind pigs over on our side of town, and there's always folks making their own and drinking with friends. But for a place where you might want to wear your nice clothes, maybe take a lady friend, or even your wife, Dutton's has always been it."

"Were there any white customers at all?"

"No, not last night. But that'll change if this place catches on." It was Shotwell's turn to smile. "And if the band stays."

Buckner stared at the ceiling some more. Then he thought of something. "Any sign of gambling going on? That'd put the stopper in the bottle, if they decided to take over gambling on that side of town."

"I couldn't tell anything about that," Shotwell replied. "And we hung around for quite a while." He chuckled. "We must've danced every dance there for a couple hours."

"Danced? I thought Augusta considered dancing to be … well, you know … just short of, well, outright …"

"Yeah, that's what I thought, too. But the music seemed to get to her."

"Well, maybe she was just helping you out with your investigation."

"Sure. But it turns out, she dances just fine. But she also made sure I understood this was a special occasion. That, and she's a friend of Helene, Buster's sister. And, of course, Buster's a deacon."

"Right. Of course." Buckner thought about Buster as a church deacon. The more he thought about it, the more obvious it was. He'd always thought of Buster as the man who walked behind Elroy Dutton, the man who kept the lid on at Dutton's place of business. But he was notorious for never drinking anything stronger than lemonade. And there was a reserved quiet to Buster as he stood by the door at Dutton's that would fit right in as he stood by the door in church: polite, observant, courteous.

"All right," Buckner said. "But you may have to go up there again. Where is this place exactly?"

"Just right outside city limits, up north there, where the train tracks make that big turn."

"Right, I know it. That big old house up on Crane's Hill, used to belong to whatsisname—Bell, sold rope and harness, things like that. His family, anyway." Buckner thought a minute. "So that's what's been going on up there."

"What do you mean?"

"Oh," Buckner explained, "I noticed some work going on up there a couple weeks ago. I just figured it was new owners fixing the place up."

"In a way," Shotwell agreed. "I asked around. This new outfit moved in real quiet about six months ago, bought the place, took out some walls, opened up the whole downstairs for a dance floor and tables, with the bar where the kitchen used to be because that's where all the plumbing was. According to what I found out, they're from Kansas City—Kansas side—but nobody knows for sure. They hired only colored workers locally … kept the whole thing real quiet."

"From me, anyway, that's for sure. But Dutton must've known what was going on."

"He had to. But I think they surprised him with this attack on Buster, and on his liquor supply. Kind of caught him off guard."

"And he got careless," Buckner agreed. "And that's why he's worried now."

"Yes."

"Well, tell Augusta this is important, and you may have to go there again, and she'll have to accompany you to provide cover. We may even have to deputize her."

Shotwell just laughed at that.

"And I'll have Carter back you up," Buckner went on. "If these folks jumped Buster, I want to know about it. But I also don't want this town getting caught in a brawl between Dutton and some new outfit trying to muscle in on his operation."

"I'll appeal to Augusta's sense of civic responsibility."

"All right. Let me know when you're going, and maybe I'll stop in."

Shotwell raised his eyebrows in surprise.

"Well," Buckner explained. "They have to know I'm a customer at Dutton's. Maybe they'll try to win me over to their place."

"Maybe." Shotwell was skeptical. "You dance?"

"No."

"Right. Well, tonight'd be a good time."

"See you there."

 **10**

The close, oppressive weather brought people out in search of relief as the sun went down. Buckner stopped at home long enough to change into a suit and tie; then he took the short walk across town. As he neared his destination, he noticed several couples headed the same way. Their goal was a large, three-story house on a slight rise at the end of a street, but it was obviously no longer a residence. There were bright electric lights strung all around, and the exterior had been freshly painted. Two large black men in evening wear greeted people at the door. They spotted Buckner at once and watched him come up the walk for a moment; then one went inside. By the time Buckner had mounted the steps to the broad gallery, the man was back with a third man, slightly older, nearly as large, also in evening wear. The three stood in a line across the door.

"You don't have any jurisdiction here, Chief," said the older man. "You didn't once you crossed the street out there. We're in the county."

"I just stopped in to listen to the music," Buckner said, smiling.

"In that case, come on in," the man said. The corners of his mouth turned up slightly, but his eyes didn't smile at all as he stepped aside.

Buckner went in. The entire downstairs was one large room. The band, looking uncomfortable in evening wear, performed on a raised platform at one end, and a long bar ran the length of the opposite wall. Tables were scattered around a central dance floor that was well stocked with people dancing. A waiter appeared and showed Buckner to a small table in a corner. As they crossed the floor, Buckner spotted Shotwell and his wife as well as Officer Carter, who was sitting with an attractive young woman at a larger table near the dance floor. He nodded in their direction, and they returned the greeting briefly. He noticed a few white faces in the crowd. Buckner was much more surprised to see another familiar face—Jackson, the waiter from Dutton's place, was just disappearing through a door behind the bar.

Buckner sat and looked around. When the waiter asked if he wanted anything to drink, he shook his head, and the waiter went away. He sat alone like that for a half hour, until the older man from the doorway came over.

"You sure you wouldn't like something to drink, Chief? We serve the best stuff."

"A cup of coffee would be good," Buckner said.

"A cup of coffee it is," the man said with a smile. A gesture brought the waiter back, and Buckner placed his order. The man spoke again. "So you only drink Elroy Dutton's whiskey? You might have to … ah … reevaluate your position on that, as I understand he's havin' some problems over his place."

"That's what I hear too," Buckner said.

The waiter brought coffee in a white china cup and saucer. Buckner sipped carefully.

"That's on the house," the man said.

"I'd just as soon pay," Buckner answered. He put a quarter on the table.

"Well, you want anything more than coffee, you let me know," the man said. He bowed slightly and went away. Buckner sipped coffee and watched the people dancing. After a while, Carter came over and sat opposite.

"Evenin', Buck."

Buckner nodded.

"They got a wheel upstairs and a craps table, and a feller dealin' faro. Everything's real quiet, everybody's real polite, and there's a couple more of those big fellers standin' around to make sure everything stays that way."

"All right. A first-class operation, in other words."

"No doubt about that. And I got the details on that knife fight at Dutton's. Seems pretty clear them two fellas wasn't trying very hard to cut each other, accordin' to folks who saw it. It was them two that met you at the front door, by the way. And another thing, Buster's healin' up real fast, and it looks like his sister's gonna let him go back to work pretty soon."

"Thanks. Have a good time. I'll see you tomorrow."

Carter went back to his table, and Buckner got to his feet and started for the door. The older black man was there ahead of him.

"You leaving already, Chief?"

"Nice place you've got here," Buckner said.

"Thank you." He held out his hand. "My name's Fitzwalter. Charles Fitzwalter. Just down from Kansas City. You're welcome here any time, Chief. Any time at all."

"Thanks." Buckner shook the offered hand. "So you plan to be here a while?"

"Oh, yes. We plan to be here for a long time." Fitzwalter's smile was confident, triumphant even. "Corinth is a lovely little town, just the sort of place I've been looking for."

"Won't you miss the excitement of the big city?"

"Not at all," Fitzwalter said. "Grew up on a farm over in Saline County. I'm just a country boy at heart."

"Well, Corinth is a very quiet little town," Buckner said. "And we work real hard to make sure it stays like that."

"I wouldn't have it any other way, Chief. It's why I came here in the first place. That, and the fact that it's ripe for change. You're not against change, are you, Chief Buckner?"

"Not at all. As long as it doesn't shake things up too much."

"Shaking things up," Fitzwalter said, frowning slightly. "That's not good for business. And business is the only thing I'm interested in."

"All right. Well, good evening, Mr. Fitzwalter. I expect I'll be seeing you again, real soon."

Buckner walked home. His mother was sitting on the front porch fanning herself and drinking ice water.

"This weather's got to break soon," she said as he came up the walk. "This just isn't natural for this time of year.'

"That's for sure. You can feel a storm building up somewhere."

"You been visiting Elroy Dutton?"

"Nope." Buckner sat down. "Been visiting the competition."

"Elroy Dutton has competition?" Buckner told his mother about Buster and the whiskey and the dance band. Then he told her about Charles Fitzwalter. "Yes," she said. "That sounds like Dutton's got a real problem."

"He's even got a gambling parlor on the second floor, according to what Carter told me."

"And he's in the old Bell place, just outside town?"

"Yep."

"Wow," said his mother.

"My thoughts exactly."

"What's Mr. Dutton going to do about it? He never struck me as the kind of man to take something like this lying down."

"I think he's just waiting for Buster to get well before he moves. I was over there the other night, and I noticed he had on that double shoulder rig he wears when he's expecting trouble."

"Shoulder rig?"

"Two .32 caliber pistols, one under each arm."

"Oh, dear. What are you going to do about that?"

"First thing in the morning, I'm going to make a telephone call," Buckner said. Then he got up, went inside, and went to bed.

The next morning, Buckner waited until eight o'clock before placing a long-distance telephone call to a private law office in the state capitol. Eventually, Davis Jackson came on the line.

"Hey, Buck! How are you doing? How's Marthy?"

The three of them had been friends through childhood, and Davis Jackson and Martha Jane Buckner had been an item briefly, long ago. As far as Buckner knew, Jackson was interested in reviving that relationship.

"I'm doing fine … Marthy's fine. You must be doing all right, too, since I had to wade through a receptionist and a secretary just to get you on the line."

"Well, you know how it is, Buck. Gotta provide jobs for the Party faithful." Jackson's voice was remote and metallic. "This must be pretty serious for you to be telephoning."

"Too much information for a wire," Buckner said. "And I don't want everybody in the world knowing about this, all right?"

"Sure. What's up?"

"First off, I know Stillson Foote's running for state assembly. How's his campaign going?"

"All right," Jackson said. A former deputy attorney general and scion of an old Missouri family, Davis Jackson was now a partner in a powerful law firm in Jefferson City. The firm was notoriously Democratic, maintaining close ties with the Democratic machines in Kansas City and St. Louis. Its partners would slide smoothly into high government offices if the Party ever got back into power. "Ever since Bob Nussbaum got all banged up when his auto ran off the road after the Fourth of July picnic, the seat's been pretty much up for grabs," he was saying. "The Republicans have a high opinion of Foote on account of he's got a reputation for being tough on crime, so he got the nod."

"What about your gang?"

"Well, that's just it. The Republicans figured to have it all their own way, but we've nominated Harry Boyer."

"Harry Boyer! He doesn't even live in the district."

"Actually, he does, ever since the last redistricting, after the Republicans got into power in twenty."

"Back when you lost your easy job with the state government."

"Don't count us out," Jackson replied, ignoring the jab. "Harry Boyer's just the kind of fellow we're looking for. He's run up quite a record as county sheriff over there, busting up the gambling operations, the stills … the bootleggers. He's closed more saloons and speakeasies than any other law enforcement officer in the state."

"And since law and order was Foote's big campaign issue—" Buckner began.

"Right. Harry's snatched it right out from under his nose." Jackson laughed. "I'm telling you, Buck, right now it looks like it's going to be a real horse race, and Foote's not too happy about that, especially since he expected to just stroll right into office."

"So he's scrambling for votes?" Buckner asked.

"Right now he is, yes."

"Great. That's what I wanted to know. Thanks, Davis."

"Any time, Buck. Why the sudden interest? Say, you're not going to get involved in politics over there, are you? I thought you were dead set against police officers in politics."

"I am, Davis. But I have a little problem over here, and Stillson Foote might be the man to solve it for me."

"Uh-huh. And what was the other thing you wanted to ask about?"

"Oh, right. What can you tell me about a gambler and saloon owner named Charles Fitzwalter out of Kansas City, Kansas?"

"White Fitzwalter or colored Fitzwalter?"

"Colored."

"Solid businessman," Jackson said. "Runs a good operation. Doesn't water the whiskey too much, his wheel's honest and so are his dice, and he doesn't take too big a percentage. He knows who to pay off, and he's generous about it. But the boys over on the Kansas side also figure him to be behind a couple of shootings that conveniently removed some major competition when he was just coming up."

"Right. A bad man to tangle with."

"I've never had anything to do with him, since he's strictly Kansas side, but, yeah, that'd be my assessment. Why?"

"No reason. Thanks. Oh, one thing more, can you tell me the number of Foote's campaign headquarters there in town?"

"Another long-distance call? You sure your budget can handle it?"

"I expect it'll pay off in the long run," Buckner said. He got the number from Jackson and hung up. *At least I hope it will*, he thought. He picked up the earpiece and jiggled the handle. "Mae?" he said when the operator came on. "Get me Stillson Foote's office. Here's the number."

Shortly before noon, Buckner got a telegram: "Arriving 4:10 eastbound. Need cell. Harris."

Driven by curiosity as much as anything else, Buckner met the 4:10 train. He was puzzled when no passengers got off. Then the door to the mail car slid open and Detective Harris, with surprising agility, hopped down. In a moment, a railroad policeman appeared in the doorway with Peralta, hands cuffed behind his back. The policeman gave Peralta a shove and he sprawled onto the platform at Harris's feet.

"Thanks," Harris said as he watched Peralta struggle to stand up.

"Don't mention it," the policeman said as he slid the door shut.

Harris grinned at Buckner. "You got room for this one?"

"Sure. Where's the Binkley girl?"

"Dunno," Harris replied. "He says she left him. Took off, and he doesn't know where she's gone."

"Really?"

"It's the truth, goddammit," Peralta said. "I swear she took off."

"Shut up," Harris said. Then, to Buckner, "Yeah, sounded fishy to me, too."

With Peralta between them, the two men walked into town.

"Why have you brought him here?" Buckner asked. "I thought you were being paid to find the girl."

"I am. I just need someplace where I can keep this dago on ice for a while. I've gotta go back to St. Louis, take care of a coupla things there. Then I want to talk to him about the girl."

"Where'd you find him?"

"Just over the line down in Arkansas. He was trying to get a stake by shooting dice with a line crew down in Corning, only he was using a pair of shaved dice he'd palmed."

"That wasn't too smart."

"No, it wasn't. Those boys in Arkansas had just started to figure out they were being cheated when I showed up. Hell, you could say I saved his life. For what that's worth."

"Well, you won't mind if I talk to him while he's a guest in my jail," Buckner said. "I need to ask him some questions about the dead girl up in Taylor."

"Hey!" Peralta said. "I didn't have nothing to do with that. I swear to God I didn't have nothing to do with any of that."

"Huh," Harris grunted. "A completely innocent man."

"There aren't many of those," Buckner agreed.

Buckner locked Peralta in a cell while Harris gave Mullen the information to log in the new prisoner. Harris joined him outside the cell.

"I gotta go tell those folks in St. Louis I found their man," Harris said.

"They going to be satisfied with Peralta?" Buckner asked.

"One way or another, I figure I'm halfway there." Harris glanced at his watch. "There's another eastbound through in an hour; then there's nothing until after midnight, and I don't want to spend the night in Corinth."

"We'll try to keep Mr. Peralta comfortable until you get back." Buckner turned and smiled at the prisoner.

"You can't keep me here," Peralta said, pointing at Harris. "He's nothing but a hired thug. He ain't no cop. He's got some phony badge says he's a St. Louis County deputy sheriff, but, hell, you can get one of those in a box of Cracker Jacks! It don't mean nothing."

"You're probably right," Buckner said. "Only it doesn't matter right now, because right now you are a prisoner in *my* jail, and I have some questions for you."

"Don't bang him around too much," Harris said. He sketched a salute and strode down the hall and was gone. Buckner just stood and watched Peralta.

"This is about that dead body," Peralta said after a while.

"That's right."

"I told you I didn't have nothing to do with that."

"Yes, you did." He continued looking at Peralta, a slight frown of curiosity on his face. Unable to meet Buckner's gaze, Peralta fidgeted, scratched himself, began to pace the cell.

Buckner said, "She was your woman, wasn't she? You picked her up someplace, probably St. Louis, got her hooked on cocaine, and then you dragged her around with you, selling her to anybody with ready cash to stake your gambling. Because that's your line, isn't it?"

"Look," Peralta stopped pacing and said, "I don't know nothing about that woman. You can't prove I had anything to do with her at all. All that about her being with me, you're just making that up."

"You came to town a couple of years ago—Taylor this was—accompanied by a young woman that fits the general description." Buckner read from his notebook. "About five feet two inches tall, blond hair, good figure, according to plenty of people who saw you with her. Then, about a year or so ago—nobody seems to be sure just when—the woman disappeared."

Peralta paced some more, talking hurriedly as he paced. "Hold it a second," he said. "If I try to help you ... tell you what I know ... maybe you could figure out some way to keep that Harris off me.

How does that sound? I mean, I'm serious. I didn't kill nobody, but maybe I can help you out some, if you help me."

Buckner shrugged. "Well, I could always talk to Harris."

"Right, right," Peralta said. He stopped pacing. "Look, I was with a woman that looked like that." He indicated Buckner's notebook. "Blond, good figure, all that. We were together for a while."

"What happened to her?"

"She disappeared. Honest, she just up and left me. I never knew where she went."

"What was her name?"

"Angelica. Angelica Cosimo. Everybody called her Angela."

"Where was she from?"

"I met her in St. Louis, like you said. I guess she was from there. Said she was, anyway. She was working at the L&M cigarette plant when I met her. Said she'd quit school and got a job on account of she wanted nice clothes, and her mother wouldn't buy her nothing."

"Do you know where her parents live?"

"Huh," Peralta snorted. "Not likely."

"So you introduced her to cocaine."

"Hell no, I didn't. She was already on the stuff when I ran into her."

"But you thought it would be a good idea to start pimping her."

Peralta shrugged. "She was already doing that, too, only she didn't have nobody to look out for her."

"So you were doing her a favor then?"

"Yeah, I was. She was getting taken advantage of, wasn't making any money, kept getting beat up, so, yeah, I took care of her."

"And kept whatever she earned."

"Her family'd kicked her out. She was sleeping in doorways and back alleys, wearing rags. With me she had a roof over her head, regular meals, nice things. And, yeah, I gotta be … uh … you know, uh … compensated for my time and all."

"The workman is worthy of his hire, right?"

"Yeah, sure. Why not?"

"Why'd you leave St. Louis and travel to this neck of the woods?"

"Well, you know how it is, if you're good at cards and dice, some fellas don't like losing … think maybe because you make a living with cards and dice, maybe you're a pushover."

"But you're not a pushover."

"No, I ain't, and some fellas had to learn that the hard way, but, you know, they got friends, and their friends got friends, so we decided to head south for a spell." Peralta grinned. "Truth is, we only had enough money for tickets this far."

"Truth is, you got thrown off the train for gambling," Buckner guessed.

Peralta shrugged and tried a thin smile.

"So, one way or another, you made it to Taylor and set up in business there."

"Sure. It was easy to catch a ride with Angela standing there smiling. Some old farmer picked us up, run us all the way to Taylor. Though, I gotta tell you, how we got there without him driving us into a ditch, I'll never know. He couldn't take his eyes off of her. Anyway, when we got there, brother, I tell you, it was like hitting the jackpot. Lots of single men looking for company, a little fun, a card game every now and then. And you could see why. I checked out some of the other places up there, and they had some of the homeliest women." Peralta shook his head in amazement. "Ugly and old. So Angela was a big hit right from the start. And I set up quick, mostly at Shorty's, providing a good clean game of chance."

"Like on payday."

"Sure. They're feeling flush, and you catch them before they get home to the old lady, or drink it all up."

"So what happened with that girl, Angela? She get tired of staking you? Her habit get too expensive?"

"Nothing happened to her, far as I was concerned," Peralta insisted. "I keep telling you. We was doing just fine, everything was going good, and then one day she just up and disappeared. Hell, I thought she'd gone back to St. Louis."

"Had she been giving you trouble?"

"No."

Buckner thought a minute. "She have many customers? I wouldn't have thought a little town like Taylor could support you for very long."

"You'd be surprised," Peralta said. "Lot of single fellows pass through, work a spell, move on."

"Any regulars?"

"Yeah, a few. That old man lived at the boarding house, Thrasher, he went with her whenever he had the money. And them two company cops was always sniffing around. One or two other fellas thought they had something special going with her."

"Company cops? Kelson and Garber?"

"Sure. Cops like to get their ashes hauled like anybody else, I figure, and that was a good way of making sure they left me alone." Peralta had resumed pacing.

"Remember the names of those other fellows?"

"Not right off."

"Think about it," Buckner suggested. "Anybody like to beat up on women?"

"Hell no. That didn't go as far as I was concerned."

"Taking care of your investment?"

"Damned right. Nobody'd go with her if she was all beat up, and the time it took her to heal was time she wasn't working."

"All right," Buckner said. Talking to Peralta, watching him pacing back and forth in the tiny cell, was wearing him down. "Let's talk about this latest girl, Rachael Binkley. What happened to her?"

"She run out on me too."

"In Arkansas?"

"Somewheres down there, yeah."

"You've been having terrible luck with your women."

"Listen, Chief, there's always plenty of 'em around. You got no idea. I get out of here, get back up to the city, I wouldn't—"

"You probably shouldn't go to St. Louis any time soon."

"Hell, it don't matter," Peralta said. He stopped pacing and stepped close to the bars. His voice was soft, insinuating. "Memphis, Chicago, KC, Little Rock, any big city, there's these girls come right off the farm, corn-fed and pretty as you please, and looking for the glamorous life. They're a dime a dozen. I'll be back in business in no time. And there's plenty of places like Taylor with men lookin' for some fun, and money in their pockets." He laughed, a short, hard bark. "It's a great life, Chief, take my word for it."

"Except that you're in jail on suspicion of murder," Buckner said. He stood looking at Peralta for a long time. It didn't take long for Peralta's confidence to drain away. He licked his lips, and a worried look clouded his face. His eyes darted anywhere and everywhere. He stepped back and started pacing again. Buckner watched him for a few minutes longer and then walked away.

 **11**

The next morning, Buckner was on his second cup of coffee when Harris strolled in. "I've got news for you," he said. "That girl used to go around with Peralta—not the first one, the second one, Binkley—she went home."

"Home?"

"Yeah. I went up there to talk to her father, and he told me she come back on her own. She'd put by enough nickels and dimes to buy a one-way. She managed to get loose from Peralta when they got off the train in Poplar Bluff. Her father said she hid out until the train was about to leave; then she got herself a ticket to St. Louis, hit town, and walked into her father's tailor shop just a few hours ahead of me."

"So I guess you didn't make any money on that deal."

"I sure as hell didn't. I tried to convince the old man I oughta get something for the work I done, but he didn't agree, and he had a couple of his friends show me the door. Hell, it wasn't worth getting busted up over, so I went."

"The girl's father didn't want a piece of Peralta's hide?"

"He was mostly glad to have his little girl back, but, yeah, he made it real clear to me that Peralta's a dead man if he shows up in St. Louis."

"Tough luck. You tell them where he was?"

"Hell no. Not doing them no favors. But it turns out there's a reward for the other girl. Just for information on her." Harris checked his notebook. "Her name's Angela Cosimo. Friend of mine on the cops up there told me about her. Five hundred for information on her and the man she was seen getting on the westbound with. This friend of mine, he says the girl was pretty wild, and she run off—either that or the family kicked her out. Anyway, they wanted her back and went to the cops. The cops weren't exactly killing themselves working on another runaway girl case, so they don't mind a bit if somebody like me comes along to take it off their hands."

"You went to see the family?"

"Sure. They wasn't getting no satisfaction, and I persuaded them to try something themselves. The family's not connected, which is funny, considering they're Italian, but they run one of the big brickyards up there. They ain't rich, but they want their daughter found real bad. So they can afford to pay me. Anyway, the man that was seen with their daughter matched Peralta's description. And then there's this story in the papers up there." Harris took out a folded newspaper and put it on the desk. "It's by one of their hot crime reporters, name of Buckner." He grinned. "All about this here mystery dead woman down in the Lead Belt."

"If it wasn't for the police and the newspapers, you'd be out of work," Buckner said.

"That's the truth." Harris laughed. "But, hell, according to this friend of mine, if the cops went looking for every girl run away from home, they wouldn't have time for anything else. And he said most of 'em come back eventually, when they find out they ain't gonna be the next Mary Pickford, and it ain't much fun being out on your own. Anyway, if I show up with Peralta and whatever information you've got on that dead woman up in Taylor, I might just come out ahead on this."

"If I decide to let you have Peralta."

"You gonna charge him? With what? You got no proof he had anything to do with that woman ending up in the cellar wall. Or proof of anything else, for that matter."

"He told me yesterday the woman he was with—the first one—was named Cosimo, and the description fits."

"Well, there you go, then. All you got to do is turn him over to me. I'll take him to St. Louis, and they can deal with him there."

"If they were legally married, the courts won't be interested in trying him for leading her astray, especially since you've got no evidence at all to persuade a prosecutor otherwise. But down here, maybe we can get him for murder."

"Hell, I don't care about no trial. Convincing the grieving family is a hell of a lot easier than convincing a jury, and you know it. And if I've got Peralta and a body they can give a good Christian burial to, that'd go a long way toward convincing them."

"All right," Buckner said. "But all this means is that you'll make some money and nobody up there is interested in holding Peralta without proof, so they'll turn him loose. So he gets away with murder. I wouldn't like to see that happen."

"I don't see how you're involved in this at all. It was up in Taylor. You haven't got a lot of evidence the dead woman is this Cosimo, or that Peralta killed her, but I can use what Peralta told you to convince her family. You've got no jurisdiction up there anyway, so how are you going to explain arresting him in the first place?"

"What do you care?"

"I care about making my score," Harris insisted. "I can't work for free. I got a wife and kids to support."

"Wait a minute. Just hold on a minute. I want to prove the dead body is Cosimo and that Peralta killed her and that he won't get away with that."

"You're a saint."

"And you want to make some money, and you think if you can prove the dead woman is Cosimo, you can put the squeeze on the family."

"I ain't squeezin' nobody," Harris protested. Suspicion clouded his face. "Hey, you talking about cutting in on my action? Is that what this is about? You want a piece of whatever I get out of the family?" Harris smiled then, exposing tobacco-stained teeth. "I think we ought to be able to work something out."

"No, I don't want a piece of your action. I just want to get this cleared up … get it off my desk, but I do want to see Peralta in jail for murder."

"All right," Harris said. He thought about it for a moment. "Maybe we're not running on separate tracks after all. It looks to me like the first thing we gotta do is make sure that dead body over at Murtaugh's is this Cosimo."

"All right," Buckner said, suddenly curious. "Then what?"

"Well, then I can go tell her family you've found their daughter, and she's been murdered, and here's the body so you can bury her. Oh, and she was pregnant, too. According to the newspapers, anyway."

"I don't see how that'd get you any money."

"We'll see," Harris replied. "Sometimes folks just need to know."

"Fine, but I'll be holding on to Peralta," Buckner insisted. "And I'll get McLaws, here in town, or maybe Strachan, the county prosecutor, to bring charges. I've got a friend, used to be in the attorney general's office over in Jefferson City, and he might help out. That'd put pressure on the folks in the county seat.

After some thought, Harris said, "Yeah, that might work."

"It looks to me like it's the only chance you've got here, since I've got Peralta, and since I'm going to hold on to him. And the first thing we've got to do is find out from the family if the girl ever broke her arm. Peck said the dead woman broke her arm some time in the past." He remembered Peck's report. "Left radius, I think he said."

"Yeah." Harris had his notebook out. He pointed to his arm. "That's this one here. The other one's the ulna."

"Uh-huh," Buckner said. "Well, that's our connection, then. It isn't much, but it's about all the proof we've got."

"Sure. Now all you got to do is prove Peralta killed her."

"Yeah. And I guess that means I've got to go back to Taylor and start talking to people again."

"Mr. Powers gonna let you get away with that?"

"I don't know."

"Well, better you than me." Harris stood. "I'll be in touch."

"You headed back to St. Louis?"

"I think I might stay around a day or so, look up some friends of mine, you know, from the old days."

"That shouldn't take long," Buckner said. "As I recall, you didn't have many friends. At least none that would admit to it."

"You never know, Chief. You never know." Harris walked out laughing.

Buckner went back to the cells. He grabbed the turnkey's stool, opened Peralta's cell, plunked the stool in the doorway, and sat down.

"You say you didn't kill Angela Cosimo."

"That's right, I didn't." Peralta was sitting on the bunk, watching suspiciously. His hands moved nervously on their own, twitching, clutching, picking at each other.

"Why don't you try to convince me of that," Buckner said.

"Why should I bother? I'm innocent until proven guilty."

"Yes, in court. But this isn't court, this is just the two of us setting here talking. And it would help a lot if you could point me in the direction of somebody else. Assuming you didn't do it."

"You mean if I can get you to pin this on somebody else, you'll let me out?"

"Not exactly. Anything I pin on anybody's got to stick. And there's still some questions about you and the other girl, Binkley. I may have to let Harris take you back to St. Louis."

"Jesus Christ, don't do that." Peralta was genuinely terrified. "I wouldn't last ten minutes up there, not even in jail. I'd be dead. That little bitch got away from me, and I know sure as hell she ran home to Daddy, and Daddy's got some bad friends. Don't send me back to St. Louis."

"Fine, but you've got to give me a reason to keep you here." Buckner took out his notebook. "Tell me about Angela Cosimo."

"What's to tell? She wanted to get away from home, have some fun."

"According to you, she was already using cocaine, and she was also going with men for the money."

"Yeah, but that was small-time stuff. And she had to do it on the q.t. because of her family. They had money—owned that brickyard. She'd gone out on her own, but she had to keep it quiet. Mostly just with brothers of her girlfriends, or their fathers."

"And you were just offering to help."

"Sure. She needed somebody to watch out for her."

"So you got to Corinth when?"

"Lessee." Peralta hesitated, frowning. "Had to be about two years ago, maybe September. Took the train here and thumbed a ride up to Taylor, like I told you."

"And when did Cosimo get away from you?"

"She didn't get away from me." Peralta was shaking his head. "She just flat vanished one day … well, one night, really. Said she was going out and she'd see me when she got back, and that was it. I never saw her again."

"When she said she was going out, did she mean for work? Was she meeting somebody?"

"She didn't say. And I wasn't working her much, since I'd been doing all right at the tables and I was pretty flush." He shrugged. "For all I know, she was going out for a walk."

"You don't seem to have kept a very close eye on your business."

"Like I said, I was flush." He smiled, remembering. "I was on the best winning streak I'd had in years. If she wanted to go for a walk, what did I care? Where was she going to go anyway, up there in the hills with no auto?"

"What did you think when she didn't come back?"

"Nothing. Not right off, anyway. It was night. I had to go to work, and I didn't get back for almost twenty-four hours. I remember that real good. The cards was running all my way, and

I didn't want to stop. Course, the reason I was so late, I had to stick around until I started losing a few hands. The boys don't like it if you get up from the table with all their money. You've got to let them win some of it back, you know, so they feel like they've won something."

"Very generous of you."

"No, no. You don't understand, Chief. If you really clean them out, you hurt their feelings cause you've made 'em look bad in front of their friends. And that could get you hurt. Worse, it might mean they won't want to play cards with you next payday. So you let them win back some of their money, make a big deal out of how they're killing you, and then leave. You've got most of their paycheck, but they won the last few hands, they feel pretty good, and they can't wait to take you on next time."

"All right. So Angela goes out one night. What time?"

"I don't know. Eight, maybe. Nine. It was dark. My game started at ten, and she was gone before that."

"So you're gone for the next twenty-four hours, away from your room."

"Something like that, yeah."

"And you get back, and she's gone. What'd you do?"

"Well, I asked around after her, of course, but nobody knew anything about her or where she'd gone."

"Did she have any friends?"

"What'd she need with friends? She had me, didn't she?"

"Of course," Buckner said. "So you asked around. Then what?"

"After a couple of days, I figured I needed to find her, you know, in case the cards turned against me."

"And did they?"

"No, not right off. Then, when they did, and she was gone, why, I got up to town as quick as I could and started looking around."

"Why St. Louis?"

"Nearest big city." Peralta shrugged.

"And you didn't find Cosimo, but you found this Binkley girl."

"Yeah." Peralta smiled and sighed. "She was something, I'll tell you. Really enjoyed the work."

"She couldn't've enjoyed it that much."

"What do you mean?"

"She ran out on you too."

"Oh, that's nothing. They get homesick sometimes. Best to just let 'em go. If they ain't happy, that shows in their work, and that means the customers ain't happy, and that's bad for business."

"That's really all this is to you, isn't it? Business. Playing cards, selling women's bodies. Just business."

"Sure." Peralta was smiling again, confidence returning, on the verge of laughter. "Hell, it's what made this country great—business. It's how come we beat the Hun. It's how come we're the richest country in the world—the strongest, the best. Business, pure and simple."

Buckner got to his feet so suddenly that Peralta was startled. He leaned back, hands half-raised in defense. But Buckner just went down to hall, grabbed his coffee cup and filled it. "You all right, Buck?" Mullen asked.

Buckner nodded, saying nothing, and returned to Peralta's cell.

"Say, I don't suppose I could have a cup of that?" Peralta said.

"So Angela Cosimo disappeared, and a little while later you picked up Rachael Binkley."

"Yeah." Peralta tried again. "That coffee looks mighty good. Can I get a cup?"

"No. Let's go over Angela's regular customers again."

"All right."

"What were their names?"

"I'd remember better with a cup of coffee. Coffee helps me think."

Buckner looked at Peralta for a long time, until the man was squirming. He opened his mouth to speak, but Buckner held up a hand. He went down the hall and returned with a cup of coffee. Peralta took it and drank. "Thanks. That's pretty good stuff."

"I'll tell Officer Mullen. Now, about those names."

Peralta rattled off several names, which Buckner wrote down.

"What about Powers?" Buckner asked. "He ever do any business with her?"

Peralta smiled slyly. "He might've, yeah. He was always tryin' to get her to go to church with him. Least that's what she told me. I told her if he wanted anything more, it was on the cuff. Gotta keep the folks on top happy."

"And did he?"

"Not that I know of."

"All right, what about Kelson and Garber? Did you have some kind of arrangement with them?"

"Yeah, sure. Mostly we just avoided each other—you know, they wasn't where we was. Except when I had Angela check on one or another of them. At a reduced rate, of course." Peralta grinned. "That's just the way the cops work, Chief. I bet you've got yourself a little piece on the side."

Just as Peralta was bringing the coffee cup to his mouth, Buckner reached out and slapped him. The slap sent the cup flying, half its contents splashing up into his face. Peralta yelped and fell sideways, banging his head hard against the stone wall of the cell before collapsing to the floor.

Buckner sat and looked at him as he lay on the floor screaming and holding his hands up to his face. Mullen came pounding down the hallway. "What's the matter with him?" he asked.

"The coffee was a little too hot and it burned him," Buckner said.

"He going to be all right? Do I need to call Dr. Peck?"

"He'll be fine in a minute or two. The coffee wasn't that hot."

"All right." Mullen turned to go, hesitated, and said, "I thought you might be in trouble."

"No. No trouble," Buckner said, sipping at his coffee and watching as Peralta's screaming subsided into soft whimpering.

"He hit me," Peralta said from the floor. "Jesus Christ, he hit me."

Mullen looked at Buckner. Buckner shrugged and handed Mullen his empty cup.

"You want a refill?"

Buckner just shook his head, and Mullen went away. Finally, Peralta sat up and leaned his back against the edge of the bunk. He touched his face gingerly. It glowed bright red.

"Jesus Christ," he said. "You didn't have to do that. I was helping you, wasn't I? Jesus. You're gonna knock me around, I think maybe I ain't got nothing more to tell you."

"All right." Buckner stood up. Peralta shrank away, hands up. "We're holding you for murdering Angela Cosimo."

"But I told you—"

"Not another word," Buckner said. Peralta opened his mouth. "I mean it." Peralta clamped his mouth shut. Buckner put the stool back and locked the door, leaving Peralta sitting on the floor of his cell.

He returned to his office and looked at the names Peralta had given him … names of men who had paid him for the services of Angela Cosimo. Thrasher, the old man up in the hills; Kelson and Garber, the Company policemen; three others he'd never heard of. Tom would know where to find them. If he decided to bother with them at all. Wasn't this just Peralta's way of throwing suspicion from himself onto others? Almost certainly. But did that also mean he was guilty? After all, that was what guilty people did.

He sat for a long time staring at the wall. He thought about what had happened in the cell. It surprised him, really. He'd never hit a prisoner before. He thought about that for a long time. Was it his way of getting back at Mrs. Belmont? After all, she was pretty much in the same line of business as Peralta, only without the gambling. But with powerful people behind her, providing protection that made her untouchable. For some reason, maybe that reason, this case had eaten at him. What had begun as an annoyance—doing the bidding of the town fathers to assist the Company—was beginning to feel more like a mission. Maybe it was just as he'd told Aubuchon: somebody had to stand up for the dead woman. Somebody had to get her some justice so her soul could find rest.

He laughed at himself, shook his head, and said quietly, "Probably shouldn't make a habit of it, though." And a cop with a mission, rather than a job, could be a dangerous thing.

Buckner was in the office early the next morning. Mullen had hot coffee waiting.

"Where you headed today?"

"What makes you think I'm going anywhere, Michael?"

"You're wearing your old cavalry clothes from before the war. That means you're riding, not driving." Mullen thought a moment. "Up in the hills above Taylor," he said. "To, uh ... what was that fella's name? Thrasher. You're going to pay Mr. Thrasher a visit."

"What if I was just going out riding for pleasure?"

Mullen said nothing, just looked at him, eyebrows raised.

"All right," Buckner went on. "But I'm not going to talk to him. I want to search his place. I telephoned the Company, and he's working underground this week, so he won't be around to complain if I don't put everything back just right."

"I knew it," Mullen said. "And you're just here to pick up your camera and ... let's see, your gun."

"No gun, Michael." Buckner grinned and went to his office where he picked up his camera. He loaded it and went back out, stopping at Mullen's desk. He handed Mullen a piece of paper. "Send these wires to these men."

"Right." Mullen scanned Buckner's scrawl. "Uh, this is Sergeant John, uh—"

"Lieutenant John Morris, St. Louis Police Department. He used to be with Pinkerton a while back."

"All right. And what's this word—Nessus?"

"Memphis, Michael. In Tennessee."

"Oh, yes. I see."

"Just get those off this morning, and be sure to tell whoever's in the telegraph office to get the responses over here as soon as they come in.

Buckner headed up the stairs. Carter, just off duty, was coming down.

"You going to take a ride up to Ratliff's Fork, Buck?" he said.

"Shut up, Carter."

"Right, Buck. Long as you ain't askin' me to go long with you."

The morning air was finally crisp, the horse was full of ginger, and Buckner was at Thrasher's place before the sun was high.

The door was locked but yielded easily to a skeleton key. The inside still smelled of bacon grease—probably always did—but the place was fairly neat. There were no crusted dishes in the washtub that served as a sink, no food rotting on shelves. Buckner wondered how Thrasher got back and forth to and from the mine. There was no sign of a horse, or of an auto. Thrasher probably walked the five or so miles to Taylor.

The kitchen and a small pantry took up one half of the dog trot, the other half contained little more than a bed, carefully made, a large easy chair, and several ladder-back chairs with woven rush bottoms that didn't look new. A small bureau stood against one wall. A table held a Bible, an almanac, and several old issues of *Collier's*. There was also a large trunk. The floor was made of ten-inch planks worn smooth, and covered with only a few worn throw rugs. The outside of the building had been covered with clapboards, but inside the massive oak logs, squared off and chinked with plaster mixed with horsehair, were open to view. Buckner guessed the place to be less than a hundred years old, but probably not built by the French. This kind of log construction wasn't their style. In fact, it looked German, and there hadn't been Germans in this part of the state until the late 1830s.

Buckner searched carefully for an hour. He had absolutely no reason to think Thrasher would have brought one of Peralta's women up here, and he was fairly sure Peralta would not have allowed it, but you could never tell what kind of souvenirs a man might keep. And so he was not surprised to find a pair of black silk stockings in a drawer of the bureau. Buckner looked harder but found nothing else, so he gave up. He checked to make sure he had left no signs of his visit, locked the door, and rode away.

After a while, the woods gave way to open ground sloping away toward the west. He wanted to stop in Taylor and talk to those other men who had been regular customers of Peralta's women. He didn't hurry, and an hour later he looped the reins over a pump handle behind the Company's offices.

According to Tom's card file, one of the three men he was looking for had left town, and two others were at work.

"Mike Devin and Bill Gamble. Devin's a drill operator, Gamble's a millwright."

"Can you bring them up?" Buckner asked. "I can talk to them here."

"I'd need to get Mr. Powers' permission to do that. And it'd take a while just to get them up here." Tom clearly was not in a helpful mood. "You can just take the elevator down and ask the gang boss to talk to them," he said.

"Look, I don't know my way around down there. It'd go a lot quicker if you led the way," Buckner said.

"I'll have to check," Tom said with a frown. He nodded in the direction of the inner office. "He expects me to be out here as long as he's in there."

"Fine." Buckner shrugged. "Like I said, it'll go quicker and cost the Company less lost time, if you lead the way."

Tom knocked on the office door and went in. He was back in a minute.

"All right. Let's go. And make it quick." They walked up the hill behind the offices to the mine head and the steel structure that housed the elevator that took men down to their work. The cage was large enough to carry half a dozen men. It had a wood floor and was wrapped in wire mesh. Tom stepped in next to the operator, and the two of them looked at Buckner, who had hesitated.

Buckner hesitated, suddenly reluctant ... suddenly—and surprisingly—terrified.

"You comin' or not?" the operator demanded.

Buckner stepped in and snugged into one corner. The operator pulled his lever, and the elevator shuddered and began its slow descent.

Immediately, the instant the elevator shuddered into motion, Buckner felt a giant hand grab his chest and squeeze. His heart began to pound, and he found himself struggling to breathe. He put his hands behind him, where the others could not see, and gripped the steel frame tightly. The shaft though which they traveled was lighted intermittently with dim electric lamps. The single overhead light in the elevator cage itself revealed rough rock walls. The elevator was impossibly slow, and it took several minutes to complete the trip. By the time it thumped heavily at the bottom, Buckner was sweating and trying hard not to scream and beg Tom to take them back up.

Tom and the elevator operator glanced at him, puzzled, but otherwise paid no attention. Buckner followed Tom out of the elevator.

"You want me to wait?" the operator asked.

"Yeah," Tom said. "This won't take but a minute."

"All right. But if I get a call, I gotta go back up."

"I know."

Buckner waited in the pool of light by the elevator while Tom asked the gang boss where the men were working. It took several minutes for Tom to locate the men, and Buckner clenched his fists in his trouser pockets and concentrated on breathing slowly ... calmly. He was only partly successful.

The earth down here had been gouged and carved into enormous, high-ceilinged rooms supported by massive pillars of rock. Dust hung in the air, and electrical wiring ran along the rock walls. Mules pulled ore carts along tracks that crisscrossed the rock floor. The rooms were brightly lit. Two hundred feet up, Buckner could see gangs of men standing on wooden planks suspended from the ceiling—"trapeze miners." The noise of the drills and the rattling of the ore carts, together with the rumbling of the elevators moving ore and people only accentuated Buckner's sensation of being crushed by the very earth itself. It was hot underground, and his breath was coming in short, light gasps that he seemed unable to control.

The men working at the rock face, filling the ore carts, barely glanced his way. Buckner watched Tom approach the two men he was looking for. One was operating a drill; the other, at the opposite end of one large room, was repairing a damaged ore cart. Tom brought them to where Buckner waited.

Desperate to escape and terrified of showing his fear, Buckner gulped air and shouted his questions, wrote down the shouted responses, and thanked the men. Yes, they had gone with Peralta's woman. Which one, the blond or the dark-haired one? Both of them … either one of them. The men shrugged. What difference did it make? Did they go with other women? Sure. Where? Back alleys … anyplace. Did you like putting your hands around her neck, choking her while you were doing it? The men seemed puzzled.

Buckner could not think of any more questions to ask, his whole attention focused on escape. He stood and stared at the men and finally sent them away.

"Is that it?" Tom asked when the men had gone back to work.

"Yes," Buckner replied.

"Fine. Let's go." Tom turned and angrily stomped into the elevator. Buckner followed slowly, each step an effort. He wanted desperately to get out into open air, to get away from this sensation of being crushed, but he felt as though he was running through molasses. Tom was frowning at him, watching him closely with something like a look of triumph dawning in his eyes. "You get used to it after a while, Chief," he said with a smile.

Buckner said nothing.

The long ride up through the narrow shaft seemed to Buckner to take an hour. He leaned heavily into the corner of the elevator cage and tried to control his breathing. Tom watched him closely the whole way up. He seemed to be enjoying every minute of Buckner's agony. The elevator operator hummed to himself and paid no attention.

By the time the elevator reached the surface, Buckner was on the verge of screaming. The elevator door clanged open, and he stumbled out and inhaled deeply. The elevator operator and the two or three men working nearby looked at him in surprise.

"Looks like the Chief here's a bit claustrophobic," Tom said with a chuckle.

Buckner ignored their laughter and made his way back toward the office.

"You want to talk to Mr. Powers?" Tom asked, his tone as mocking as his smile.

Buckner just shook his head. He untied his horse, mounted, and turned the animal down the road, resisting an urge to spur it into a fast gallop.

By the time Buckner got to the junction with the Corinth road, he had stopped trembling and was breathing normally.

A short way down the road to Corinth stood a nameless roadhouse. Back before the War Between the States it had been a wagon belonging to a liquor dealer who sold to the local Indians. The wagon had somehow taken root there and had evolved into a building that had been added to, burnt down, and rebuilt over the years. The original owner had come to a bad end, tortured and killed by Osages who thought alcohol was destroying their people. But the place remained, passing to various owners until it became the property of the current proprietor, Corrado Nirchio.

Nirchio had left the hitching rail in place, and Buckner left his horse there and went inside. Nirchio, a powerfully built man with one empty sleeve, looked at him in surprise.

"Deputy Buckner. Haven't seen you in a while." Nirchio chuckled. Corrado Nirchio had been a lead miner in Italy and in America, losing an arm in the process. But he had saved enough money to buy this place, and had the leisure time to dabble in local politics. He headed the local chapter of the Socialist Party, and had run for several county offices, winning none.

Buckner went to the bar. "I'd like a glass of whiskey, please," he said.

"Sure thing, Deputy." Nirchio, carefully observing Buckner's face, poured a tumbler half full.

Buckner picked it up carefully, slowly, making sure his hand didn't shake too much. He sipped carefully and sighed as the liquor burned its way down. It wasn't Neb Healy's, but it would do. He took another sip and set the tumbler back on the bar. Nirchio just watched quietly. Buckner drank some more, finished the whiskey, and put the tumbler down.

"You want some more, Deputy?"

"Chief of police now," Buckner said. "No, no more. Thanks." He reached into his pocket. "How much?"

"Deputy ... chief, no matter. It's on the house for you."

Buckner said, "Thanks." He left a dollar on the bar and walked out. He mounted and resumed his ride. The horse's easy gait seemed to relax him ... soothe him.

By the time he had returned the horse to the livery stable and walked to the town hall, Buckner's hands were no longer shaking. But he couldn't let go of what had happened. That feeling of terror that had gripped him the moment he stepped into the elevator ... the suffocating, paralyzing sensation that weakened him so that he had to hold on to the cage to keep from collapsing—that had never happened to him before. Except once, a long time ago.

Buckner shook his head to drive away the thought ... the memory that suddenly loomed up out of his past. He felt beads of perspiration pop out suddenly on his forehead, his armpits.

He stopped and looked around. He was on the corner of the town square across from the town hall. People passing by nodded, greeted him by name. He smiled vaguely in return. He took out his watch and looked at it.

"You late for a meeting, Chief?" someone said, laughing.

He put the watch back in his pocket and went on without answering.

He found a telegram on his desk. Whatever was happening to him—his surprising, sudden panic, his terror—it would have to wait.

His ex-Pinkerton friend on the St. Louis police department had replied in language so terse it was almost incomprehensible. It was a hallmark of the Pinkertons, who didn't like to spend a lot of money on telegrams. "Garber left suspected expense account fraud (stop) You owe me."

That answers the question of Garber's background, anyway, Buckner thought as he put the yellow Western Union half-sheet in what was now the Cosimo folder. It didn't exactly help explain the murder, though. And who would have suspected Garber of financial malfeasance, especially since the man looked like a typical Pinkerton strike-breaking thug? Maybe the police chiefs in Memphis and Little Rock would be more helpful.

Mullen brought more wires later in the day, one from each town. Both messages were roughly the same—no information was available regarding the individual Buckner had asked about.

"What the hell does that mean?" Buckner wondered aloud.

"It could mean they have information but they won't give it to you," Mullen said.

"That's what I'm afraid of." Buckner thought a moment and then said, "Looks like I'm going to have to go get it myself."

"Get it yourself? You mean go all they way down to Little Rock and Memphis?"

"Looks that way."

"All right," Mullen said. "Is Shotwell in charge?"

"Yeah, same as before. Where is he?"

"Home in bed, I expect," Mullen said. "He's on nights this week."

"All right. I'll go talk to him before I go."

"When are you leaving?"

"Soon as I can pack a bag." Buckner glanced at his watch. "There's a westbound in an hour." He got up and headed down the hall, Mullen tagging after. "Don't expect to hear from me till I get back."

"Right."

The bag Buckner carried to the station held fresh underwear and socks, a clean shirt, razor, tooth powder, and toothbrush. Young Clarence was happy to sell him tickets and to hold the bag while Buckner ran his other errand.

Augusta Shotwell, barely five feet tall, wearing a housedress with an apron over it, was not happy to see him. "He's asleep. He's on nights this week," she said. The apron was dusted with flour, and there was a smudge of flour on one cheek.

"I know, ma'am," Buckner replied. "But I have to leave town, and he's in charge while I'm gone, and I need to talk to him before I go."

She looked at him for a moment, her mouth set in a hard line, but eventually decided to go wake up her husband. Buckner sat in the small, tidy parlor and waited. The room was sparsely furnished, but the few pieces were all good quality and carefully kept. A few photographs sat on a low table, serious people in dark clothes standing in front of a church. In a few minutes, Shotwell emerged, wrapping a robe around pajamas.

"Sorry about this," Buckner said, standing. "I need to get down to Little Rock and then Memphis to follow up on something, and I want to get down there and get back as quickly as I can."

"All right," Shotwell said. He was rubbing his eyes. "You have a whole police department that you're in charge of. Couldn't you send one of us?"

"If this works out like I want it to, I'm going to be interrogating the police chiefs of those two cities—or anyway, high ranking officers."

"Ah," said Shotwell, nodding. "And they wouldn't be the sort to tolerate being interrogated by the likes of me."

"Right. So you're in charge here again."

"All right."

"And there's something really important you have to do while I'm gone."

"Sure."

"Go talk to Buster's sister and tell her to keep Buster in bed until I get back. I don't have any idea how long all this is going to take me, but I figure that will be fine with her anyway."

"I expect you're right. So you want to make sure Dutton doesn't go on the warpath while you're gone."

"Yep," Buckner said. "Any questions?"

"No," said Shotwell after a moment's thought.

"Fine. Tell your wife I'm sorry I had to bust in on you all like this."

"She'll probably forgive you."

"Good. See you in a couple of days."

Buckner returned to the train station.

13

The St. Louis, Iron Mountain, & Southern Railroad that ran through Corinth continued directly to Little Rock and then on down into Texas and points west. The westbound pulled in moments after Buckner had retrieved his bag. As usual, the rattle and swaying of the train put him to sleep almost at once, and the conductor had to wake him at his destination, Little Rock. The station was empty at this hour except for a dozing clerk who managed to wake up enough to give Buckner directions to the police department. It was a short walk from the station, housed in its own building, which was only right for the police department in the state capitol.

Buckner gave his name to the desk officer and the reason for his visit, leaving out Kelson's name.

"A former officer in this department?"

"I believe so, yes," Buckner said.

"Well," said the officer, "it's two in the morning, and the chief's home in bed, and I ain't about to telephone him and wake him up at this hour."

"Don't expect you to," Buckner said. "I can talk to the commander of the night shift."

"I can't promise anything," the desk officer said. "He's pretty busy."

"I don't need to take up a lot of his time," Buckner said.

The desk officer nodded.

Buckner sat on a bench and waited, his bag between his feet. After about an hour, he was escorted through a fog of tobacco smoke, across a mostly empty bullpen, and into an office. The handful of officers at the scattered desks barely acknowledged his presence. The man at the desk in the office was pounding on a typewriter and didn't look up for several minutes. Buckner leaned against the doorjamb and waited.

The night shift commander was a big man, almost completely bald. His uniform jacket was unbuttoned, exposing a vast expanse of freshly pressed white shirt. He rolled the paper out of the typewriter, tossed it into a tray marked "out," and turned to Buckner. "Bill out there tells me you're chief of police from up in Missouri, and you're looking for information on a former officer in this department. That right?"

"Yes, it is. His name's Kelson, Jack Kelson."

"Kelson." The man thought a moment. "Yeah, I think I remember him. Have a seat." He gestured toward a chair, and Buckner sat. The night shift commander went out and came back with a file folder. "Well, I haven't got much to give you. Is he a suspect in something?"

Buckner laughed. "I've got more suspects than I know what to do with right now. I just want to know whether to cut him out of the herd or leave him alone."

"I know what that's like," the man said. He scanned the file folder. "About all I can tell you about Kelson is that he was with the department for a couple of years back before the war." He leaned forward and glanced again at the folder. "Nineteen fourteen and fifteen. Says here he was over in Memphis before that."

"Say why he left?"

"Here or Memphis?"

"Either one?"

The man consulted the file. "Nope."

"Do you happen to remember?"

"Nope." He glanced at the file again. "Nothing in here about any trouble." He thought a bit. "Only thing I can remember about him was he had a reputation for going after hookers."

"What does that mean?" Buckner asked. "Going after how?"

"Well, he wasn't no beat cop, on account of his time in Memphis. He was plainclothes, working burglaries, robberies, that sort of thing. But he always seemed to me to be a bit too fond of the hookers. A bit too fond for a police officer, if you see what I mean."

Buckner nodded. "Any of them ever turn up dead?"

"Who? The hookers?"

"Yes."

"Oh, hell. I don't know. Every now and then, I guess. But we got enough to do around here without getting too worked up about a prostitute winding up dead."

Buckner said, "Uh-huh."

"That what you got up there in … uh, in …"

"Corinth. Missouri."

"Yeah, Corinth. You got a dead whore? That what brought you down here?" The night shift commander shook his head in amazement. "Sorry. I can't help you there. What I mean is, yeah, Jack Kelson hung around with whores, and sometimes a whore turned up dead, but I can't make a connection between those two things on account of there ain't one, so I think you might've made the trip down here for nothing." The man pulled out a fat silver watch and gazed at it.

"Right," Buckner said. He recognized the sign of dismissal. "One more question. I sent a telegram down here asking for information on Kelson and the reply said no information was available. Can you think of any reason for that?"

The man just shrugged. "Well, we don't usually trouble with telegrams asking for help from other departments. My guess is, whoever got it just didn't know him. Never heard of him."

"Or was a friend of his," Buckner said.

The night shift commander just looked at Buckner, saying nothing.

Buckner got up and stuck out a hand. "Well, thanks anyway."

The man ignored Buckner's hand, nodded, and began studiously reading a blank report form.

Getting to Memphis was slightly more difficult. There was a line that ran from Ft. Smith through Little Rock and on to Memphis, but it ran eastbound only once a day, and Buckner had missed it. He debated getting a room for the night in Little Rock, but there was an eastbound coming through, so he caught the Iron Mountain back up to Bald Knob and just made his connection into Memphis. It was morning and raining when he got off the train, but he had managed to get an hour or two of sleep. City hall was not far from the train station. He was thoroughly wet by the time he got there.

"Chief's not in yet," the deskman informed him.

"But you've got somebody on night duty," Buckner said.

"Well, sure. But he's pretty busy right now."

"I'm sure he is," Buckner said. He was tired and wet and shivering now, and everybody was too busy to talk to him. The smart thing to do would be to get a room and a bath. Instead, he said, "I'm just looking for a little inter-departmental cooperation, is all."

The desk officer was not impressed.

"What's this in regard to?"

"I need to talk to somebody in charge who was in this department before the war, say nineteen ten … nineteen twelve—along in there."

"Oh." The desk officer grinned. "Well, I was here back then. Will I do?"

"You might," Buckner admitted. "But how do you think your boss is going to react when some out-of-town feller like me comes around asking a lot of questions without stopping in to pay his respects first? And how do you think he's going to feel about somebody—you for instance—answering this feller's questions?"

The deskman nodded sagely. "Yep. See your point there, Chief … uh, Buckner." He pushed a button on a box on his desk and spoke into it. "Can you ask Cap'n Maklin to come out here for a second? There's a Chief Buckner from up North would like to talk with him."

The box squawked.

"Send him on back? Right." The desk officer grinned and pointed. "Right through them doors there and turn right. Name's painted on the door."

Captain Maklin was short and wiry and wore a suit that was at least a size too big. His wide, bright tie was spotted with dark stains. He was chewing tobacco, which probably accounted for the stains. It certainly explained the brown teeth he showed when he smiled.

"What can I do for you, Chief?" He gestured Buckner to a chair. "You look like you're mos' drowned."

"I'm looking for a little background information on a man who used to be with this department," Buckner said, settling into the chair. He was too tired for pleasantries. "His name's Jack Kelson. He's involved in a case I'm working on."

Maklin didn't say anything right away, just looked at Buckner and chewed his tobacco. He had a sharp, narrow face and chewed with his front teeth. Buckner thought it made him look like a contemplative rabbit.

"Kelson," Maklin finally said.

Buckner nodded. "Jack Kelson."

"Reach behind you and shut that door," Maklin said after another long pause. He leaned over and spat into something behind his desk that Buckner couldn't see.

Buckner got up, shut the door, sat back down, and waited.

"You got something solid on Kelson?" Maklin asked in a soft voice.

Buckner, surprised, said, "He's just one name on a list of men who spent time with the same prostitute—a prostitute who later turned up dead."

Maklin frowned. "I need more than that. I need to make sure this won't come back and bite me in the ass."

"Well, I can't promise anything," Buckner said, puzzled now. "Except that your name will never come up. I can guarantee that. Why? What's the problem here? I'm just asking for information on a former officer."

"Well, hell," Maklin said, his voice still quiet. "Kelson's got kin here. All 'round here—in town ... out in the country. Hell, they own half the damn county. There's three or four of his relatives—cousins and such—on the force. Got a uncle that's a municipal judge; another that's in the state legislature. His father used to sit right here in this office."

"That probably explains the answer to my telegram," Buckner said. He took it out and handed it to Maklin. Maklin read it and handed it back.

"That'd do it," he agreed. "All right," he said, leaning forward, his voice now very soft. "Jack Kelson and hookers, right?" Buckner nodded. "He was on the force here for quite a few years, back before the war this was. Started in ought eight, left in thirteen, fourteen, 'long in there. Hell, he was my partner when he first started. We pounded a beat together his whole first year."

"Was he especially fond of prostitutes back then?" Buckner found himself whispering and leaning forward as well.

"Oh, yeah, he was. Seemed to think like it was one of the privileges of being a cop, along with the free lunches and carrying a gun."

"But he left the department."

"Yeah, he did."

"What happened?"

"Couple of his favorite hookers wound up dead," Maklin answered.

"Strangled?"

"Yep. Bodies were found buried in the cellar of a building one of his uncle's rented out," Maklin said. "Kelson had lived there off and on; then he found himself a new place. Anyway, they found them bodies kinda by accident, really. The uncle was havin' the place tore down so's he could build a new one, and that's when the bodies were discovered."

"And that was it?"

"Oh, hell, I think everybody in the department had their suspicions. Nobody could touch him, of course, but I guess he figured the town was just a little to warm for his ... ah, his constitution."

"So he went to Little Rock."

"That's right. The family knew somebody over there, pulled some strings, and they put him right onto the force, right into plain clothes."

"Right," Buckner said. "Until prostitutes started turning up dead in Little Rock."

"Well," said Maklin, spreading his hands. "Prostitutes are always turning up dead. It's kind of a occupational hazard, you might say." He spat tobacco. "You say he's on your force now?"

"No," Buckner said. "He's been working for American Protective at least since nineteen seventeen, working security at a mining operation up in my neck of the woods."

"Company cop," Maklin said. "Yeah, that'd be 'bout right, somebody like him. What're you interested in him for?"

"Under the circumstances," Buckner said, "do you really want me to tell you?"

Maklin smiled at that and shook his head. "Prob'ly just as well if I remain in ignorance."

Buckner got up to go. He stuck out his hand. Maklin got up and shook it. "You know, you're damn lucky I was on duty tonight," he said. "It was anybody else, you wouldn't've got a thing."

"Well, I appreciate it, Captain," Buckner said.

"Just make sure you nail that son of a bitch. I been waiting for years for this to catch up with him. You just make damn sure it sticks—I don't want this coming back on me."

"Like I said, there's no reason why your name should ever come up," Buckner said. He thanked Maklin again and walked out.

Men in uniform and in plain clothes were changing places in the hallways and at the front desk. The duty officer who had greeted Buckner was putting on a raincoat, preparing to leave. "Find out what you was lookin' for, Chief?" he asked.

"Nope," Buckner said. "'Fraid not."

"Well, better luck next time."

Buckner went out into the street. It was full morning, but the sky was still dark. The wind cut razor sharp through his wet clothes, and the rain stung his face. He was shivering again by the time he got to the train station. He bought a ticket for Bald Knob, Arkansas, and went into the station restroom, where he took off his wet clothes and put on dry underwear and socks—the only dry clothing he had in his small bag. Then he put his wet shirt and trousers back on, went out into the waiting room, and sat shivering until the westbound train pulled in just before two in the afternoon. The car was nearly empty, but it was heated, so Buckner's shivering subsided, and he was able to sleep a little.

The clerk in Bald Knob was sound asleep at his window when Buckner walked in, and he woke up in a bad mood. "There's a fast liner through here, pulls into Union Station in St. Louis at ten in the evening," he told Buckner. "It's the Businessman's Special, but it don't usually stop here. Nor in Corinth, for that matter."

Buckner was exhausted and cold. His clothes were still damp, and he had started shaking again. He could feel heat coming from somewhere behind the ticket clerk, pouring through the small window, but the waiting room was dark and chilly. "I need to get to Corinth as soon as possible," Buckner said. He took his billfold form his trouser pocket and opened it, revealing the badge he'd gotten when he became chief of police. "Are you going to sell me a ticket, or not?"

The ticket clerk, as an employee of the large and powerful Missouri Pacific Railroad, did not seem impressed by a chief of police from Corinth, Missouri, a mere whistle stop. But he sold Buckner a ticket anyway. And he agreed to signal the liner to stop.

As the wind drove rain against the thin waiting room walls, Buckner paced to keep warm until the eastbound liner finally puffed in. The conductor was clearly irritated at having to make the stop. He glowered as Buckner, wearing damp clothes and carrying his small bag, climbed wearily up into the car. He waited until Buckner, huddled against the heating element, had begun to doze and then woke him with a smile and asked for his ticket. "Corinth, huh?" he said. "Don't b'lieve this train's ever stopped in Corinth."

Buckner ignored him. He looked out the window as the afternoon sun struggled to break through the heavy clouds, watching the darkening towns flash by. Poplar Bluff didn't even rate a stop.

When Buckner stumbled down onto the platform in Corinth, it was just six o'clock, but the sky was pitch black. As the liner pulled out, Young Clarence came around the corner of the waiting room. "Well, hello, Buck," he said. "I figured it must've been something important for the liner to stop."

"First time in history, according to the conductor," Buckner said.

"Second time," Young Clarence said. "Bryan stopped and give a speech off the rear platform. First time he run, this was. Ninety-six. He never bothered with us after that one time. Guess he figured we was all Democrats already."

"Was there anybody here to listen to the speech?" Buckner asked.

"Not many," Clarence agreed. "Me and a few others."

"Probably why he didn't bother after that."

"Prob'ly."

Buckner stopped at the office. Bill Newland was on the desk, and he still had some hot coffee left in the pot. It was burnt and bitter, but Buckner drank the first cup as quickly as he could, sighing as the heat spread through his body.

"You're back pretty quick," said Bill.

"Figured I'd better just keep moving," Buckner said. "I'm not here long, though. Soon as I finish this, I've got to get home, take a bath, get into some dry clothes." He sipped more coffee. "I'll be heading up to Taylor."

"Taylor? You got some new information?"

Buckner just nodded. He headed up the stairs and then made his way across town.

He met his mother coming out of the house as he was going in.

"I'll be at church," she said, adding, "You look like a drowned rat."

"Storm's coming up the river," he replied. "You might want to take an umbrella."

His mother stopped, looked him up and down, and nodded. She took an umbrella from the stand just inside the door, nodded again, and strode off down the walk.

Buckner ran the bath as hot as he could stand and soaked in it for half an hour, adding hot water as needed. When he was warm and dry and clean, he dressed in an aged pair of dark-gray trousers that matched a suit coat he had once owned but could no longer locate. He pulled on a dark-gray sweater and slipped into a pair of black canvas basketball shoes he hadn't worn since high school. He put on a gray cloth cap and went to the kitchen. He dug an old cork out of a drawer and charred it black at the stove. He wrapped the cork in his handkerchief, got his small flashlight, and headed for the livery stable.

Buckner ignored Greene's bursting curiosity and rode out of town. He took back roads and narrow dirt tracks through farm gates and across fields, staying well away from the road to Taylor. Finally he came to the edge of the woods above the town.

He dismounted and sat with his back against a tree. The horse chomped grass quietly behind him.

The air was still and heavy and warm. He was tired from his train trip and fell asleep almost at once. A dream—barely a flash—of being buried deep underground, jolted him awake. He felt he'd been asleep for only a matter of moments, but his watch told him it was after midnight. He took out the cork and blacked his cheekbones, nose ridge, and brow, plus his ears and the backs of his hands—any part of his anatomy that might catch what little light there was in the town. Then he got up and moved closer to the buildings.

The smelter roared and thumped tirelessly, and men moved to and from work with the shift change. Eventually everybody got settled, and, outside the domes of light from the smelter and mine head, the town darkened.

Buckner moved in closer, pulling his cap low to shield his eyes from the powerful lights at the Company's works. He paused under the cover of a fat maple tree that seemed to have wandered off by itself. From barely twenty yards away, he watched Garber rattling doorknobs, chatting with the few people still out. He saw no sign of Kelson. He stood motionless for a long time—long enough for the pain in his leg to spread from hip to ankle. The slight shifting of weight that he felt was safe provided no relief.

Finally, around about two, he saw Kelson come through the door of a small house. After turning and locking the door, he walked down the porch steps into the street. He hitched his trousers, felt under his jacket for his pistol, and walked down the hill.

Buckner waited another fifteen minutes and then headed for the back door of the small house. The blade of his folding knife fitted easily between the door and the jamb, and the lock slipped open with a soft click. He entered quickly and left the door unlocked. The windows of the one-story building were curtained, and Buckner pulled out his small flashlight, prepared to use it only sparingly. His eyes were fully accustomed to the dark, and what he saw was the usual four-room company house, sparsely furnished, and not particularly tidy. Clothing lay scattered across the bed and the chair in the bedroom. Unwashed dishes sat on the kitchen table and in the sink. Open envelopes on the table revealed that Kelson had received a letter from somebody in Memphis, and several bills. Thick dust coated unused surfaces and lay piled in corners. A cheap cardboard suitcase lay open on the narrow bed. It contained a few items of clothing.

Buckner moved quickly, going through drawers and cupboards and pockets, reaching under the mattress, listening constantly, finding nothing. He was quickly reduced to crawling painfully around on hands and knees, feeling for loose floorboards. He found none, but he did aim his light at the underside of the easy chair in the bedroom. That's where he found the cigar box.

It was tin, six inches by four, and half an inch thick. It had been shoved edgewise between the springs and the chair frame at the back. The hinged lid was secured with a large rubber band. Buckner reminded himself to bring gloves next time he burgled a suspect's home. Then he pulled his sleeve down over his hand and teased the box out of its hiding place. He held it by the edges and sat on the floor, pulled off the band, and opened the box. Inside he found trinkets—over a dozen pieces of cheap costume jewelry in different styles. They were all ear bobs. There was only one of each.

He closed the box and thought about that for a bit; then he replaced the rubber band and put the box back where he'd found it. He left by the back door. Since he had no way of relocking it, he left it unlocked and hoped Kelson would chalk it up to absent-mindedness.

He returned to his horse, remounted, and headed quickly straight back to Corinth. On the way, he stopped at Little Tavern Creek where he dismounted and scrubbed most of the cork from his hands and face.

Walter Greene was not in yet at the livery. Buckner unsaddled the horse, rubbed him down, and left him in a stall. He put two dollars on Greene's desk and headed across town to the Corinth Café.

Jeff Peck sat bolt upright, head back against the wall, staring grimly into some unreachable middle distance. In his right hand he clutched an empty glass. He was the only customer. "Kinda late for you," he said when Buckner sat down. "Whaddya want?"

"I figured you'd be here, since even Dutton closes up after a while. Unless you're getting a jump on the day."

"As I said before, whaddya want?"

"I need to ask you a question."

"Of course you do. It's all you ever do. It is the basis—the sole and entire basis—of our relationship. Indeed, it is its entirety. If you never asked me questions, we would never speak." He held up his empty glass. Buckner took it and got it filled by the beefy man who sat in a corner with his elbow resting on a case of beer. Buckner also got a drink for himself.

"How much?" he asked the man.

"We keep a tab on him and bill him at the end of the month, but yours'll be fifty cents."

Buckner put a dollar on the counter, returned to Peck's table, and placed one drink before him. Peck stared at it for a full minute, face blank, eyes empty, and then he picked it up and took a delicate sip. But he didn't put it back down. "Ask your question," he said with a slight smile. "I figure you've got about two minutes."

"What happens in two minutes?" Buckner drank. The whiskey burned a path down.

"Well, in one minute, I'm gonna finish this drink. And in two minutes I will be leaving."

"All right. You want help getting back to your place?"

"I'll manage, thank you."

"All right. Tell me about the marks on Kelson's hand."

"Glad to. What marks? Who's Kelson?"

"Company cop up in Taylor. When we were up there the other day, you said something about him needing to have somebody look at his hand. What did you mean?"

"Oh, yes." Peck sipped at his drink. "He has a bad patch on the back of one hand, something he's kept worrying at, picking at. I didn't get a very good look at it, but I thought it might be a cancer. I suspect it's just an old injury, though."

"Just the one hand? What about the other one?"

"I didn't see the other one. And he didn't exactly let me conduct a complete medical examination of the one I did see."

"Uh-huh. Could the mark have been caused by acid splashing on his hand?"

"I suppose so," Peck said after a moment's thought. "Is that what was nagging at you?"

"Yeah," Buckner said. He sipped his own drink. "Thanks."

"Doesn't mean a damn thing, you know."

"I know. But Kelson kept popping into my head, and I couldn't figure out why, and that's the reason—those marks." Buckner fell silent, struggling to find some words. Peck just gave him a puzzled stare.

"Well?"

"Another question."

"I might have to bill the town."

"Sure." Buckner hesitated.

"For Christ's sake, get it out," Peck urged. "I've got places to go."

"Course you do." Buckner paused and then spoke. "Over there …" he began. "In France … where'd you live?"

"What?" Peck's astonishment at the question seemed to wake him up. "What do you mean, where did I live? I lived in a hole in the ground, like everybody else within reach of the Boche artillery. Bunkers. Dugouts. Where the hell do you think I lived?"

"Right. Right." Buckner nodded, sipped some more whiskey, resumed. "Ever have one collapse on you?"

"No," Peck replied. "We took over a section of the French line, and their trenches and dugouts were crap, so we practically had to start over. And we did it right—had the engineers in, everything. So, no, never had one fall in one me, even in the worst shelling. And I'm telling you, that spring offensive in eighteen … the shelling got pretty bad."

"Yeah, I heard."

"Oh, that's right," Peck said. "You'd already been invalided home." He looked closely at Buckner. "What the hell is this all about?"

"I was just curious, that's all."

"Bullshit."

"I was," Buckner said after a long pause.

"You were what?"

"It was summer, nineteen fifteen ... August. We hadn't figured out how to do it yet, dig safe dugouts. I don't think the generals wanted us to get too comfortable."

"Yeah, they were still thinking about the next big push, the breakthrough, cavalry charges with sabers drawn. Dumb fuckers." Peck watched Buckner some more. "So you were in a dugout."

"Yes. This was after I got hit. The stretcher bearers put me there, mostly to keep me out of the way ... to keep the trench clear. There were already some other wounded in there, some on stretchers, some just lying on the ground in the mud." Buckner stopped and stared into his glass.

Finally, Peck said, "And it got blown in on top of you."

"Yes."

"Well," said Peck. "It couldn't have been that bad, 'cause here you are."

"There was some timbering, and that kept the dirt from covering me up, and I could breathe, but it was like I was in a box. A very small box." Buckner shuddered and drank. He went on. "And they must've forgotten me or something, because I lay there a long time."

"You're lucky you didn't bleed to death."

"They'd bandaged me up pretty good," Buckner explained. "But I was in there for a long time, and I guess it festered—my leg—and it's never really recovered."

"Uh-huh." Peck finished his drink. "And that wakes you up in the middle of the night."

"I thought I was going to go crazy," Buckner said. "I couldn't move. I was too weak to dig myself out. I could barely call for help. I think I was unconscious a lot of the time, but I can't really remember. All I remember is the pain and lying there in the dark and thinking any minute the entire earth was going to settle down on my chest—not fall, just settle, ever so slowly, and slowly, and squeeze the breath out of me an inch at a time." He drank some more. "Anyway, they eventually got me out. I guess somebody remembered a dugout full of wounded and wondered where we'd all got to."

"And those other wounded?"

"I never knew. Later, after they'd operated on my leg back in Rouen, one of the doctors told me I was babbling incoherently—raving, he said—when they brought me in. I asked him about the others, and he said he didn't know for sure, but thought most of them had died."

"All right," Peck said. "So why are you telling me all this? I already know about your leg. I've seen it. They didn't do such a bad job, you know."

"This isn't about my leg, goddammit. A couple of days ago, I had to question two workers up in Taylor—men who were known to be special customers of Peralta's women."

"Uh-huh. And?"

"They were underground, working, and Tom wouldn't bring them up so I could question them," Buckner said. And stopped.

"And you had to go underground to talk to them," Peck said. "Ah, yes. I see. You panicked."

"Damn near," Buckner admitted.

"Ever happen to you before?"

"No. Never. Took me by surprise, but, thinking about it, I've never really been anyplace like that, not since I got home. Certainly never underground, not once. I have dreams about it every now and then, and that wakes me up pretty quick, I can tell you, but, no. Never anything like what happened up there."

"Anybody notice?"

"It felt like the whole goddamned world noticed."

"And was laughing."

"Yes," Buckner said, remembering the look on Tom's face. And remembering the aching desire he had to smash that face into pulp. And remembering hitting Peralta.

"Mm," Peck said.

"That's it? You're just going to grunt at me?"

"What the hell do you want? I'm no goddamned psychiatrist."

"I thought that doctor was a friend of yours—that German doctor."

"Sigmund Freud? Hell no. I just met him once, heard him speak ... hell, years ago now. It's all a load of crap, far as I'm concerned. All that analysis ... dreams, all that. Anyway, I got my own problems. And my own dreams. So I don't have a lot of room for worrying about yours."

"All right." Buckner nodded curtly and stood up. "Thanks. Sorry I bothered you."

"No goddamned bother," Peck said angrily.

"All right," Buckner said, just as angry now, jeering. "You sure you don't want some help getting somewhere? Home? Anywhere?"

"You're offering to help me?" Peck was scornful.

"Yes."

"Well, no, I don't need your help." Peck got to his feet slowly with a drunk's exaggerated caution. When Buckner reached out a hand to steady him, he brushed it away and walked out the back door and into the dark street. Buckner glanced at his watch and followed. "Good morning, then," he offered.

Peck did not respond; just kept walking into the darkness.

A few soft drops of rain fell, plopping loudly into the dusty street.

 14

Buckner walked across town to the town square. Michael Mullen's father owned and operated a dry goods store on the square and lived in an apartment on the floor above. Mullen had a room of his own on the same floor. Buckner climbed the back stairs and knocked on the door. Mullen, in a long nightshirt and bare feet, answered the knock.

"Buck? Everything all right? What time is it?"

"Time to get up. Listen, I need you to get dressed, draw a weapon, and get over to the train station."

"Right." Mullen suddenly spun on his heel and pounded down the hallway. In a minute he was back, buttoning his trousers and tucking in his shirt. He looked so eager, Buckner had to smile. "What's up?" Mullen asked as he locked the door and they went back down the stairs.

"I need you to get to the train station and stay there."

"All right. Why?"

"Do you know Kelson, that company guard up in Taylor?"

"Well, I know him by sight, sure, but I've never spoken a word to him."

"That's good enough. Just stay at the train station, and if he tries to buy a ticket out of town—I mean a ticket to anywhere at all—you arrest him."

"Uh, sure, Buck. What charge?"

"I don't care. Think of something. Spitting on the sidewalk. Carrying a concealed weapon in town. Anything. Just do not let him leave."

"Ah, right. I see."

The two men walked across the square and down the stairs into the department. Bill Newland stared goggle eyed at them as they came through the doors. His eyes widened further when Mullen opened the weapon locker and grabbed one of the department's twelve-gauge riot guns.

"I think a pistol should do the job, Michael," Buckner said.

"Oh, right. Sure."

Mullen buckled on the pistol belt, loaded the weapon, and holstered it.

"See you later, Bill," Buckner said. He and Mullen left, parting company on the town hall steps.

"Just don't let him leave town by train, Michael."

"I won't, Buck. I promise."

"I know you won't."

Buckner went home to bed. He lay awake for what seemed the rest of the night, until the sounds of his mother in the kitchen stirred him.

He dressed, skipped breakfast, and went to the town hall. He walked straight around back, cranked up one of the Fords, and drove to Taylor. The sky was dark and heavy with rain. A few drops fell, and thunder grumbled in the southwest. Buckner parked next to a large touring car parked outside the company office. As he reached into the back of the Model T for his raincoat, he noticed a driver dozing at the wheel of the big car. He put on his raincoat and headed for the office. More fat drops of rain began to hit the tin roof of the building.

"I need to see Powers," Buckner said as he stood at Tom's desk.

Tom was not delighted to see him. Looking confused and unhappy, he took refuge in staring at the ceiling. Raised, angry voices were coming through the door to the inner office.

"He's busy," Tom said.

"Sounds like it," Buckner agreed. "And somebody pretty important, I expect, judging by that big Oldsmobile parked out front."

The door to the inner office banged opened suddenly, and a tall man with a General Pershing moustache and the military bearing to go with it, strode out. Powers hurried right behind. Both of them stopped and looked at Buckner.

"Good morning," said the man with the moustache.

"What do you want?" demanded Powers.

"I'm pretty sure I know who killed Angela Cosimo," Buckner said. "And I want your permission to search his house." He turned to the man with the moustache. "Good morning. I'm James Buckner. I'm chief of police down in Corinth."

"I'm Vernon Elgar, American Protective Agency. We handle company security. I'm down from the St. Louis office with explicit orders to look into this matter. We've, ah … received word, you see, about the corpse in the boarding house cellar. Is that the Angela Cosimo you spoke of?"

"Yes, sir, it is," Buckner said. The man's entire demeanor made Buckner want to stand up straighter, perhaps salute.

"Let's go back in," Elgar suggested. Without asking Powers' permission, he turned and led the way back into Powers' office. Once inside, the door shut, he asked Buckner, "All right. What have you got?"

"A man named Kelson, who works here as a company guard, was known to have spent a considerable amount of time and money on the dead woman. The medical evidence showed that the woman's body had been immersed in sulfuric acid for a short time after death. There's usually a lot of that stuff stored here, and Kelson had access to it."

"Along with a dozen other people," Powers said.

"Yes," Buckner agreed. "Kelson also had access to the cellar where the woman's body was found."

"Along with half the population of Taylor—" Powers began.

"That's pretty thin stuff, Chief," Elgar agreed.

"Yes, it is. But it was enough to get me to take a quick train ride down to Little Rock and to Memphis."

"Kelson was a police officer in both places," Elgar said, nodding. "He cited them as references when he applied for a job with us." His mouth split in a grin so shy that it almost made him look human. "I looked up the situation down here before I came," he confessed, adding, "Don't keep that sort of thing in my head."

Buckner continued, "According to what I was able to learn from some not-very-helpful people down that way, Kelson had a reputation for spending time with prostitutes while he was in Memphis and Little Rock. And after one of his favorite whores turned up dead in Little Rock, he suddenly quit and headed north. Nobody followed up on it, since it was 'just some prostitute, after all.'" Buckner looked closely at Elgar. "Did you check his references when he applied for the job?"

"No," Elgar admitted. "I wasn't with American Protective at that time—I'd taken a leave of absence to go back to the army. But I gather, what with all the labor trouble they were having back then, they wanted men and weren't too picky about where they got them. And what about Memphis?"

"That was pretty interesting," Buckner said. "Kelson's from Memphis originally, and he's got a lot of kin down there, some of them on the force. The fellow I talked to was reluctant to get involved, but I guess he had some kind of grudge against Kelson, so he told me his suspicions, as long as I promised to keep his name out of it. Anyway, he's pretty sure Kelson is responsible for the death of at least one prostitute that he knows of, but he can't do anything about it on account of Kelson's kin folk."

"How sure is this fellow?" Elgar asked.

"He's near certain as he can be, under the circumstances. Hasn't got any proof, of course."

Elgar turned to Josiah Powers. "I think that's enough. Maybe not enough for a warrant from a judge, but enough to justify the Company looking into the activities of an employee. Specifically, it is enough for you, Mr. Powers, to officially request, in your capacity as the man in charge down here, that I investigate further, even if that means searching the company housing where this employee lives."

"I do so request," Powers said unhappily. "But what about Foote?"

"Who's Foote?" Elgar asked.

"County sheriff," Buckner said. "Taylor is an unincorporated community, so according to state law, it lies within the jurisdiction of the Highland County sheriff."

"So you're here …?" He glanced at Buckner.

"On loan from the town of Corinth," Buckner said. "As a favor to the Company."

"As a way to keep a lid on the whole thing," Elgar said, ignoring Powers' embarrassment. "Good thing I read the St. Louis papers, I guess. Anyway, if we turn up something and wind up having to arrest Kelson, we'll just be handing him over to the sheriff for custody and trial. But until then, let's just keep this a company matter."

Powers, looking relieved, nodded.

"That's all right with me," Buckner said. "As long as we get whoever did it and he gets what's coming to him."

Elgar seemed surprised at Buckner's sudden vehemence. He looked closely at him for a moment and then said, "Shall we go take a look at where Kelson lives?"

"I'll have Tom show you where it is," Powers said.

"All right," Buckner said. "Can we borrow Garber, just in case Kelson shows up and decides to object to having his rooms searched?"

"Yes," Powers replied. "I'll tell Tom. And try to keep all this as quiet as possible, will you? I don't want the whole town standing around gawking."

"Do my best," Elgar said.

Tom was standing by his desk, hat in hand, when they came through the door. He grinned and took a small revolver from his pocket."

"Just in case," he said.

"Put that pea-shooter away," Elgar said. "We're not going to have any shooting. Bullets flying around up here, somebody could get hurt."

"But *he's* got a gun," Tom said, gesturing at Buckner.

"So have I," Elgar replied. "A real one. But I'm going to try to avoid using it if I can, and I don't want to have to worry about you, too."

"But what if he runs?" asked the disappointed Tom after making his pistol disappear into a desk drawer.

"We'll chase him," Buckner said. "Not a lot of places he can go. But for right now, do you know where he is?"

"On patrol, I guess. That's where he's supposed to be. But I couldn't say exactly where."

"Find out," Elgar said. "And keep him busy with something that will keep him away from his place while we search it. Oh, and find Garber and have him meet us at Kelson's place."

"All right." Tom turned to go and then turned back. "Kelson's place is about halfway down the street there, then two doors to the right, back up against that big maple tree."

Buckner and Elgar headed down into the street. Elgar stopped and took a raincoat from the Oldsmobile. Buckner led the way up to the door of Kelson's house.

"Been here before, have you?" Elgar asked softly.

Buckner said, "I spent a fair amount of time up here when I was a deputy sheriff."

"I meant this house."

Buckner shrugged, said nothing. Elgar pointed. Garber was coming up the street.

"Tom said you wanted to talk to me about something," he said.

"Yes." Elgar produced a badge and ID card. "I'm Vernon Elgar from American Protective. We have Mr. Powers' permission to search Kelson's place, and I want you to open it for us and then serve as a witness."

"What for?"

"To see if we find any connection between Kelson and Angelina Cosimo."

"Is that the girl in the cellar? She used to … You think Kelson did for her?"

"I think we're going to go inside and look around," Elgar said. "Do you have any objection to that? You two have been working together for a long time, so you don't have to do any searching, just be a witness."

"We haven't worked together all that long," Garber said. "Besides, just 'cause we work together don't make us friends."

"So you'll help? You'll search too?"

"Sure. Let's get to it."

Elgar ignored Garber's offered key and unlocked the door with a key from his own pocket. Buckner wondered if the American Protective people could unlock any door on any company building. Probably could, he decided.

"What are you looking for?" Garber asked as they entered.

"Anything that will connect Kelson with the girl."

"Well, hell, I saw him with her plenty of times," Garber said. "He was a regular customer."

"Sure," Elgar said. "But we need physical evidence to tie it all up nice and neat."

They went inside. Elgar and Garber spotted the suitcase immediately. It was closed now and sitting just behind the door. Elgar picked it up and opened it on the bed. It was fully packed.

"He say anything to you about leaving town?" Elgar asked Garber.

"No."

"Well, let's look around."

Buckner went through the motions while the other two searched. He concentrated on the kitchen, finding nothing. Then he heard Garber's voice.

"Found something." He didn't sound happy.

Buckner and Elgar went to look.

"A cigar tin?" Elgar said. "Where'd you find it?"

"Tucked up in the bottom of that chair," Garber said. "Look what's inside."

Buckner took a pair of cotton gardening gloves from his hip pocket, put them on, and took the box from Garber. Elgar watched silently while Garber just looked puzzled. Buckner flipped back the lid.

"Jewelry," Elgar muttered. "Women's jewelry. Earrings." He poked through the contents. "Looks like a dozen or more pieces."

"Yeah," Garber said. "But none of 'em match. They're all singles."

"Not all of them," Buckner said. He reached into his shirt pocket.

"Hey," Garber said. "Ain't that the one you found in the cellar where we dug out that body?"

"It matches this one here," Elgar said. He took out a cheap imitation pearl earbob and held it up next to the one Buckner was holding. "Matches perfectly."

Garber said, "Damn," very softly.

"Better keep looking," Buckner said. "We don't want to miss anything." He took out a handkerchief and carefully wrapped the cigar tin in it, holding the handkerchief in place with the rubber band.

"I'll hang onto that," Elgar said, taking the cigar tin. He gave Buckner a long, serious look. "Seeing as it was found on company property and all." He grinned. "And don't worry. I've got a fingerprint kit in my motor." He indicated the earbob Buckner was still holding. "What do you want to do with that one?"

"I'd like to hang onto this one for a while, if you don't mind." He had run a bit of thread through the loop and attached an identification tag. "But I think we ought to keep them separate for right now."

"All right." Elgar continued watching Buckner as he tucked the cigar tin in a jacket pocket. "I'll leave this with your department down in Corinth after I check it for prints."

Buckner returned to the kitchen and they all searched for another half hour. Finally, Elgar called a halt.

"Nothing else, I guess. Let's go show Powers what we've got. And we ought to take Kelson into custody. You got yourselves a jail up here?"

"Not really," Garber said.

"What do you do with the Saturday night drunks?"

"Mostly we just send 'em home, let their wives take care of 'em."

"I bet their wives appreciate that."

"If that don't work—or if they're not married—we lock 'em in a spare room somewhere." He shrugged. "Buckner's got a jail, though."

"That might have to do," Elgar agreed.

"Let's see what Powers has to say," Buckner suggested. "We might need his permission."

"What for?" Elgar asked.

"It might be a good idea to dig out the rest of that boarding house foundation," he answered. "There was a lot of jewelry in that cigar box."

The two men looked at him and suddenly realized what he was talking about. Garber looked stunned. Elgar only looked sad.

Powers seemed to be waiting for them. His desk was clear of papers, and his office door was open. But he was not ready to be convinced just yet.

"It's just women's jewelry, from what you say."

"It's enough to hold on to Kelson, Mr. Powers," Elgar said.

"And there's nothing to stop us from digging out the rest of the boarding house cellar," Buckner added.

"You'll have to talk to Charboneau about that," Powers said. "He owns it." He was shaking his head. "Seems like a lot of trouble to go to over a dead whore. I tried to help her, you know. But she wouldn't listen. It comes as not surprise she ended up like that."

Elgar and Garber went to find Kelson. Buckner found Charboneau at his sister-in-law's house, but he refused to come to the door ... refused to talk about the house at all. Buckner went back up the street and got a long, heavy screwdriver from the Ford's boot and began poking it into the cellar wall.

It took him less than five minutes to find a second body. The masonry was better here, more solid, less affected by the fire, as though the mason had had more time to work. He removed just enough stone to allow him a quick look. This one had been in the wall longer than the first. Or had been in the acid longer. Anyway, it was mostly bones with scraps of flesh that looked like old rags, and Buckner detected no smell at all.

He resumed his search.

The third corpse was just bones. Buckner kept poking into the cellar wall, but found nothing more. He stopped searching after that. He sat on the cellar wall and gazed off into the trees while rain drizzled down on him, pattering on his hat brim. He didn't seem to notice.

After the armies had been entrenched along the Western Front for a year and more, bodies that had been buried in shell holes or collapsed dugouts, or hastily interred by fast-moving forces in the early weeks, when armies still moved across the land before they went underground, began to emerge as though they were being squeezed out by an earth that rejected them. Some were suddenly exposed by shellfire, some by men digging new trenches or bunkers, some simply appeared where nothing had been before.

Buckner thought about them as he sat on the cellar wall. He could see them still, half covered in mud and filth, empty eyes looking at him.

He sat on the cellar wall because he did not want to find any more dead bodies. But his work had attracted attention. Some people had gathered to watch, huddling under umbrellas or watching from porches.

"You still looking?" someone asked.

"Not right now," he answered.

"Finding anything?"

"Yes."

"More a them hoors?" A woman's voice. "Good riddance, you ask me."

"Somebody been doin' the town a favor," another woman agreed.

There were one or two men, but they said nothing, shuffled their feet, looked closely at the ground as though there was something there they wanted to find. Then they wandered away, leaving the women to watch.

Buckner got up and climbed out of the cellar.

"You gonna leave 'em in there?" one of the women asked.

He did not answer; just headed toward the office. Tom was still out, and Powers' door was closed. Buckner called Coy's drugstore using Tom's telephone and asked Mrs. Coy to find Jeff Peck and send him to Taylor.

"How'll he get there, Chief? You know he don't drive."

"Tell him I need him up here and to find a way. Murtaugh's truck maybe. Tell him he'll need it anyway." He ignored Mrs. Coy's urgent questions, hung up, and made another call.

"Corinth Police Department," said Bill Newland.

"Bill, it's me. Thanks for sticking around. Send somebody over to the Iron Mountain depot to fetch Mullen and tell him there's a prisoner coming in. Just lock him up and we'll deal with the paperwork later. Thanks." He hung up and went out onto the office porch. Garber, Elgar, and Tom were bringing Kelson up the street. Somebody's handcuffs had locked Kelson's hands behind his back. Everybody went up onto the office porch to get out of the rain, which was coming down quite heavily now.

"You can take him back to town in that fancy motor of yours," Buckner said to Elgar. "My desk officer is Michael Mullen. Tell him to give you the loan of a cell." He turned to Garber. "You're going to have to put a guard on that boarding house cellar again."

"You find another body?" Elgar asked.

"Two more. Both look to have been in the ground longer than Angela Cosimo. I've sent for Peck—Dr. Peck—to take a look at them. Tom, you better tell Mr. Powers about all this."

Tom, looking horrified, fascinated, and scared all at once, hurried inside.

"You ain't never gonna be able to prove a thing, Chief, you oughtta know that," said Kelson with an easy smile.

"If we find any earrings in those holes that match any in that cigar box of yours, you're going to have some serious explaining to do," said Elgar.

"Don't know nuthin' 'bout jewelry," said Kelson. "'Cept that cheap whores wear cheap crap, and you can get that stuff anyplace."

"True enough," said Elgar. "And you just happen to be a collector."

"I don't know nothin' 'bout what you found in my place—*say* you found. Hell, you prob'ly planted something on account of you ain't got no idea what happened to that little tramp and you're just lookin' to pin it on me to save your jobs."

Buckner turned sharply to face Kelson. "Which tramp would that be, Kelson? Which one of the dozen or so would that be?"

Kelson stepped back. Elgar quickly dragged Kelson into the street, opened the door of his car, and shoved him in. He slammed the door and turned to Buckner. "I'll take care of him. I'll put him in one of your cells, and then I'll be back to help you up here."

"I can handle this," Buckner said, indicating the cellar. "You're going to have to keep an eye on Powers."

"Don't worry. I'll handle Powers too." He was looking at Kelson, who sat smiling in the backseat of the Oldsmobile. "You know, Buckner," he observed, "we might have some kind of jurisdictional problem here. I'm just a private cop working for a private company."

"And I'm not much more than town constable," Buckner said. "And not in this town, which, as I said, is under Sheriff Foote's jurisdiction. But he's so busy running for state assembly, he hasn't got time—or the interest—to get involved in this. According to Powers, he figures it's a company matter."

"So what'll happen to Kelson after I lock him up in your jail?" Elgar asked.

"I don't know, for sure. I'll talk to the prosecutor. See what he has to say. And I've got a friend over in the state capitol." Buckner shrugged. "We'll just have to see what works."

"So in addition to the first woman you found," Elgar said. "You've got two more in the cellar here, at least one in Little Rock, maybe a couple more in Memphis. How many all together, you figure?"

"No way to tell. There's at least a dozen pieces in that cigar box."

"One way or another," Elgar said, "Angela Cosimo is the last one."

"Maybe," Buckner said. He watched as Elgar drove away and then went back into the street, into the rain, to the cellar, where he poked around, finding nothing of interest. Finally he sat down again and waited. As the already-dark sky darkened into evening, the rain increased. Buckner was finally driven back up onto the office porch. He watched people run through the rain during the shift change; then things quieted down. Neither Tom nor his boss appeared. Buckner paced the length of the porch to keep his leg from bothering him too much.

Finally, Jeff Peck arrived in the flatbed truck from Murtaugh's Funeral Parlor. The driver was Murtaugh's wife's younger brother. Buckner noticed that his acne seemed to be clearing up. He was helpful as always, and never said a word. He had brought tools and blankets and a lantern, and the three worked through the darkness and the rain to uncover and dig out the two corpses, wrap them carefully, and load them onto the truck. The wind came up, and the rain lashed at them. They worked alone and undisturbed. The watching women had gone home. Powers had granted permission with a wave of his hand and then disappeared. Tom had closed and locked the offices. Bob Charboneau came out onto his sister's front stoop, watched for a few seconds, and went back inside. He did not reappear.

When they were finished, they stood for a few minutes under the shelter of the office porch. The driver smoked a cigarette and stared at nothing. The town seemed deserted.

To no one in particular Buckner said, "I thought I'd never have to do that again."

And no one responded. When the driver had finished his cigarette, he and Jeff Peck got into the truck and drove away. Covered in mud and soaked to the skin, Buckner didn't move. He could feel the chill working its way into his bones and knew that soon he would start shivering.

Elgar pulled up in his big Oldsmobile and rolled down the window.

"You want me to open up so you can get in and wash up?" he asked.

"No."

"Can I give you a ride somewhere?"

"No."

"All right. One thing more, and it's got nothing to do with any of this. Hell, ain't even my business, but I thought I'd ask."

"All right," Buckner said.

"Did you get that bum leg in France?"

"Yes."

"Who'd you serve with?"

"Canadians. First Division. Went over in fifteen, was back home by seventeen. Fifth US Cavalry before that, though. Down along the Border."

"Yeah," Elgar said. "That's what I heard."

"You?"

"Rainbow Division, chief of staff under MacArthur. Cuba and the Philippines before that, with Pershing. Then I retired, went to work for American Protective. Pershing brought me back for the war because he said he needed somebody to keep an eye on MacArthur—Douglas I mean … General MacArthur's boy." He laughed. "Didn't do much good. Nobody tells Doug what to do."

"Uh-huh." Buckner recognized the name. General Arthur MacArthur was famous, and the army in Buckner's day was small, barely 65,000 officers and men. It wouldn't exceed 100,000 until after Buckner left to join the Canadians. So everybody knew everybody else, or had served with somebody who did. MacArthur had won his Congressional Medal at Missionary Ridge when he was barely nineteen.

"Be seeing you." Elgar sketched a salute and drove away. Buckner headed down the hill in the department's Model T. When he got to town, he pulled around back to Murtaugh's loading dock. He spoke briefly to Murtaugh. "Send the bill to Powers up in Taylor," he said. "The bodies were found on company property. Or as near as, anyway."

"I don't know, Buck," Murtaugh said. He was a pale, balding man, and Buckner always felt as though he was about to start praying. "Getting money out of the Company's like pulling teeth on a tiger. You know, you gotta—"

"Yeah, you gotta catch the tiger first. Give it a try anyway. If it doesn't work, let me know." He thought a moment. "Peck working on them now?"

"No. He said they'd keep till morning."

"Right." Buckner drove to the town hall and parked. He found Mullen back at his desk. "I've got the prisoner all signed in, Buck. Elgar left this box of jewelry for you. He said he dusted it and then he took the prisoner's fingerprints. He found Garber's prints, but that was all. Now what?"

"I'll talk to Peck after he does his autopsies, then go see McLaws, see what we can put together to get an indictment on Kelson."

He went home and tried to wash off the smell of mud and corpses. He was convinced he had failed, but his mother said nothing as he joined her in the kitchen. She offered him sherry.

"I need something a bit stronger than that," he said.

"Well, you know where it is," she replied.

Buckner got the bottle from the pantry and a tumbler from the cupboard, sat, and poured. He drank off the first helping and immediately poured a second. His mother just watched.

"I found two more bodies in the cellar of Bob Charboneau's boarding house in Taylor," he said. He sipped slowly at the bourbon.

"Oh." She poured herself a bourbon and sat down.

"They're over at Murtaugh's. Peck's going to look at them in the morning, see if he can find out anything about them that we don't already know."

His mother nodded.

"I think he's been doing it for a long time," Buckner said.

"He?"

"Kelson. Company cop." Buckner sipped some more in the silence that followed. He refilled the tumbler when he had emptied it. "Gonna try to get him indicted for this latest one, get him hung for it."

His mother only nodded again, and they sat in silence drinking for several more minutes.

"Weather finally broke," Buckner said.

"I can hear it," agreed his mother. She watched as he finished the bourbon and poured more. "What are you trying to do? You don't usually drink that much." She sounded genuinely curious. "At least not where I can watch you doing it."

"Trying to make sure I don't have any dreams."

"I see." She pointed at the half-empty whiskey bottle. "That going to work?"

"Dunno. Hope so."

"Good luck," she said, and then she got to her feet and left the room.

Sometime later—he did not notice or remember when—Buckner also went to bed.

 **15**

Buckner's mother was humming softly when he went into the kitchen the next morning.

"Well?" she said as he poured coffee.

"Well what?" His voice was rough, and he tried to clear his throat.

"Did it work? Did you dream?"

He thought about it as he drank his coffee. "Can't remember."

"Well, I suppose that counts," she said.

"I suppose."

"Are you going back to Taylor today?"

"I don't think so. Jeff Peck is going to do autopsies on the two bodies we found. But first I have to go talk to Mrs. Janeworthy."

"Oh," said his mother. "I don't envy you that."

He finished his coffee and went out, walking quickly across town. The rain had stopped, but the sky continued dark and threatening. There was no wind, and the temperature had dropped twenty degrees. From the sidewalk in front of the Mouser's home, Buckner could see a figure in the attic window. As he turned in at the gate, the figure drew back.

Mrs. Mouser answered the door herself. Her smile was so bright, so infectious, he almost smiled himself.

"I need to speak with Miz Janeworthy, if she's in."

"My mother is always in, Chief Buckner." The bright smile faded just a little. "She never leaves." She stepped back to let him in. "You know the way."

"Miz Janeworthy?" Buckner called as he climbed to the attic. "It's Chief Buckner, ma'am. I need a moment of your time." He found her in the same chair, wearing the same too-big robe. She did not speak when he sat down, but her eyes watched him closely … searching.

"Sorry to bother you, ma'am, first thing in the morning like this."

"No you're not. Bothering folks is what you do. I expect you enjoy it." She leaned back and turned her gaze to the window and the yard below. "What do you want?"

"I want to talk to you some more about the fire." When she was silent, he went on. "You see, one of my officers has learned that your brother had the boarding house insured against fire for $1,000. Unfortunately, over the years, he had trouble making the payments, and just recently the policy lapsed. So the boarding house was not insured when it burned down." He waited briefly for a response. None came. "And it seems the policy lapsed just a week before the fire."

"Too bad," she said grimly.

"Yes, ma'am. Too bad. But I was just wondering, did you know about that? Did you know your bother had insurance on the place? And did you know that insurance had lapsed? Did you know about that?"

She turned to look at him now. Her heavy brow shaded her deep-set eyes, and a hint of a grim smile stretched her thin lips. "No, Chief Buckner, I didn't know about it." Her smiled widened maliciously. "And you can't prove otherwise."

"Well, I thought I'd ask. More to satisfy myself than anything else. It just struck me that it would be a good way for you to get back at your brother. You know, for charging you rent to live in your own home."

The woman's grin twisted slowly, as though she tasted bile, but she said nothing.

"We did find out a few things, though," Buckner continued. "The fire chief up there is pretty sure the whole thing started when somebody put a candle too close to a curtain in the parlor." He watched for her reaction, and got back nothing but her continuing rancor. "He's even found the candlestick. Was hardly damaged at all. It's even got fingerprints on it."

"Fingerprints?" She was frowning now. Buckner recognized puzzlement, and he thought he recognized a suggestion of fear.

"Yes, ma'am. Marks left by your fingers when you touch something. Everybody's fingerprints are different—no two alike. That's been accepted in court for years now."

"I don't believe you. You're just talking nonsense to try to scare me."

"No, ma'am. It's true. Criminals know all about fingerprints, and some of them have even gone so far as to try to burn them off with acid, or cover them up with skin grafts." Buckner smiled now. "Soon as I get around to taking the fingerprints of everybody that lived in the boarding house, I think I'll have a pretty good idea of who started the fire."

"Nonsense," she snapped. "Besides, that doesn't prove a thing." Her old confidence seemed to return. "Just because somebody touched a candlestick doesn't mean anything at all about how the fire got started. Why, I've probably touched most everything in that house at one time or another, and so has everybody else that lived there. So even if my so-called fingerprints are on a candlestick, it doesn't mean a thing. And how does the fire chief up there know that's how the fire started anyway? Isn't he that Big Foot … that Indian? Why, he doesn't have a lick of sense." She shook her head and turned to stare out the window again, clutching together the edges of the robe. "You run along, Chief Buckner. I don't know about the sort of people you're used to dealing with, but I don't bluff that easily. What you may or may not have doesn't prove a thing."

"No, ma'am, not by itself, but it's a good place to start. Probably get an indictment for arson out of it. Even if that doesn't guarantee a conviction, there's sure to be a trial." He got to his feet. "No matter how it turns out, I guess in a way I ought to thank whoever did start the fire. If it hadn't been for that, we'd never have found those dead girls. So there was some good came out of it."

The possibility that she might have done some good to somebody only seemed to anger the woman even more. She hunched her bony shoulders and continued to stare through the window.

Buckner went downstairs.

"I'm sorry, Chief Buckner," said Mrs. Mouser. She was at the front door as though waiting for Buckner to return. "I hope she was not too unpleasant." She frowned her gentle, placid frown. "I don't know what we're going to do. My husband says she can't stay, she's just so unpleasant. She's so mean to Elsie, and now Elsie won't go up there anymore, so I have to serve her hand and foot. But she hasn't anyplace else to go, and no money to live on even if she did." She stopped suddenly and gave Buckner a startled look. "Oh, I am so sorry, Chief Buckner, going on like that." She opened the door hurriedly. "You don't want to hear about my troubles."

"Don't think a thing about it, Miz Mouser." Buckner tried a reassuring smile. "Family can be like that sometimes."

By the time Buckner got to Murtaugh's, Jeff Peck had finished and gone. He asked Mr. Murtaugh to hold the bodies for a while, at least until he tried to get identities and locate survivors, if any, so they could be notified.

"You don't expect much along that line, do you, Chief Buckner?" Murtaugh asked. "Women like that?"

"No, but I'd like to try."

"Fine. We'll hold them for a week, but after that, well, we'll have to bill the department."

"Sure."

Buckner left and crossed the square to Coy's Drug Store. When he reached the top of the rickety staircase leading to Jeff Peck's office, he found an envelope thumbtacked to the door with his name in pencil scrawled below the words "Do Not Distrub."

The note inside combined the doctor's bad handwriting and worse spelling, but Buckner could make out the gist of it. Peck had worked on both bodies, was unable to learn anything at all about them beyond the fact that they were women who had died at around the age of twenty. Both had been strangled, and that was probably the cause of death, because he couldn't find any other, but he wouldn't swear to it in court. He had found traces of acid on both corpses, but no jewelry of any kind.

Buckner pocketed the note and returned to the town hall.

Hampton McLaws worked for the attorney general of the State of Missouri out of a small office two floors above the police station. Roughly the same size as Buckner's own office, it always seemed much smaller because it was bursting with file cabinets and bookcases, all stuffed to capacity. Additional books and papers spilled across any level surface, so there was barely room to walk, and none to sit. Buckner felt intimidated by the chaos, as though one wrong step—even a wrong gesture, or a loud word—might set the whole mass into motion, and so he hesitated in the doorway, silently thanking Michael Mullen for the obsessive tidiness that kept his own office relatively clear.

"You ought to take some time off for lunch," Buckner said.

"This is lunch," McLaws replied. He gulped coffee and peered at Buckner through a cloud of pipe smoke. He nodded while Buckner spoke, outlining the evidence he had gathered in the case of the dead girls. McLaws occasionally jotted down a note or asked a question. He looked at the earring from Buckner's pocket and the ones in the cigar tin. He quickly scanned Buckner's photos and sketches of the crime scene. He read Peck's notes on the two fresh corpses and the earlier one on Angela Cosimo.

"This is it?" he asked when he was finished.

"Yes."

"You said Elgar—that Company detective—was going to look for fingerprints."

"Yes, well, all he found was smudges, nothing that would match up with Kelson. Or anybody else."

"All right." McLaws sighed heavily. "I'll get in touch with the county seat, see what Strachan wants to do about this, if anything." Norven Strachan was the county prosecutor and McLaws's immediate, though mostly nominal, superior. "But I gotta be honest with you, Buck, I don't think he's going to be interested. There's a grand jury sitting now, but I'd be willing to give you odds of ten to one—hell, hundred to one—that he'll never even take this to them." He gestured at the reports and the jewelry. "Stuff like that you can pick up at Woolworth's. No fingerprints on the cigar tin. Peck's got nothing on the two new bodies. You say you've got witnesses that'll swear Kelson kept company with Angela Cosimo. So what? She was a prostitute. That's what you'd expect, isn't it? Cop and a whore? I mean, a cop like that. Present company definitely excepted." McLaws hurried on. "You see what I'm saying here, Buck? There just isn't enough for an indictment, much less a conviction, and Strachan isn't about to go spending state money if he can't get a conviction. Marks him down as a loser." He bundled up Buckner's evidence and handed it to him. "Now, maybe if it was somebody important got killed up there, maybe he'd give it a try, just for the publicity value of the thing, but, well, no, not for three prostitutes." McLaws shook his head. "It just don't make good sense from an economic standpoint or from a political point of view."

Buckner said, "You mean I'm going to have to let Kelson go."

"You got anything better to hold him on?"

"I'm waiting to see if I can get some evidence from Memphis. He used to be with the department down there but left under some pretty heavy suspicion for killing a prostitute. He's got a lot of kin down that way, and nobody wants to go up against them, but there's one police officer I might be able to count on to send me anything solid he's got." Buckner shrugged. "But, after all, it was just prostitutes."

"Yeah." McLaws frowned slightly. "I know you're not too happy about this Buck, but there's really nothing I can do. You just don't have any evidence."

"You know I'm going to call Davis Jackson about this," Buckner said.

"Sure. But he's in private practice now, and all he'll do is tell you the same thing I'm telling you."

"God dammit, Hamp!" Buckner said. McLaws looked startled. "The man has murdered a dozen women! He got tired of them, and he strangled them."

"You don't know that. And, anyway, however bad it is, it's still a dozen prostitutes, Buck. And I know whores've got the same rights to life, liberty, and the pursuit of et cetera as anybody else, but you know that some folks'll be perfectly happy there's twelve fewer of them around."

Buckner stared at McLaws. McLaws returned the look, shrugged helplessly, and finally said, "Sorry, Buck."

Buckner nodded and went back downstairs. As he had promised, he put in a telephone call to Davis Jackson in Jefferson City. Eventually, Jackson came on the line.

"Hey, Buck. Two telephone calls in one week. How you doing?"

"Fine, Davis, just fine."

"What can I do for you today?"

Buckner told his story as quickly and succinctly as he could, including a full accounting of the evidence he had gathered.

"Oh, right," Jackson said. "The papers here picked up Marthy's story for the *Post-Dispatch*. Congratulations on making an arrest. Sounds like this gambler—Perino?—sounds like he's just a no good murderer as well as a pimp."

"Peralta's a gambler and a pimp, but I don't think he's a murderer," Buckner said. He explained.

"Gosh. A company guard." There was silence for a moment. "And you want me to see about putting some pressure on Strachan … try to get an indictment. Is that it?"

Buckner said that it was.

"I don't know, Buck. From what you say, it sounds to me like your evidence is pretty thin." More silence. "Look, Buck, I'll be honest with you. I've known Strachan for a long time, and he owes me a couple, no question about it. But the fact is, it's not really worth it to me to call in those markers just on account of some dead prostitute. I hope you understand."

"It's not one dead prostitute, Davis. It's a whole lot of them. I believe the man has killed at least a dozen women, if the earrings we found are an accurate count. Here, in Little Rock, in Memphis ... who knows where else. And if he goes free because you goddamned lawyers are choking on a gnat, then he's going to kill more women, because I think he likes doing it."

After a long silence, Jackson said, "I understand your frustration, Buck, but ... well, with the evidence you say you've got, there's nothing I can do."

"Nothing you *will* do, Davis. Which is not the same thing."

"Well, Buck, maybe if you policemen could communicate with each other a little better, this thing wouldn't've got this far. You ever think about that?"

"Yes, Davis, I have. Thank you for your advice. Good-bye."

Buckner hung up and sat for a moment. The day had not gone well. His pathetic attempt to bluff Mrs. Janeworthy into confessing to starting the boarding house fire had failed. He was going to have to let Kelson go, and he no longer had any reason to hold Peralta.

At least he could do something about that, he decided. He got the keys to the cells from Mullen and unlocked Peralta's cell door. Peralta's surprise turned to naked suspicion tinged with fear. He got to his feet slowly ... reluctantly, looking ready to run despite the fact that he had no place to run to.

Buckner pushed the door as wide open as it would go and stepped back.

"Come on. I'm not feeding you any more. Get out of here. You can collect your property at the front desk."

Peralta stepped quickly, almost delicately—a man walking across a minefield—through the cell door and then down the hall, moving faster now, until he disappeared around the corner. Buckner closed and locked the cell door. Kelson, who had watched the entire process closely, smiled. "You're gonna be doing the same thing with this one before too long, Chief, so why don't you save yourself the walk and do it now?"

Buckner ignored him and followed Peralta down the hall. He found the man stuffing a billfold into his pocket.

"He have any money?" Buckner asked Mullen.

"He had a ten dollar bill and some change."

"All right." Buckner took out his own billfold and extracted a ten. He handed it to Peralta. "That's twenty dollars, and plenty enough for a train ticket to almost anyplace within a hundred miles. Go to the station right now and spend it all on a ticket on the next train passing through, no matter where it's going. Do not let me find you in this town after sunset. If you're still around tonight, or if I hear about you operating up in Taylor, or in any of the other towns in the Lead Belt, I will find you and beat you to within an inch of your life. Do you understand?"

"Yes, sir, I understand."

Buckner caught the hint of self-assurance in Peralta's reply ... the trace of a smile. *Well*, he thought, *if the man really is that stupid, there's no help for him.*

"Good. Go away. I never want to see you again."

Peralta disappeared quickly up the stairs.

Mullen must have seen something, too. "He'll be back," he said. "He's gonna find a game somewhere, and he's just dumb enough to think he can get away with it."

Buckner shrugged. "I want to talk to Harris. He's still around, I think. He said he was going to look up some old friends. So tell everybody to keep an eye out for him, and if they see him, tell him to come see me."

"Right." Mullen made a note. "I didn't know he had any friends in town."

"It's just what he told me." Buckner got coffee and returned to his office. He was on his third cup when Harris walked in and sat down. Buckner got up at once. "Come with me," he said, and walked down to the cells. He still had Mullen's keys, and he unlocked the door where Kelson sat. "You got cuffs?" Buckner asked Harris.

"Sure."

"Put them on him."

Kelson jumped to his feet, and Harris, with his sudden, surprising agility, stepped in and punched him in the stomach. Kelson collapsed to the floor gasping for air. Harris put the cuffs on him and hauled him to his feet.

"All right," Harris said to Buckner. "Now what?"

"He's all yours," Buckner said.

"Hold it a minute," Kelson protested. Harris punched him in the gut again and turned to Buckner as Kelson again folded up onto the floor.

"Mine?"

Buckner nodded. "You said you could make some money from Angela Cosimo's family if you brought back the girl's body and the man who killed her. I've already put in a call to Murtaugh's about the body." He indicated Kelson, who had apparently decided he was safer on the floor. "Now you can have him too."

Harris grinned. "Perfect." He looked closely to Buckner. "You know I won't exactly be turning him over to the police up there."

"I know that."

"Right. And there's the Binkley girl's family."

"And her father's friends," Buckner added.

"They're not gonna like what he done to their little girl, 'specially if I dress up the story some." Harris agreed. He frowned. "You still say you don't want a cut of my action? I'm gonna do pretty well out of bringing Kelson in."

"That's right, I don't."

"I notice that dago you was holding is gone," Harris said. "So you're just sorta cleaning house here. Mucking out your stalls, as you might say."

"That's right."

"Well, I've hauled plenty of shit in my time." Harris looked at Buckner for a while. He seemed puzzled, curious, looking for something. Buckner looked back, expressionless, and said nothing. With a final shake of his head, Harris reached down and effortlessly hauled Kelson back into an upright position. "Let's go, friend. We've got some traveling to do."

"Jesus, Chief," Kelson said, his voice how high pitched and thin with fear. "Jesus, Chief. You can't do this. You can't let him take me."

Harris slapped him hard across the mouth.

"You're gonna keep quiet," he said harshly, "or I'll make this the longest train ride of your life."

Kelson's lips were already bleeding and starting to swell. His eyes were on Buckner—wide, terrified eyes—as Harris led him away.

After a while, Buckner locked the cell door and returned the keys to Michael Mullen, who hung them back in their place, but avoided looking Buckner in the eye.

The rain had picked up again, driven by a hard northeast wind, and Buckner leaned into it as he walked. The house was empty when he got there. He lighted the stove and heated water for tea. He filled the tea ball with enough leaves for one cup, and when the kettle started singing, he poured. He found some bread in the bread box, and while the tea was steeping, he sliced a piece, spread it with jam from the ice box, and ate. When he finished his small meal, he rinsed the cup and the knife and left it all to dry. He stood leaning against the kitchen sink for a long time and then went to his room, undressed, and went to bed.

In the morning, Michael Mullen, who generally got in before anybody else, was surprised to find coffee made and Buckner standing in the front office staring morosely into his empty cup. After a brief "'Mornin," Mullen practically tiptoed to his desk. Buckner filled his cup and went back down the hall. Leaving the office door open, he sat at his desk and sipped coffee. He could hear Shotwell, on nights this week, check in before heading home. And he heard Carter, yawning cavernously, clump noisily down the stairs.

"Keep it quiet," Mullen cautioned, pointing in the general direction of Buckner's office.

"Trouble?" Carter asked softly.

"I don't know," Mullen answered. "Something, anyway."

"Well, he might wanta come outside, 'cause there's something he's gonna wanta see."

"It better be good," Mullen said. "Cause I don't think he's in the mood for fun."

"It's good."

Mullen went back down the hall and leaned in through the open door. "Carter says he's got something to show you."

"It better damn well be worth my time."

"He says it is."

Buckner followed Mullen to the front desk, where Carter was still grinning hugely. "How 'bout a little walk," he said.

"You look like the damned cat that swallowed the damned canary," Buckner grumbled.

"You just wait," Carter said, ignoring Buckner's mood. "Come on." And he led Buckner up the stairs and out.

"Where the hell are we going?" Buckner demanded.

"You'll see," Carter answered merrily.

"You're awful damned cheerful for being on days."

"Yep. And you're gonna see why."

As they walked, Buckner began to hear shouting in the distance—laughter, cheering.

"Where're we headed?" Buckner asked.

"The old Bell place," Carter said.

"The Bell place? That's where—"

"That's right," Carter answered. "That new speak those fellows from KC are trying to start up."

"Then what's all the commotion?"

"You'll see."

The walk took several minutes. People were gathering, hurrying past them, headed in the same direction. Buckner heard more cheering and saw balloons rising in the sky. Then they rounded the last corner and saw the source of all the commotion.

"Well, I'll be. It looks like it might be a political rally," Buckner said.

"It sure does," Carter responded. He looked closely at Buckner, frowning. Buckner returned the look and smiled innocently.

The rain had stopped, and the air was bright and crisp—a perfect autumn morning. The old Bell house, lately converted into a fancy nightspot by certain elements from Kansas City, was the center of what did, indeed, seem to be a political rally. Several county police sedans were parked in front, each one bearing on its door a sign saying "Vote Foote! He'll kick 'em out!" and a photo of the county sheriff looking grimly determined. Each of the sedans flew a bunch of balloons—red, white, and blue—from short staffs tied to its roof. Sheriff's deputies wore boot-shaped lapel pins saying "Foote for Assembly" and handed out flyers while other sheriff's deputies were busy escorting large men in pajamas and robes to the waiting sedans. One of them was Charles Fitzwalter, wearing elegant satin pajamas and a long black satin robe. His wide, flat feet were stuffed into scuffed leather slippers, and he was in a boiling rage. As soon as he spotted Buckner, he broke away and stormed over, fists balled, shoulders hunched. Deputies scurried to catch up. One grabbed Fitzwalter's arm, but Fitzwalter shook him off and kept coming.

Carter said "Uh-oh," and braced himself. Buckner smiled. "Howdy, Mr. Fitzwalter." He put out a hand. Fitzwalter, surprised, slowed down, which allowed half a dozen deputies to catch up with him. Stillson Foote, hatchet faced and wearing a tailored uniform complete with flared cavalry breeches and high, shiny boots, was smiling happily.

"Now, then, Mr. Fitzwalter, let's try to keep calm about all this."

"You set me up, Buckner, goddammit, all so you could protect your friend Dutton. How much is he paying you for this?"

Buckner continued smiling. That's when Fitzwalter launched a massive left in the direction of Buckner's head. Buckner stepped back quickly, and the blow landed solidly on Stillson Foote's shoulder, rocking the sheriff, nearly knocking him over. The sheriff's deputies immediately applied their nightsticks to Fitzwalter's head and ribs. As he sagged to the ground, they hoisted him and dumped him in the back of one of the sedans. Foote turned calmly to the assembled citizens and smiled broadly. "Folks," the sheriff said in his best public-speaking voice, "this is just the kind of law enforcement you have come to expect from me during my years as your county sheriff. And you can bet it's the kind of work I'll be carrying out once I'm in Jefferson City. The day of the gambler, the bootlegger, the moonshiner is over. I'm going to make sure that every speakeasy in this state is closed down, shuttered, and locked up tight. I'm going to put the criminals in jail, and I'm going to run the immigrants out of Missouri so fast they won't have time to telegraph the pope to come help them out."

This was greeted with laughter. Buckner kept smiling. When he heard Carter mutter "What the hell?" he gently stepped on his toe. Carter fell suddenly silent.

"I know most of you folks down this way have been loyal Democrats for a mighty long time," Foote continued, "but maybe it's time for you to make a change ... time for you to start thinking about which political party is the political party of decent, God-fearing, clean-living Americans ... about which political party is going to make the streets safe for you and your children ... about which political party is going to protect this great nation of ours from filthy foreigners and their filthy foreign ideas."

This was rewarded with scattered applause.

Foote checked on the progress of his deputies, both those handing out fliers and those arresting Fitzwalter's employees.

Buckner noticed that Jackson, Dutton's former employee, was one of the last to be escorted out. And he saw a deputy give Foote a quick nod.

"Now, I'm not going to try to tell you folks how to vote," Foote resumed. He grinned modestly when this was greeted with much laughter. "But I do want you to remember what I've said here today when you come to cast your vote in November, and I want you to remember what you've seen here today as well, because if you vote for me, you're going to see a lot more of the same kind of thing."

Foote gave one last wave to the cheering crowd. He gave Buckner a quick nod, climbed into the lead sedan, and led the convoy out of town.

"That was quite a show," Carter said as he and Buckner walked back toward the town hall. "I hope Dutton appreciates it."

"I noticed he had the good sense not to show up," Buckner said. "I just hope he doesn't think this was all on his behalf."

"He's smarter than that, for sure," Carter said. "But I wonder how he's going to explain to Jackson's mother about her boy getting arrested."

"Jackson's just lucky Dutton didn't have Buster work him over for putting soap in the whiskey."

"How'd you figure that one?"

"Wasn't anybody else could've done it," Buckner said.

"He won't have Buster go over Jackson like that, would he?"

Buckner shrugged. He turned and started back into town. Carter joined him.

Buckner returned to his office. As the clock in the tower above him was striking six, Vernon Elgar stuck his head in the door.

"You got a minute, Chief?"

"Sure," Buckner said. "Come on in. Have a seat."

"I'm heading back up to town. Thought I'd stop by first, see how things wound up."

Buckner explained what he'd done with Peralta and Kelson.

"Not exactly by the book," Elgar said when he'd finished. "But it does kind of put a capper on things."

"What about Taylor?" Buckner asked. "Powers tried to keep a lid on all this, but it didn't work out the way he'd hoped."

"No, but that won't matter much to the folks in the big offices," Elgar said. "Operations continued smoothly right along, which means the money kept rolling in right on schedule. And that's the main thing, far as they're concerned. So, no, I don't think Powers is going to have any trouble over this."

Buckner said, "Uh-huh."

Elgar seemed to have more to say, so Buckner waited for it. "There was one other thing," he said. "I like the way you handled all this, working with Powers, figuring out it was Kelson. How did you figure that out, by the way?"

"I hate to disappoint you," Buckner said, smiling. "I didn't really figure it out at all. I never really paid much attention to Kelson or Garber, mostly since they were Company police, and I guess I made a mistake there. Anyway, what got me interested in Kelson was when I remembered those sores on his hands, and when it occurred to me they might be from old acid burns. I decided to check up on him and Garber, just to make sure." Buckner explained the telegrams and the trips south. "Once I found out about Kelson's past—his time in Little Rock and Memphis—I decided it was time to do some serious investigating."

"So you searched his place," Elgar said.

"Yes," Buckner admitted.

"And you found that cigar tin and then you put it back."

"Yes."

Elgar laughed. "What were you going to do if Garber didn't find it—or me, for that matter?"

"Well," Buckner said. "I guess I'd've had to find it myself."

"But it still wasn't enough for an indictment," Elgar said.

"No," Buckner admitted. "But there was just no way in hell I was going to let that man loose, knowing as I do that he's killed a dozen women and he's going to go right on doing it unless I stop him."

"Not going by the book, anyway," Elgar said. "That's kind of the way you do things around here, isn't it? I checked up on you before I came down here, and I've been asking questions since I got here. There's your saloon-keeper buddy over in Darktown, with his high-priced whiskey and low-stakes gambling, and that woman runs that fancy whorehouse too."

"That's right," Buckner agreed. "One of the first things I learned when I started in here, back when I was a deputy sheriff, was that when it comes to law and order, most folks are more interested in the order part of that. They really don't much care who's breaking which law, especially since plenty of them are breaking one law or another, just so long as things are nice and quiet and peaceful."

"And this new fellow, Fitzwalter, he threatened to cause trouble?"

"I don't need some kind of gang war going on around here."

"Kind of tough on Fitzwalter, though."

Buckner shrugged. "I doubt if he'll spend ten minutes in jail. All that with Foote was for show. It was politics. He'll run Fitzwalter back to Kansas City, and everybody will think he's hell on lawbreakers and he'll get elected to the state assembly."

"And be out of your hair, anyway."

Buckner just grinned.

Then Elgar said, "You ever get bored, being a small-town cop?"

"Sometimes," Buckner said. "Why do you ask?"

"Because American Protective is always on the lookout for good men," Elgar said.

"Oh, I don't think so." Buckner was surprised. "I don't think I'm cut out to be a company guard."

"Hell no," Elgar said, waving that away. "They do hire a lot of ex-military fellows like you for security work, but they wouldn't waste a talent like yours on small-time stuff like that. You've got a real gift for investigative work. That's where they'd use you. Plainclothes investigation. Only it'd be a considerable notch or two above this." Elgar's gesture took in the office, the department, all of Corinth, and most of Highland County. "American Protective has got laboratories and scientists using all the latest techniques for analyzing evidence. They got lawyers whose sole occupation is protecting the company's investigators and then making damn sure the criminals they bring in wind up in jail. Or in the electric chair. Hell, the regular police departments in this country are out-manned and out-gunned by the criminals, and they're damned glad to see an operative from American Protective show up and give them a hand. Plus we operate nation wide, so a fellow like this Kelson, he wouldn't've got this far before we'd've found out about him and spread the word to our people across the country."

Buckner thought about it for a while … about his mother … about Judith Lee. Elgar seized the opportunity. "Pays damned good too," he said. "Probably twice what you're getting here, although I'm pretty sure you're not in it for the money."

"Well, that's true enough," Buckner said with a laugh. "But, no, I don't think so. I appreciate what you're saying, but … well …" he groped for words. "I just don't think I'm ready for that big a change in my life right now."

"All right," Elgar said. He got up and stuck out his hand. "Lemme know if you change your mind. You know where to find me."

Buckner got up, shook Elgar's hand, and walked him down the hall. "Be seeing you," he said.

"I hope so," Elgar said, and walked through the double doors and up the stairs.

After his footsteps had died out, Buckner said, "I'll be home if anybody wants me."

Mullen, intent on writing something in a ledger, muttered, "Uh-huh," and kept writing.

 16

That night, Buckner went to Elroy Dutton's. The old man in the barbershop greeted him happily, shook his hand, and thanked him. Buster grinned at him through the open door at the top of the stairs and pointed him in the direction of Dutton's table. Dutton had company. Jeff Peck sat clutching his whiskey glass, and Martha Jane Buckner sat next to Dutton and smiled as Buckner came over. As soon as he sat down, Jackson's replacement, looking immensely pleased with himself, appeared with his bourbon.

Buckner thanked him and raised his glass to Dutton.

"Everybody back where they're supposed to be, I see. Almost everybody." He gestured at the bandstand, where the musicians were tuning up. Couples were already on their feet and heading for the dance floor. "That was pretty quick."

"Yeah," Dutton admitted. "Is that why you're here? To hear me say thanks? Or was it to make sure I didn't leave Jackson lying in a ditch someplace?"

Buckner said, "It occurred to me you might do something like that."

"I couldn't. He's kin. Besides, you know I don't work that way."

"So where is he?"

"Back there." Dutton aimed a thumb over his shoulder. "Washing dishes, scrubbing floors. Tomorrow he's going to start on the new paint job this place needs. It's going to be a long damn time before he gets to work out front again."

Buckner said. "Foote was talking about closing down every speakeasy in the state. Aren't you even a little worried?"

"Nope." Dutton laughed out loud. "Look," he said, "folks want to drink and they want to dance and have a good time, and making that stuff into a crime is just plain stupid."

"Well," Buckner said, "I can't say as I care much for what the band's playing. Why don't they play ragtime, like they used to?"

"Because folks want to dance to the new music and listen to the new music, and I'm in the business of providing folks with what they want," Dutton said. "Ragtime is too old fashioned."

"I don't care. I like it."

Dutton opened his mouth to reply and then clamped it shut and shook his head in frustration.

"I heard you settled things in the Taylor case," said Martha Jane, groping for a safe topic. Dutton hadn't heard what had happened, so she filled him in. He just laughed. "You sure don't mind ignoring protocol when it suits you," he said to Buckner.

"What the hell does that mean?"

"I mean sending Kelson up to St. Louis with Harris. All nice and tidy, even if it wasn't strictly legal."

"I tried doing it by the book," Buckner said. "And going by the book wasn't going to get justice for the women Kelson murdered. And it sure wasn't going to keep him from doing it again. So I took care of it the best way I could."

Dutton shook his head and sipped his champagne.

"Why in hell you ever expect to find justice in this world is something I don't understand," he said.

"Folks in St. Louis will take care of Kelson, and one of these day's Peralta's going to deal seconds to the wrong man and get himself killed, so I guess it'll all work out."

"I expect you know that little stunt you pulled on Fitzwalter means you just handed the election to Stillson Foote," Dutton continued.

"Yes, I do."

"Of course, Foote going off to the state assembly, that'll mean a new county sheriff," said Martha Jane.

"Yes, it will," Buckner agreed, smiling now.

"So we might do pretty well out of this deal. New sheriff and all."

"Couldn't do worse."

Dutton and Martha Jane turned to Buckner.

"No," he said firmly. "Being chief of police of Corinth is about all I can handle. Besides, being sheriff is mostly about politics, and I have no interest at all in going into politics at this point in my life."

"Shame, really," said Martha Jane.

"Yes," Dutton agreed. "Can't you just see him, smiling and shaking voters' hands ... kissing babies?"

"Well you can just put that right out of your mind," Buckner said.

Dutton waved the waiter over and ordered another round. The band had started up, something nice and slow, with the trumpet and the clarinet trading melancholy leads.

"What about you two?" Buckner said with a short, harsh laugh.

"What do you mean, us two?" Martha Jane said.

"Well, you two looking all cozy like you are."

"What are you getting at, Chief?" Dutton said, his voice carefully soft and friendly.

"What the hell do you think I'm getting at?" Buckner demanded. "The two of you, carrying on like you do. I guess what I'm doing is, I'm asking you what are your intentions regarding my sister?"

"What?"

Even Peck looked surprised at that. But Martha Jane exploded. "You are not in charge of me, big brother! Never have been and never will be! And my relationship with Mr. Dutton none of your damn business."

"Mr. Dutton!" Buckner was on his feet. "As long as you're my sister, that makes it my business. I've been watching the two of you carrying on for a few years now, and I'm getting tired of it."

"We are not carrying on," Martha Jane responded. "We are friends, and we are having a drink together with another friend, Doctor Peck here."

"Keep me out of it," Peck protested. Everybody ignored him.

Buckner glared, speechless, at everybody and then abruptly turned and stalked out, oblivious of the fact that the entire room—the band members included—had stopped what they were doing and stared at him as he crossed the floor and went through the door Buster had already open for him.

"Good grief," Peck said. "He comes in here like a bear with a sore nose, tries to pick a fight over Prohibition, how he handled the Kelson case, complaining about the music."

"Yeah. What the hell was that all about?" Dutton asked, astonished.

"Oh," said Martha Jane. "I think I know."

The others turned to look at her.

"Judith Lee's not coming back."

"Oh," said Elroy Dutton.

"Good grief," said Jeff Peck again.

Buckner went down the stairs and out into the street. The air was cold and wet with a slight drizzle, and the dark street was empty. He walked back toward the Iron Mountain tracks. Mrs. Belmont's place was brightly lighted, and music and singing poured through the high windows. Buckner stopped at the foot of the steps and looked up at the door. It opened slowly, and Isaac Joe stepped out onto the stoop.

"Evenin', Chief," he said softly.

Buckner said, "Evening, Isaac."

"You thinkin' 'bout comin' in, Chief?" Isaac Joe said. "Lot warmer inside than out here."

Buckner didn't say anything for a long time and then finally just shook his head. "Not tonight, Isaac."

"Boss'll be disappointed."

"I know."

Buckner stood motionless for a moment longer, finally turned and continued across the tracks.

"Be seein' you, Chief," Isaac called.

Buckner waved without turning.

Bill Newland looked up from his newspaper as Buckner came through the department's swinging doors.

"I won't be long, Bill," he said.

"Okay, Buck."

Two files lay on Buckner's desk. He opened the one labeled "Peralta" and took out the arrest report. Across the bottom, he scrawled "Released for lack of evidence," and added the date. He opened the file labeled "Kelson" and took out the arrest report. Across the bottom he wrote, "Remanded to the custody of ..." and stopped. After a moment, he added "other jurisdiction," and closed the file.

Then he got up, went out, and walked home.